MW00680181

THE END OF TIME IS UPON US
THIS IS THE FACE
OF THE ANTICHRIST

Here is the extraordinary, true, and controversial story of the prophesied Antichrist.

But contrary to the dire warnings that have come from the pulpits for the past 2000 years, Mabus the Antichrist is not out to destroy the world. His mission is to save it.

Hunted by shadowy conspirators and persecuted by religious zealots, the Antichrist escapes their grasp and works towards his aim of global liberation—not from evil, but from superstition, repressive politics, and anti-science demagoguery. His message is clear and threatening to the powers-that-be: Religion was created to distract humankind from discovering the wondrous truths and enlightening secrets of the universe. And nothing will stop Mabus from spreading his incendiary gospel–not even attempts to kill him.

His beautiful companion by his side, Mabus must first come to grips with his supernatural, superhuman nature. Next he has to accept his place as Leader of the New World Order. Then, to fulfill his mission, he must elude a deadly female adversary with designs of her own. Finally, Mabus must face the greatest challenge of all: to save the future of humankind, he must find a way to travel back in time.

Blending top-flight speculative fiction and Biblical prophecy, *The Antichrist: Version 666* may be the timeliest book of the decade and a thriller like none other you've ever read.

"This book rocks! It leaves *Left Behind* and *The Da Vinci Code* in the dust! More than just a fast-paced sci-fi thriller, THE ANTICHRIST: VERSION 666 tackles cutting-edge scientific theories, biblical prophecies, where we come from, where we're going, and much, much more . . . Don't miss it! Buy it!"

–Vivian Garcia, author of *REC:ord*

"A fantastic take on just who is the Anti-Christ. The author does an admirable job of providing fact-based research at the same time giving us a first-rate thriller."

–John Pellicano, NYPD (ret.), author of *Conquer or Die*

(for more reviews turn page)

THE FATHER

THE SON

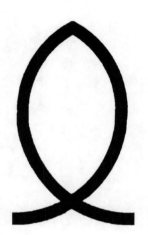

THE HOLY GHOST

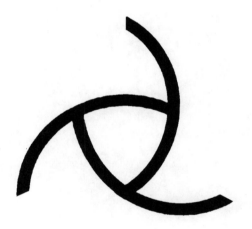

THE HOLY TRINITY

The Antichrist: Version 666

BY

CLOISE ORAND II

Port Orchard Publishing

The Antichrist: Version 666
by Cloise Orand II

For further information, contact the author at:
Port Orchard Publishing
P.O. Box 1746
Port Orchard, WA 98366
portorchardpublishing@yahoo.com

Book designed by:
The Floating Gallery
244 Madison Avenue, #254
New York, NY 10016
www.thefloatinggallery.com

PRINTED IN CANADA

The Antichrist: Version 666
Cloise Orand II

1. Author 2. Title 3. Science Fiction
Library of Congress Control Number 2005901211
ISBN 0-9766131-0-7 (Hardcover)

Disclaimer

THIS BOOK IS INTENDED SOLELY as a work of fiction. Claims made herein about various institutions, groups and individuals are not intended to be taken as entirely based in fact. However, this will not, we hope, interfere with the casual reader's evaluation of the text as a potentially realistic appraisal of the advent of the one true Antichrist and other events portrayed in this book.

We have endeavored to not present any evidence of questionable actions that might impugn or malign any extant groups. However, if there is anyone in the Illuminati, NASA, or any other U.S. Government entity who might take offense in any form, legal or personal, to what we have stated herein, we recommend that he or she take our disclaimer at face value. We do not consider any of the fictive events in this book to be of a nature that could cause us (the creator, writer, editor, and/or publisher of this book) to be held legally or personally liable regarding the portrayal of any actual persons, organizations or events portrayed in this book. Once again, this book is solely to be considered a work of fiction.

Dedication

I would like to dedicate this book to: my foster parents, Chris and Mike Miller; my wife's parents, Pauline and Vern Cornelius; my beautiful children: Christopher Craig, Stefan Nicholas, Alexander LuJacque, and Savannah Jordyn; and my wife, Michelle,who gave me unconditional love,hope for the future, and the fulfillment of my dreams.

Acknowledgments

I would like to give a special thanks to all the people who helped me put together this project:

The staff at The Floating Gallery: Larry Leichman, Joel Hochman, Olga Vladimirov, and Sharon Smalls Williams; my editors: Wendy Bonadio, Jonathan Cohen, Pauline Cornelius, Karen Cole Peralta, and Brian Smart; my friends and advisors: Jeremy St. James, Shawn Bailey, Jeremy Tatum, Jake Lanphier, Dawn Crawford, Billy Armstrong, Tom Cowan, Christina Cowan, Rick Davis, Mike Smith, Pat Smith, Kasey Waters, Brandon Wayne, Peter Updegrove, Sam Blevins, Tim Updegrove, Jeremy Hunnel, Joshua Ehrhardt, Joe Krecker, Christie Miller, Mike Miller, John Wagner, Mike Holbrook, and Megan Gjertsen; and most especially, my wife Michelle.

Prologue

MANY WORLD CULTURES ARE BASED on a cycle of birth, destruction, and rebirth. The symbol of the Ouroboros, a serpent or dragon swallowing its own tail, has existed since the dawn of civilization. Yet no one is completely sure where it comes from. We only know that it signifies eternity. The ancient Mayan Sacred Calendar places Earth in a final cycle of life that will end near the winter solstice of 2012 AD. Many other civilizations and faiths maintain a belief in reincarnation, continuous birth, and return. Only three world religions use the concept of linear time instead of cyclical time: Judaism, Christianity, and Islam.

What if we have all lived the same lives and done the same things countless times? What if the world is trapped within a bubble in time where everyone is doomed to repeat the same actions over and over again? Would worldwide religions and governments want you to know about this, or would there be a monumental conspiracy to cover it all up?

Some people currently think that the Illuminati, a highly secretive group—believed by many to be a wayward branch of the Society of Freemasons—is responsible for such a conspiracy. They believe that the Illuminati have infiltrated every branch of government, including NASA and all of its works, and every religion on the face of the planet. It is said that Fatalism, the religious doctrine of a preordained and immutable future, is being used to control our hearts, minds, and spirits. Religion is being used to keep us unaware of what is really happening in order to maintain a power structure of the elite ruling over us until our deaths, and possibly until the death of the entire world.

This book explores the possibility that life as we know it is going to end on December 27th of the year 2012 AD, as outlined by the ancient Mayan culture of central Mexico. Their most sacred and accurate calendar, the Tzolk'in, which is based on the 26,000-year cycle of the Pleiades, states that thirteen cycles of 400 Mayan years will pass before the calendar ends. It begins in 3114 BC on August 1st (roughly 3750 BC in "our" calendar), which is very near the time of creation as perceived by the Jews.

If you count every century as a single "day," as some Biblical scholars do, the world's first day could have begun with the century of 3700 BC, and the last day, or the day of completion, would have been the century of 3100 BC. This juxtaposition seems to be much more than coincidental. However, these are merely calendar estimates concerning Biblical Creationism, and as most scientists now know, our world is much older than that.

In fact, this book relates to a timeline that is an endless cycle beginning roughly 1,000,000,000 years ago, before the first appearance of mankind. This cycle has no real beginning or absolute end, and thus is a manifestation of the Ouroboros—the snake/dragon swallowing its own tail and perpetually manifesting an infinite and eternal universe. It culminates in the year 2012 AD, when the Earth is hit by a giant asteroid and is changed forever, slowly turning into an uninhabitable, frozen orb which eventually must become the planet Mars. Before this happens, a group of intrepid, technologically advanced people known as the Antis, led by the actual Antichrist, must travel back in time to the planet Venus, to begin life anew and to perpetuate an eternal cycle which will keep mankind forever evolving and alive indefinitely.

We have much established research pinpointing the Cydonia region of Mars as corresponding to the Giza region of Egypt, where the five Great Pyramids reside. On Mars lie the ruins of incredibly similar structures that are obviously artificial, as they encompass many straight lines and right angles that cannot be formed through natural means. These structures, along with the famous "Martian Face"–which, remarkably, appears to be the crumbled ruins of the Egyptian Sphinx– pointedly correspond almost exactly to the Great Pyramids of Egypt. This validates a current scientific theory, postulated and detailed in this book, that Mars is indeed the planet Earth in the not-too-distant future. If this is so, then the planet Venus, known to the Romans as Lucifer, or the Morning Star, must also be Earth in its distant past. We have found much scientific evidence indicating the potential validity of this remarkable theory.

We propose now to show you an entirely realistic history within this book, based on hundreds of hours of solid current scientific research and factual data from a wide variety of interrelated and extremely credible resources. We suggest that the prophesied Antichrist of the Bible will appear very soon in our times and establish a New World Order, fulfilling many of the soundest Biblical prophecies. Then he will leave in a spaceship with the twelve people of his eternal destiny, known as the Antis, to begin life anew on Venus just before the predicted cataclysm engulfs our forewarned but doomed planet on December 27th of the year 2012 AD (or, as it is known and dated by some Christian scholars, AC 2012).

Chapter One

I T IS TIME,> THOUGHT ONE Grey to another Grey, who merely nodded.

Without any marvels, heavenly signs in the cosmos, or anything out of the ordinary except one recurring number in the date, a child was born in the early morning of June 6th, 1976 AD—in other words, AC 06-06-76.

Somebody, surely, was number 666 during the Holocaust. Mabus? Maybe. There are several such names, and there are several such…phone numbers.

It was precisely ten years after his parents had married on June 6th, 1966. At that point, a decade later, Mabus entered our modern world. But his father was not present at the birth.

Outwardly, that sometime gentleman was calmly attending an employee meeting. He was a government worker whose whole life revolved around a strange, particularized version of Roman Catholicism. It had been passed down through many generations, and he was neither a calm nor a gentle man when it came to his family. His wife had been a Reform Jew, but her husband had forced her to convert when she married him.

His bosses at work were members of a secret religious society, called the Illuminati. Their sole purpose was to destroy the soon-to-come prophesied Christ. Some thought this group was associated with the higher levels of the Freemasons. It was rumored that they had woven their way into almost every branch of the US government. Slowly, they had worked their way into other governments also.

They bothered and tormented Mabus's father constantly. But little did he know that he had been injected with a microchip device that had wormed its way up to his central cortex and tapped straight into his brain. He had carried this implant for quite a while, unbeknownst to him. These implant devices were developed by underground scientists, agents of the Illuminati. With these devices, the person implanted would become a puppet to whoever was at the controls. They needled their way into the farthest corners of his mind. As people sharing his religious preference, they were able to control him down to his bottomless soul. This caused him to do all kinds of horrible things in the name of God.

Mabus's father brushed it off as voices in his head. At first he thought he was going mad, but his religion slowly blended in with his insanity. Soon he thought it was God himself speaking straight to him.

Mostly, he verbally and physically abused his firstborn child. When Mabus was brought home from the hospital, his father stared harshly at the innocent baby's face.

"Son of Perdition," he muttered under his beer-tainted breath. "This is no child of mine. He'll come to no good end."

Mabus's family had originally come from the Middle East, and they tended to be dark-haired white people. Yet the boy was extremely fair, with blond, curly hair and green eyes. And so his father thought he was not his own, blaming the child and not the mother for his loss of true fatherhood. He began plotting how he would one day kill the boy and cover up the crime, as his bosses at work continued to torment him daily.

At the tender age of two, unbeknownst to his mother, Mabus was locked into a tight, filthy closet by his angry father for over ten hours. Being so young, he naturally fell asleep, and thus began his endless dreams of building pyramids and a fiery red ball destroying them. They were to recur every night of his life, with an ever-expanding, unspeakable quality that would mirror the growing nightmare of his abused life until he was twenty-nine years old.

Mabus's father wore him down and would often torment the child into submission. When the handsome and clever boy first began to walk, his father called him "The Lawless One," right out of the description of the Antichrist in 2 Thessalonians 2:8, chasing him into dark corners of the house where he would repeatedly slap him and taunt him as the seed of Satan. Mabus cried out in pain and frustration, wondering what was happening, but his hapless mother never responded. All she did was to serve him toast with butter and honey for breakfast, under the theory that thus "he [might] know to refuse the evil, and choose the good." He was beaten nearly every day, with the poundings increasing in severity until he was black and blue all over his body.

Mabus wasn't sure how to handle this. At first he tried appealing to his mother, which was fruitless, for she was afraid to defy her husband. Then, having learned in church about Jesus and God, Mabus tried praying to them. He constantly entreated his God to help him, and asked Him why his life was so unbearable.

"God? I spoke with the priest, and he told me that if I asked you to show me a sign, you would. So, I'm asking you, please, give me a sign that you can hear me. I really need you. I don't think I'm gonna make it. I can't take this abuse. I'm only ten years old, and my father has beaten me daily since I can remember. I don't feel like I'm bad. What did I do to deserve this? Please, God, if you can hear me, please say something. It's me, Mabus."

At night as he knelt by his bedside, saying his prayers, he begged this "God" to tell him exactly why he must suffer so much, and if his father was finally going to kill him someday. He never got any answers, and after a while, he began to realize that the only person he would ever have to rely on was himself.

He learned how to be reticent, and he hardly ever complained. At school he was well-liked by the other children. He was charismatic and charming, and soon became very popular.

One day at school, Mabus's teacher noticed some welts on his lower back. "Mabus! What happened to your back? You look like you've been beaten."

"I never said I was beaten! No! I wasn't beaten! I don't know how I got the marks." The teacher was suspicious at that point because she had recalled bruises on him before. She felt the principal should be notified.

"Mrs. Steamer, we have a problem with one of our students."

"And who might that be?"

"Mabus, Ma'am."

"Mabus? What on Earth did he do?"

"Well, it's not exactly what he did, it's… well, I noticed some welts on him. I asked him where they came from, and he got real defensive, and said he didn't know."

"That's odd. He doesn't know? I'll call his mother. Thank you for bringing this to my attention." For the principal it was protocol to notify the parents and CPS (Child Protective Services). CPS called Mabus's mom, and arranged for a meeting that night to discuss the marks on Mabus's back. Mabus's mom denied any knowledge of marks on his back and agreed to meet with them at her home.

Mabus was scared to go home, knowing that the school had called CPS. When he opened the door his mother and father were waiting for him in the hallway with very angry looks on their faces. "What did you tell them? Did you tell them we beat you?" shouted his father. Mabus cried out, "No!" "Do you want them to lock me up in a prison, and put you in a boys' home? Who will take care of your mother? Are you trying to break up this family?" his father screamed. "No!" cried Mabus, as he slid down the wall into a fetal position. His father walked up to him and whispered in his ear, "Then you know exactly what to say to the CPS worker. Right?"

Later that night the doorbell rang. It was the CPS worker, as expected. Mabus's mom greeted her, took her coat, and pointed her over to the dining room table. Both Mabus and Mabus's father were patiently waiting. "Thank you for coming on such short notice. We're actually kind of embarrassed at all this commotion over a misunderstanding," said Mabus's mom. The CPS worker, looking quite confused, said, "What do you mean?" "Well, we're gonna let Mabus tell you," explained his father. Mabus, embarrassed, looked at the CPS worker and began to go on about how he injured himself in a bicycle accident and that he had been trying to hide the scrapes from his parents. Because he was officially on bicycle restriction, he feared more trouble by telling the truth. "So you see, we apologize for taking up your time over a big misunderstanding like this." The CPS worker was satisfied that this was a cut-and-dried case, and dismissed the allegations.

Mabus now felt very lonely and isolated. When he was only eleven, he began running away from home. Each time he would run away, his time away from home would get longer and longer. The first time he ran away, he was gone for only a day. The second time it was for a week. His parents never went looking for him, knowing that once the cruel world had its way with him, he would come crawling back. He felt like a black sheep around his home and often contemplated suicide. He constantly pleaded to God to rescue him. And as always there was no reply. This made Mabus begin questioning whether there was a God.

Even when Mabus stopped going to church, it came to him; a strange presence followed him, haunted him, and watched from a distance. He would be walking home from school, hear footsteps, and swear he saw a large shadow, but would whirl around to see nothing. At night, he would awaken from his usual nightmare to see light streaming into his room from an unknown source. When he opened the curtains to look outside, the light would vanish, but he often saw a furtive figure—tall, human and male—disappearing into the night. Mabus would strain to see who it was, but he always disappeared too quickly. It was maddeningly frustrating.

The nightmares continued. Mabus would dream of a fiery, round object coming toward him. The screaming scarlet ball would suddenly swell, jolting him awake. Mabus tried telling his father about the dreams, but the furious, hateful man called him "The Liar." And when he was brought home one time on a charge of shoplifting, his father yelled at him again, repeatedly calling him "Deceiver!" as he soundly beat him into submission and beyond.

One way Mabus learned to cope was to laugh inwardly at his father when he sensed a beating coming on. When he would see his father reach for his weapon of choice—a long, thick, leather razor strop—he would boldly laugh in his mind and manage to keep a grip on his self-respect. But this courageous laughter would almost be the boy's undoing.

One beautiful spring day, Mabus strutted home from school. His fourth-grade class had voted him class president that day, and he couldn't wait to share the news with his mother. As he walked along, he noticed he felt unusually alive. Spring was here, and the ground seemed to be waking up—Mabus could smell it. He squinted in the warm sun and noticed happy yellow daffodils popping up in a neighbor's front yard that he hadn't seen the previous day. He felt he was coming alive, like the daffodils, and with giddiness he mused, "Today, president of my class, tomorrow, President of the country!"

As soon as he stepped into the kitchen, he told his proud mother about being voted class president. But the words had barely tumbled from his mouth when he saw his father reaching for the strop. Mabus laughed and told his mother that he didn't care what his father did anymore; he was going to become the president of the world someday—not because he even wanted to, but because everyone liked him so much.

"And when I'm voted Leader of the Universe, I'll take all of Daddy's beer away, so he doesn't get so mad!" he boasted.

"Oh, you will, Perditious One? I think it's time you learned not to laugh at your elders, Unholy One, so you will never grow up to be a Man of Sin. In fact, it's time for you to not grow up at all!"

And with that, Mabus's father grabbed him by his beautiful blonde hair, and lifted him two feet into the air. Mabus's school-books went flying to the floor as his father hauled him upstairs to the bathroom. Each step his father made up the steps, Mabus could hear popping noises of his hair ripping out of his scalp. Mabus would have cried out to his mother, but she would have just turned away, paralyzed by fear.

"Liar, liar, pants on fire!" the maniacal man chortled, as he began dunking his son's head into the toilet. "Witches like you deserve to burn. But this is the most I can do to make you pay. That's exactly what they told me, and I know they're right about you!"

Mabus gasped and choked for air and fought his father's strong grip as his head was repeatedly forced into the filthy, grimy toilet. He was starting to drown when his father, distracted, released his grip slightly and Mabus managed to gasp.

His mother had timidly crept to the top of the stairs and Mabus heard her whimper, "Phone call for you, honey. It's from work, and they say it's very important."

Mabus's father paused, then sighed. "Terrible timing," he thought, but he couldn't make the boss wait, no matter what. He released his grip on Mabus's hair and stood up. Nearly unconscious, Mabus felt his head bang against the toilet lid. It jarred him awake. Through blurry eyes, he saw his father's backside strut from the room and he righted himself on the cold tile floor, blinking. Just before his father had stopped, the aching lad had seen the fiery ball again. This time he'd also heard a voice. "Don't worry. We are going to save you," it said, sounding strangely like Mabus's own voice.

But Mabus didn't trust that anyone would save him. Fighting dizziness, he stood up and crept down the staircase. He heard his father talking on the kitchen phone as he slipped silently, unnoticed, from the house. He gently clicked the front door shut, and turned and ran as fast as he could, away from the house, his father, his mother, and the shadows in his bedroom. With every step, he felt the distance from them grow, and with the distance there grew a surprising, liberating freedom. The air felt refreshingly cool and soothing on his wet, pounding head as he ran. He knew that this was the last time he would run away from home, and that he would never return. He passed the house with the daffodils and turned for a quick glimpse of their sunny heads. They seemed to wink and say, "It's a new life for us both!"

But what a life it was! Mabus quickly learned the ways of the streets. He stole food to eat, committed petty crimes to survive and slept wherever he could—in alleyways, doorways, and abandoned cars. He stopped going to school. Though he missed his friends, he knew his father would look for him there. He had to think of his own survival.

To get around, Mabus frequently hitchhiked. Most of the people who picked him up seemed kind, but usually they wouldn't ask Mabus any personal questions, even when he felt their eyes on his dirty clothing. The one exception was a woman in a beat-up old Ford who asked, "You haven't sold your body yet, son, have you?" Mabus wasn't sure exactly what to say. He'd been tempted to once when he was really hungry. Mabus turned and noticed her leathery hands firmly grasping the steering wheel. Her steel-blue, unblinking eyes squinted straight ahead. She hadn't seemed that old when she'd picked him up, but now, as Mabus looked closely at her profile, he noticed exhaustion etched into the fine lines around her tight mouth and tired eyes. Life itself had aged her, not the years.

"Trust me, son, don't do it, no matter how bad it gets," she said before Mabus could stammer an answer. "You'll never be the same."

When she dropped him off, she reached into her worn purse and took out ten dollars, avoiding eye contact the whole time. "I wish I had more to give you. You take care of yourself," she softly murmured before driving away. She didn't glance in her mirror or look back. Mabus found other ways to survive.

When he was thirteen years old, something happened that would strip Mabus of what was left of his childhood. Like his father had often said, he would have to pay eventually for all of his petty crimes, lies, and deceptions. Most especially, he'd pay for the little white lies he had told himself over the years. In fact, he was to make the ultimate sacrifice for his "sinfulness and lawlessness."

Chapter Two

IT WAS JUNE 6TH—HIS THIRTEENTH birthday—and since it was so nice out, Mabus decided to give himself a present and hitchhike out to the countryside. He always enjoyed exploring the wide-open spaces; he would imagine what his future would be like—out in a cowfield or clover-dotted pasture. He would gaze into the skies for hours watching the clouds change into lifelike characters and cartoons. He found that just by changing his perspective, the gauzy forms he saw could transform into a whole different image, making the previous picture disappear. He was fascinated by these transformations which were at work all around him.

Life on his own had made Mabus quite strong and willful, but with no more formal schooling to his name, he was clearly headed nowhere. Even with his intelligence, good looks, and physical strength, he had no job prospects in sight. Sometimes he thought of getting a job pumping gas somewhere, but he also enjoyed being free.

He was having a hard time getting a ride that morning, even downtown, so when Mabus spotted a large, impossibly shiny black van with tinted windows, he thought, "Hey, it's my birthday, I deserve to ride in style." He got the invisible driver to pull over by jerking up his pant leg and showing off his bare calf, like he had seen the female prostitutes do.

The passenger door of the van popped open. Mabus trotted over to the van and saw the man who had leaned over to let him in. The man's deep-set eyes and upper half of his face were obscured in shadow under the brim of a black baseball cap. A few gray hairs protruded from under the cap at the temples. Mabus laughed and said he only wanted a ride out of the city.

"Fine," replied the man. His voice sounded friendly, though a little scratchy with age. "Get in, I've been expecting you. We're going to have a really good time, just the two of us."

Mabus smelled beer on the man's breath, but he wasn't afraid; since he'd left home, he hadn't been afraid of anything, not anymore. So he wasn't greatly alarmed either when the driver casually offered him a can of cold beer, even though Mabus was clearly underage.

Mabus didn't usually drink, but the day was hot and the beer was cold and free. He downed the entire can quickly while he talked and joked with the man. Soon he was downing a second can while the driver savored his. The man never offered his name nor asked Mabus for his, and Mabus didn't much care; he had learned not to make attachments to anyone too quickly, especially people he would probably never see again.

Grey pavement gave way to green, lush grass and scenery as they drove well out into the country. Mabus peered through the tinted windows and imagined many great pyramids and structures. He used to wonder to himself, trying to figure out not only how they had built the great pyramids, but why.

The landscape grew greener and greener, and the roads they drove looked less and less traveled, until finally they turned onto a dirt road. It had been about twenty minutes since they had passed the last farmhouse they'd seen. Mabus could hear small rocks kicking up under the van's sleek tires as he told the man about his structures. "Do you think aliens could have built the pyramids?" Mabus asked the man.

"Mmm, that's pretty far-fetched," muttered the driver. He seemed distracted.

It didn't bother Mabus that the driver didn't share his enthusiasm. He was happy; he was in the country in a fancy black van, feeling good. So far, it was turning out to be a great birthday.

Mabus gulped the last bit of beer in his third can. "Got any more?" he slurred. The beer was the only thing he had consumed yet that day, and the liquor hit his empty stomach hard.

The driver's mouth curled into a broad smile. "I got a great stash of twenty-year-old Scotch hidden under here," the strange man boasted, pointing under his seat. "Heh, I'm sure it's even older than you, and I know where we can enjoy it in total privacy, my dear Lawless One."

Slumped in his seat, Mabus jerked halfway upright when the driver called him that, he rationalized that it was pretty obvious he was a juvenile delinquent.

For the first time that day, Mabus felt a seed of discomfort in his belly. Yeah, he was drunk, and maybe he wasn't seeing things clearly, but still, hadn't they been on that dirt road for ages now? The van's tires still kicked up the rocks, but it was less frequent now. Mabus narrowed his eyes to listen for the "ping" as each one hit the metal underside of the van. The dirt road was drier now, and great clouds of brown dust billowed at the windows. Mabus imagined the sleek van now dull with dust and dirt, and dented and scratched on the underside from all the rocks. The seed of fear in his belly had now sprouted, and through the haze of beer and dust, he struggled to deny he felt it. "Anywhere's fine with me now, anywhere", he thought. "Nothing's gonna go wrong on such a nice day, my birthday, no less! Who cares?"

But now he also heard something whispering in his head, like many dim voices. The voices said *they* cared, and they were going to do something soon, before it was too late. Mabus thought he heard them hiss of ". . . making a deal with them," but he wasn't sure.

"Yeah, go ahead and make the deal," he mumbled under his breath. He wanted to pacify the voices and make them shut up. "Just cut me in, too. Who's it with?"

The van suddenly jerked left and swerved through the wide-open gates of a gigantic, deserted dumpsite. A faded, hand-lettered wooden sign over the gates read "Sheol Transfer Station." This was a local joke, being that there was a small town nearby called Salem, short for Jerusalem.

"Welcome to Hell," the driver slowly and dramatically cackled. "Last stop for you! Time to have fun, and to die slowly."

Laughing and snorting, the old man guided the van up to a sky-high pile of trash. He fished under the seat for the bottle of scotch and leaped out the van door and over to the passenger door with an agility and speed beyond his years. He pulled the sleepy boy out the door and to his feet, leading him to what was left of an old, lime-green couch.

"I'm going to be generous and let you sample some of this fine old scotch before the real fun begins. I don't want you to put up any fight."

"Huh?" mumbled Mabus, sliding onto the couch. It was missing most of its cushions, and cheap foam stuffing protruded like a pale tongue from a hole in one of its arms.

The man sat down next to Mabus, unscrewed the cap of the bottle and took a swig. He then put his arm around Mabus's shoulders and righted him, for he had started to slide down onto the arm of the couch where the foam tongue protruded. He supported Mabus with his right arm and lifted the bottle to his lips with his left hand.

"Come on, drink!" the man growled, and the feel of the glass bottle neck clinking against his front teeth jolted Mabus into awareness. For a brief moment, Mabus's fear cut through his drunkenness; the seed in his belly had now fully bloomed into a thorny vine. Mabus imagined the vine growing in thickness and length, feeding on the alcohol in his belly, curling around itself like a snake, shooting out sharp thorns along its entire length that cut into his insides.

The man was forcing him to drink, and Mabus choked the bitter liquid down before he drowned in it. Again and again he swallowed, until the man seemed satisfied and relaxed his grip. Mabus collapsed again over the arm of the couch and put his hand over his eyes to block out the man, the coach, and the thorns in his belly. Sleep beckoned, and he surrendered gratefully. His eyelids closed over his innocent green eyes.

"Now the preordained fun begins," sighed the old man. "It's only what you owe us, little Beast," he said to Mabus's sleeping form. "For we are the saved, and are not ever the ones to blame. Our puppet friend Jesus will be sure to forgive us."

He turned Mabus over, face up. The boy was vaguely aware of his shirt being unbuttoned and his jeans being pulled down, and he started dreaming of when his mother undressed him for bed as a young child. The dream suddenly changed; he imagined himself being tossed over onto his aching stomach and spanked hard on the backside.

The pain jerked Mabus awake long enough for him to feel the man behind him. "Yeah, yeah, that's the stuff, you Son of Perdition!" cried the man. "I haven't had sex like this in over a thousand years!" The thorny vine in Mabus's stomach now seemed to have found an escape through his anus. He surrendered again to unconsciousness, all the while picturing the thorns now tearing at his colon.

"I KNOW HOW to wake you up," the older man viciously growled, pulling out a razor-sharp five-inch Bowie knife. Gently, almost austerely, he rose from the couch, putting the knife directly under Mabus's small and beardless chin. Then he shook the boy to wake him, while grinning proudly. At last his kind would succeed in ruling all, for the world was now theirs.

"Wake up, boy, you're about to get whacked. Here's your second smile."

"No!" cried Mabus as the knife began to slice into his delicate, pale throat. He forced his chin down tightly and whimpered. It was happening all over again, and this time he felt weird and wet down around his anus. His head began spinning like a giant wheel of fire.

"It's far too late for you to save yourself," the man spat. "You're dead meat, and about to fully pay for your many mortal sins." He went on. "You think you're funny, Deceiver? Here, let me put that big smile upstairs!" and he viciously carved a wide swath straight across Mabus's terrified face, laying his cheeks open from ear to ear. "And here's some more where that came from!" the man crowed. He reached into the boy's open, screaming mouth and grabbed his tongue. The whiskey had dried it out enough for him to get a firm hold. All it took was one quick slice with the knife, and the tongue was free. The man stuffed it into Mabus's open shirt pocket.

"Now you'll be telling no one of this, Liar! You will never deny that our Jesus is the one and only Christ! And you will never order the rebuilding of the temple in Jerusalem!"

Mabus screamed even louder in pain and fear. The man finally released him from his surprisingly strong grip, and he fell back upon the green couch, struggling not to choke on his own blood.

The hideous man walked swiftly to the van, reached once more under the seat, and came back pointing a Glock 18 pistol at Mabus. "This is to make sure we win. Say 'Hi' to your buddy Satan for us," he laughed as he emptied the bullets into Mabus's narrow chest.

He paused, looking at his work. "It is finished," he sighed. "Time to report back." He turned to walk to the van and glanced back for one last look at Mabus. Noticing the knife where it had fallen in the dirt, the man rushed back to the sofa, grabbed it, and buried it up to the hilt into what was left of the boy's heaving chest. Mabus's small heart pumped and pumped to compensate for the loss of blood. With a deeply contented smile, the awful man left Mabus for dead; a twisted wrenched corpse where there had once been a sweet and loving boy. The vehicle's tires squealed as its driver fled the hideous scene.

THAT NIGHT, MABUS woke up—not in the afterlife, but in a hospital. His chest, face and throat were thickly wrapped in bandages. He licked his dry lips. His tongue had been reattached. The medical team had managed to piece him back together.

Mabus found out later that the fire department had gotten an anonymous phone call at exactly six o'clock. The tipster had described the van and its driver in great detail. While police looked for the driver, the paramedics found Mabus. Miraculously, he was still clinging to life when they arrived in their screaming white ambulance, though they at first thought he was dead.

Mabus vaguely remembered bouncing around in the back of the ambulance, one paramedic shouting over the din of the siren at the other who was driving. Then the siren stopped, and he felt his body being lifted and wheeled about. He felt many hands flitting about his body; some felt for the pulse in his wrist, while others lifted his eyelids and shone lights into his eyes. Still others pressed absorbent gauze onto his many wounds. And there were voices, too—voices shouting for gauze packs, syringes, saline. The last words Mabus remembered, though, were those of a doctor who leaned in close, transfixed by the boy's bloody face, and muttered, "Twenty years, and I've never seen anything like this. There's no way this kid should be alive!"

BUT MABUS WAS alive, and he stayed that way. In only four weeks, he regained much of his strength, although he did thin out a bit, living on a menu of juice and yogurt. The boy was unable to eat because his tongue was swollen and hard from being cut off. His speech was almost back to normal and the only obvious evidence of his ordeal were the scars that remained on his face—two broad cuts across his cheeks, three inches wide on either side of his mouth. In time, they faded into thin white lines. They vaguely resembled an old-fashioned Teutonic saber deuling scar, and Mabus would later joke about his "sword wound."

While Mabus was recuperating, the police launched an extensive search for his attacker, but all their leads turned up empty; he was never found.

Mabus's body had suffered greatly from the rape and mutilation, but the worst wounds were the ones inflicted on his psyche. Fortunately, the hospital had a staff of accomplished counselors.

Mabus found the emotional healing he needed with a very kind counselor named Christina. She was in her thirties, trim and girlish in her long tweed skirt and lacy blouse, yet her face had seen much suffering. She carefully guided him through dream imagery and helped him understand that the incident had not been his own fault. She would sneak candy bars and soda into his room. "I wouldn't do this for just anybody, Mabus. You know I could lose my job. But I tell you, Mabus, I'd do it again for ya. Besides, you could use the extra pounds. You don't tell, I won't tell. How's that?"

Though Mabus hated the memory of the kidnapping and rape, he was grateful that the incident brought him in touch with the counselor; she helped him heal from the years of abuse at the hands of his father and the tough life on the streets. She gave him faith that there were people in the world who cared, but he knew they were few and far between. He kept talking with her, sharing his adventures of the streets, and she was relieved and impressed that he was holding up so well. Surprisingly, the boy showed no signs of ever having been traumatized.

Because of all the attention of the media, CPS was on the chopping block for not investigating past complaints by the school. They were partially to blame for the boy's fate. If CPS had intervened properly before, this event might not have happened.

Shortly thereafter, Mabus was released from the hospital, into the custody of CPS. The nurses there had grown to care about the resilient boy, and they tearfully bid him farewell, especially Christina. Mabus had grown very fond of her, and she was one of the few adults that Mabus trusted.

Mabus didn't fit well in the foster homes CPS put him in. He felt like an intruder to these foster families. The streets, and the independence they conferred, were where Mabus felt he belonged. The independence of the great grey outdoors conferred upon Mabus a deep, concrete sense of belonging. He returned to the only home he knew—the streets.

Mabus was a survivor. He made decisions for his survival. He became distrustful of adults, governments, and authorities. All had let him down. He had known from an early age how to live life—on guard. Since the beginning of his existence, the people he had trusted the most, with a childlike vulnerability, had been the very ones who sought to destroy him.

In between stays with his neighborhood friends, he often found refuge in newspaper recycling boxes. One morning, Mabus awoke to find newspapers being hurled at him. Although it was a rude awakening for Mabus, he nearly gave the old man depositing the papers a heart attack.

Mabus learned how to break into vacant houses. Usually, the power was still on, as were the utilities. He had all the comforts of home at his fingertips. He found out soon enough that he couldn't stay in the houses for very long when he woke up to a real estate agent showing the house. While the agent stood there, startled and terrified, he made a dash for the back door, escaping. Luckily, he was never caught. He soon got a pretty good system down. He even seemed to be enjoying himself.

Mabus loved going to the donut store down the way. They only served up fresh donuts in the morning, so all the leftover donuts in the evening were thrown away in the dumpster. Now, Mabus loved donuts. Even the shame of eating out of a dumpster didn't stop him from tearing into those chocolate-covered donuts. One night, a chubby, brown-visored Hispanic employee noticed Mabus out there. She asked her boss if she could just give him the donuts instead of throwing them away. He rejected her plea, telling her about the store's strict policy not to give away any donuts, and saying it was unfair to the paying customers. She still felt she had to do something, given Mabus's age. She started boxing them up, and double-bagging them, so Mabus could take the donuts with him and so that they might be kept sanitary. He gave her an appreciative wave every time he saw her.

Now, that wasn't the only trick Mabus had up his sleeve. This one took a little more skill. He would call the nearest pizza place and order three large pizzas with anchovies and hot peppers, for pickup. Now, nobody likes anchovies, or hot peppers—but combining the two is even worse. Mabus didn't mind. He loved anchovies and spicy food. He would wait two hours. And soon, because they couldn't bear the smell, the pizza place's employees would throw the pizza in the dumpster. Then Mabus would once again eat like a king.

MABUS KNEW THAT a life of doughnuts and pizzas wasn't going to last. During one of his routine panhandling sessions, Mabus heard a voice shout, "Get a job!" He suddenly thought, "Yes! That's exactly what I need." He was very optimistic about finding a job. He felt the days were a bit boring, and that a job would be just what he needed to occupy his time. He took the loose change he had just panhandled and bought himself a newspaper. An ad read, "Carpenter's assistant needed. Apply in person at 1976 Old Berry Road."

Chapter Three

HE CARPENTER'S HOUSE WAS OUT in the country, down a lonely, unmarked road. Mabus remembered the last time he had been down a road so desolate—three years ago, to the day—and he felt uneasy. But this time he knew where he was going, and his friend was driving him. Mabus calmed himself with deep breaths as they drove along, all the while reminding himself that this job could be the ticket to fulfilling his dreams.

The carpenter was looking for an apprentice. Though regular jobs didn't usually appeal to him, Mabus knew he could learn a lot as a carpenter's assistant, and perhaps maybe even become a carpenter himself. "Seems like a fun job, too," Mabus thought.

They reached the house, and Mabus asked his friend to wait for him in the car. He had grown more aware of his personal safety, and he wanted to have a means of escape should he need it.

The old wooden house must have been there a long time, for it seemed that it had become very comfortable, with the lush trees and greenery around it. Mabus noticed that the house stood on stilts about three feet off the ground. To distract himself from the pounding in his chest, he imagined the house not really sitting on the ground, but defying gravity. The house seemed to float just above the Earth, the thick ivy reaching from the ground like long, leafy green fingers, holding it firm so it wouldn't float completely away.

But the steps of the house felt firm and strong beneath Mabus's feet as he climbed them to reach the door. He smoothed his clothes—he had worn the best he had—took a deep breath, and arranged his mouth into a wide, eager smile. He knocked.

17

"Yeah, who is it? If you're here for the assistant's position, I already hired someone," came a faint voice drifting through the door from deep inside.

"Just my luck," Mabus thought gloomily, "This is how my life always turns out." He considered trying again at the gas station down the street from where he was staying with one of his friends. He turned to leave, but the voice in his head—a distant, more mature version of his own voice—told him to wait.

"Hold it," the faint voice from inside said, seeming to float on the gentle breeze blowing outside the door. It merged with the other voice, the one in his head. Mabus wasn't sure which one was which.

"I forgot, that guy said he couldn't make it out today, so I'm not hiring him. Come in the back, you're not going to get through the front door with all the books I got piled up against it!"

Mabus wasn't proud and he was always willing to oblige. Besides, he wanted the job badly. His small feet flattened a narrow path in the tall grass as he moved to the back of the house. He saw a rickety-looking wooden porch. He heard the gurgle of water and noticed a shallow, wide river cutting through marking the rear of the property. Mabus slipped on the first porch step and almost fell. The steps were covered with green, slippery slime from the last time heavy rains had caused the river to overflow. No wonder the house was on stilts.

Mabus firmly held onto the rickety railing and slowly climbed the steps. With every movement, he was afraid the railing would come off in his hand. This would end up being the first challenge from the man Mabus was later to refer to as "The Master." Finally making it to the door, Mabus knocked once again.

"Come in, and enter of your own free will," boomed the voice in a theatrical Bela Lugosi monotone. The voice sounded closer than before, and now stronger than his own.

Mabus smiled at the joke. He had seen all the Bela Lugosi vampire movies, almost every vampire movie ever made. He loved vampires and couldn't understand why people thought they were scary. They could make you live forever if you wanted to. Mabus liked the idea of living forever but not the idea of growing older, so he identified with vampires.

Mabus twisted the large doorknob and the heavy, unlocked door swung open. He slowly, cautiously stepped inside, and was nearly knocked over at the sight of thick books, hundreds of them, lining the walls on shelf after shelf, stretching up to the ceiling. Although the shelves and the palatial room in general were both dusty and messy, the books all looked clean, as though they were being either constantly cared for or persistently read. "The guy living here must be a genius," Mabus thought. And then he saw the computer system.

It was a cleverly arranged network consisting of four computers, three of them desktop machines and one of them a laptop. A jumbled mass of multicolored wires and cables connected the computers to each other and a large printer like umbilical cords. The whole system covered every square inch of an imposing, old-fashioned wooden dining room table. The man with the Bela Lugosi voice was sitting at one of the interconnected terminals, busily typing away.

"Come in, come in," said the grimacing carpenter, without lifting his eyes from the monitor. "I'm just posting on a bulletin board that tells the truth about government and religious conspiracies in America. You know the government—always trying to control our minds and tell us what to do, where to go, how to wipe our asses."

Mabus didn't know what the man was talking about, since he hadn't been to school in years and didn't keep current with what was happening in the world. At the library, though, everything was free to read, and Mabus devoured books there. The only things he wouldn't read were the magazines and newspapers, because something about them scared him, and the Bible, because he regarded it as a pack of lies.

"I'll wrap this up now. Okay, kid, sit over here and tell me your life story," the man said, nodding toward a large leather chair next to the table and double-clicking the computer mouse with a flourish. There was a teetering pile of computer disks stacked on the seat of the chair. "Just shove those somewhere, kid," the man said. Mabus carefully gathered the disks, fighting the nervous trembling in his hands. He figured the disks were important and he didn't want to drop them all over the floor. He managed to stack them neatly on top of a serious-looking book on the floor next to the chair.

Mabus sat down, and the man finally looked squarely at him. The man's steel-grey hair framed a face weathered by outdoor life rather than age. That made it hard for Mabus to guess how old he was; he could have been anywhere from fifty to seventy years old.

The man's face wrinkled into a frown after a few long seconds of silence. "What's wrong with you, kid, Bush got your tongue?"

After a long moment, Mabus finally spoke. "I'm sorry, sir. I didn't get the joke. What bush?"

For a moment, the man looked as though he thought that the boy might be crazy, or mentally retarded.

"You don't know who Bush is? He's the guy who's gonna found the Bush Dynasty, establish a New World Order, and keep our minds entranced for all infinity, that's who he is. I wouldn't be surprised if his son runs for President sometime in the future, and enslaves us all. These politicians are vicious. Once they stick their bloodsucking tentacles into your wallet and get a taste, the greedier they get. Oh yah! They'll suck ya dry."

"Really? That's fascinating," Mabus said. "I didn't know anything about that. I came here to apply for the carpenter's apprentice job. If it's still open, I promise I'll stick with the job and work very hard for you."

Mabus knew exactly what to say. He had learned job search tactics at a free class offered through a homeless shelter. He had been on the streets for what felt like forever, but he was determined to have a real future. He wasn't sure yet exactly what he wanted to do for work, but he knew this job would be a stepping stone in the right direction. He considered getting his GED and earning money for college. Then again, he could remain a carpenter and spend his life reading space books and hatching theories. Yet he had a real drive to get something accomplished, especially regarding the mysteries of the pyramids. Mabus was fascinated with the Egyptians, and how they might have erected the pyramids.

"You came to the right place, but I don't know about you. You look sorta like a dumb blonde, if you don't mind my sayin' so." The man said. More silence. "You always this talkative, or did somebody stick a plunger up your butt?"

The man smiled, obviously pleased with his own humor. When he did, Mabus thought he looked like the driver of the dark van. Mabus glared at the man. His anger was slowly mounting.

"What's your name, kid? Mine's Napoleon, Bonaparte Napoleon—the exact reverse of the famous dictator. You can call me Boone, everyone else does. Say, you look about sixteen. Is that how old you are?"

Mabus was nodding before the man had finished asking. He was tightly reining in his emotions; there had been too many things so far that day—the country, this man—that reminded him of the day he was raped, and it was getting difficult to keep his composure.

He began thinking about the crying fits he often had, especially after his nightmares. He could tell now that the dreams were about the end of the world, and he was pretty sure a comet was going to collide with the Earth on a certain very important and significant day. For some reason, he wasn't sure if it was a past event that he was dreaming about, or one in the future. How this could be, he didn't know.

Mabus managed to snap himself back to attention. "I've got my GED, too," he lied. The people at the counseling center had told him that without a high school education, he would never get hired. So he was planning on lying at all of his interviews. He could read, write and do basic math, so he figured he could fool people.

Boone spoke. "Did you know that the Emperor Napoleon was only sixteen when he became an artillery officer in the French army in 1785? It didn't take him long to become dictator of France after that. Some people even think he was the first Antichrist, like Nostradamus said. I don't have any plans to rule the world, but I keep my mind clean by devouring at least five books a day, every single day. How about you?"

"I thought you were a carpenter, not a...I'm sorry, I hope I haven't said anything wrong," Mabus muttered. He noticed the web page displayed on Boone's computer screen. In large letters, he saw "666—Number of the Beast, or Number of Those Who Dominate the World?" Something about the number 666 stirred in Mabus a vague but pleasant memory—something about the beginnings of something big, something destined to change his entire outlook. He often had such déjà vu experiences, but he dismissed them. He'd read somewhere that people often mistake the present for the past.

"An ineffectual? Yeah, that's me," Boone said. "I'm a hopeless ineffectual—that's an inefficient intellectual, in case you were wondering. That's a panjandrum word, mind you, straight out of

Alice Through the Looking Glass. So's the Clinton administration, but I guess you don't know about that," said Boone, rolling his eyes. He was beginning to think he would be better off looking for someone else, someone he could actually converse with.

"Most people think that the poem 'Jabberwocky' is from *Alice in Wonderland.* But I happen to know it's not," said Mabus suddenly, the words tumbling out of him like water from a spilled cup. "It's from Lewis Carroll's other 'Alice' book, *Alice Through the Looking Glass.*" He had read both books twice at the library.

"You know, you're right. I was starting to think you were kinda empty upstairs," Boone said, tapping his temple with a calloused index finger, "but maybe you're not." He turned off his computer monitor. "Say, how do you feel about living off the land? I can't put you up in here—the back bedroom's full of books and my unpublished papers, but I've got a nice single-wide trailer with a cut-out on my land you can live in. And since this gig doesn't pay a lot, you can catch wild geese, ducks and fish, of course, out by the river. Job pays seven dollars an hour to start, and when you reach journeyman, maybe we can raise your wages. But you'll probably move on from there."

Mabus was floored. In an instant, his anger vanished, giving way to gratitude and the desire to work hard. He was suddenly aware of just how tired he was of always being one step away from jail, starvation, death, or worse. And through it all, he lived in constant fear that someone was coming after him. He didn't know who it could be, though he knew it had something to do with his father.

"Maybe this Boone guy is all right, like my street buddies," Mabus thought. "Show me the trailer," he said, trying not to sound too eager. "I'll do anything you want me to do—well, almost anything."

After talking to Boone a few more minutes, Mabus carefully descended the back porch steps and went to the front of the house to thank his friend for the ride. As he heard him driving away, he looked again at the house on stilts and imagined he was floating three feet off the ground, too.

MABUS HAD LONG ago developed a sense of situational ethics. He accommodated easily to whatever situation he found himself in, as long as it could help him get ahead, make himself some friends, or get by financially. So although Boone's trailer turned out to be filthy, Mabus had it fixed up within a few days. He cleaned it inside and out with a mop, broom, soap, and a bunch of rags he'd found in a small shed nearby. He dusted the few old pieces of furniture inside and arranged them to his liking. It was starting to feel like a home, the first home of his own.

When he was done, Mabus proudly showed Boone his handiwork. Boone was so impressed, he asked the boy to clean up the main house, too. Mabus was happy to clean the old rooms and make them as dust-free as the books. He found the cleaning work strangely appealing, almost therapeutic. When he was done with each room, he would stand in the dark oak doorway and proudly admire the way he had created order from clutter and chaos. "Perhaps," he pondered as he scrubbed and polished, "the trailer and this old house are just the beginning. Maybe it's not too late to turn my life into something great, too—maybe even the life of anyone who wants to follow my example."

MABUS BECAME BOONE'S once-per-week housekeeper while also training as his carpentry assistant. Boone showed him how to make furniture and cabinets, which were the bulk of his carpentry trade. Boone's fine, one-of-a-kind artistic pieces fetched the most money and allowed him to afford his computer equipment. Mabus loved the countryside outside Boone's home. The fresh air and wonderful smell of plants growing made him feel alive, and he would often sit riverside at the edge of Boone's property, trying to tickle a trout or two out of the water and into his hands. On the other side of the river sat the grounds of a large mansion, which Boone said belonged to a high and mighty government official. Mabus never saw anyone from there except a cowed-looking Mexican gardener, riding a lawn tractor.

Boone proved to be Mabus's opposite—a man of many rather than few words. He would often corner Mabus in odd moments, start a monologue about government conspiracies and how the Jews, Catholics and Protestants were controlling the United States.

"And there's some group I'm always hearing of called the Illuminati," he'd say. "They purportedly founded America, wrote the Declaration of Independence and the Constitution, and created the Great Seal of the USA. You can see all their stuff on the Seal, which was totally designed by the Society of Freemasons. The

Illuminati are kind of a bastard branch of the Masons, who will stop at nothing to control the world.

"There are thirteen leaves on the olive branch and in the right claw of the eagle and thirty-two long feathers on the right wing, symbolizing the basic thirty-two degrees of Freemasonry. There are thirteen granite stones in the pyramid, and its thirteen layers all represent the thirteen bloodlines of the Illuminati. Some people think that's why there were thirteen original colonies. Some really reputable people say these cats run our government, and maybe the entire world. I don't really know a lot about them. They keep things pretty secretive nowadays. But you can't hide something that big forever, you know."

"Tell me more," Mabus would beg. As Boone often didn't have the answers to all his questions, he would point out certain books to him, telling him to study them carefully.

"But don't always believe what you see. You've got to read with an open mind, but cross-check all of the references. Be very careful when something is published by a church or a government, or even NASA. They all have vested interests in keeping our minds clouded. Don't believe in anything that seems to be an attempt to control your thinking.

"Don't buy into these politics. What you see is not what you get," Boone often explained to Mabus. "These guys aren't just politicians, they're businessmen. The decisions made in the government move a lot of money. The government spends our hard-earned money on independent contracting companies that these politicians own."

"That makes so much sense, Boone," said Mabus. "That's probably why the beginning of contractor is 'con'!"

"It's not just the contractors, Mabus. These judges that get elected are known for taking kickbacks. You don't know how many times I've heard, 'I've got friends in high places.' These judges and lawyers eat their lunches together, and discuss our cases with each other. Where's the confidentiality that we're promised? Are these guys mak'in deals behind closed doors? 'I'll let you have this one, but the next case is mine.'

"We trust these people to make decisions based on evidence, and justice, not for personal gain. Yet this goes on every day. Hell, one time, I had to hire a lawyer from another state, just to make sure I was being represented with my interest in mind. These local courthouses are filled with the same lawyers and judges every day, who practically consider each other co-workers. How can you be sure that the case you just lost wasn't a favor for a co-worker whom they have to see on a daily basis?"

Boone's eyes lit up with the fire of his convictions and the flame of his anger. He went on.

"And that's not all. These so-called non-profit charity funds, they're just the same. The only way true evil can exist is through the disguise of goodness. The charity organization itself is nonprofit. And every audit would prove that to be true. But the contractors, my friend, the contractors whom these organizations hire, they profit. They profit well! And in return, the people in charge of hiring these contractors get a little kickback. We call it 'grease money.' And that's what makes the world go 'round, grease!'"

FROM BOONE, MABUS slowly learned even more about thinking for himself, asking pertinent questions, what books were the best and most honest ones to read and, most importantly, how to approach his daily life with inner strength and deep pride in himself. In Boone, Mabus found a mentor whom he felt he could finally trust. He was deeply inspired by Boone's passion when he preached about conspiracies. He loved the way he would shake his fist as he spoke. Boone would get so angry. It definitely ingrained some suspicions into Mabus about charities, governments, NASA, and religious groups.

Mabus loved books written by Jules Verne. Some people saw him as a prophet because of the amazing futuristic things he wrote about that came true—for example, *20,000 Leagues Under the Sea*, where he wrote about submarines and technologies unheard of in that time. Another example of his prescience was *Journey to the Center of the Earth*, where people were trapped in a prehistoric time. And through reading the more honest and truthful literature, Mabus found a gold mine of information to help him completely formulate his radical theories.

One day Mabus was doing his usual research on the planets when he stumbled upon a website. The site claimed pyramids had been found on the surface of Mars, and that these pyramids were in a similar formation to the ones on Earth. It also stated that a face that resembled the Sphinx was also photographed in this region of Mars, which was technically known as Cydonia, or Cydonian Mars.

Ideas started racing in Mabus's head. The nightmares of a comet destroying Earth were flashing back. He thought, "What would Earth look like if it had been hit by that comet?" Then it dawned on him that it would look similar to Mars. He finally realized the truth, and it was highly incredible, but absolutely real. The pyramids on Cydonian Mars were indeed the exact same ones, he figured, with some adjustments for the great amount of time that had passed, as the ones on Earth. Mars had not always been the Red Planet. Venus, roughly the same size as Earth, is a chemical-soaked hothouse. He began to ponder the idea of Mars being Earth in the future. He thought, "Could it be possible that Venus is Earth in the past?"

Indeed, Venus could be very hospitable to inhabitants. But it lacked one important thing: water. Mabus realized Venus also needed a comet to hit it, in order for it to sustain life. A comet would bring death to Earth, and life to Venus. The impact of the comet, which was far bigger than any space debris that Mabus had ever read about, must be the cause of the cataclysmic event. He could feel it in his bones, and he knew it well.

Now all that remained was for Mabus to prove his theory that Earth had once been Venus, and was eventually going to become the planet Mars. He decided the only true way to test the theory was to build a pyramid and see if it appeared on Mars, as the Egyptians did thousand of years ago. Mabus thought, "Maybe the Egyptians built this pyramid for that specific purpose—to warn man of his destiny. The pyramids are basically manmade mountains. Geological mountains are made of solid rock, so when the Earth shifts, the mountain crumbles. But a manmade mountain is made of thousands of individual stones perfectly stacked, which allows the pyramid to withstand the Earth's shifts and earthquakes." Mabus was certain he was onto something big.

When Mabus's head filled with such big ideas, he sometimes needed a break. He would often go to the riverbank and beguile away the time drifting his hands in the water, searching for the perfect trout to catch. One day, he was fishing and thinking by the bank when he heard a rustle in the grass on the other side of the creek. He looked up and saw a girl of about his age, dipping her bare feet in the water. She had beautiful short golden blonde hair in a neat bob, high cheekbones, fascinating narrow blue eyes, a coltish body with small, firm breasts neatly concealed under her costly silk blouse, and a smile that was at once pleasant and disarming.

"Who are you?" the girl asked.

"I'm Mabus. Who are you?"

"I'm Eva. Eva Salvatore. I live in the house back there." She pointed back toward the mansion in the far distance. "My daddy is Senator Salvatore. He's in Washington right now." Mabus bristled. He remembered what Boone had told him about government officials.

"Who are his contractors?" Mabus asked sharply.

"Contractors? I don't know what you mean. You mean the people that come over and fix our house?"

"No, I mean the ones he gives all the people's money to."

"It still sounds like you're talking about the people that come and fix our house."

"I mean the ones he helps."

"Oh. You must mean the people who come to black-tie dinners at our house. There are bankers and manufacturers and all. Most all of them need Daddy's help."

"Yeah, that's the ticket. You mean like the manufacturers who believe in 'clean coal,' and the bankers who believe in maximizing their profits on debtors for a good bottom line."

"Sure. Daddy always says that we own the environment, and that people should pay what they owe."

Mabus couldn't tell about this girl: was she as sweet as she looked, or was she as evil as her father? As he looked into her narrow eyes with their glittering blue irises, he felt uncannily like he did during his dreams, but this time, instead of wiping out his vision, the ball of fire rubbed up against him, and he could feel a shiver of warmth against his body. His street instincts, honed by years of homelessness, were what he usually trusted, but this time his gut was no use at all. He decided to play along for a while.

"I can understand that," Mabus lied. He found that if he shifted a little to the right, he could see how the sun shone through and showed him the profile of her breasts through the fabric of her blouse. He shuddered a little at his strange combination of desire and dread. "It's nice to know about your father, but what do you do?" he asked. "Oh, I'm a student at Choate. I'm just out here for break." Mabus didn't know what or where Choate was, but the way she said it made him think that it must be a very fancy place indeed.

Eva put her feet into the river and waded over to Mabus's side. Fortunately, there wasn't much of a current. Mabus didn't like the proximity, but Eva stayed a few feet away from him. "I'm a student, too," said Mabus. "I study carpentry with Boone, and I'm also studying the secret history of mankind and the universe." Eva's eyes lit up a little. "How very interesting," she said in a soft, thoughtful voice. Mabus could not tell what she thought of him, but he had a small inkling that she was going to draw him out on his beliefs just as he had done to her.

Mabus took the bait. For twenty minutes or more, he lectured her on all the things he had learned: the origin of the world; the pyramids of Cydonia; the evils of the monetary systems; the influence of the Illuminati upon NASA and all other governmental institutions; the fraudulence of religion and charities; and esoteric astronomy. Like Boone and Mabus himself, she seemed to have a taste for long discourses, and looked at him, nodding attentively, throughout his speech.

Then, Eva spoke: "And you *believe* all of this stuff? My science teachers at Choate are PhD's, and they'd tell you that you're a couple tacos shy of a combination plate. How weird. You probably believe in the Bermuda Triangle, too. But you're sweet." She moved closer to him and took his hand in hers. He was shocked. Her disbelief would have been crushing to a less confident boy, but it still was disappointing. But why was she taking his hand, then?

"I have to go, now," Eva said sweetly. "Mama is having the chef make vol-au-vents for dinner tonight, and I just *love* vol-au-vents." "Wait!" said Mabus. "Just two minutes! I'll be right back." He ran back to Boone's house and came streaking back out with a copy of F. Tupper Saussy's book *Rulers of Evil*. Mabus thrust it into her hands, saying, "Read this! You'll know the truth." Eva was taken aback, and kissed him on the cheek impulsively. Then she laughed, and ran back across the river. Truly confused, Mabus watched her small form recede into the approaching dusk.

Chapter Four

ABUS LIVED ON BOONE'S LAND, largely minding his own business, but he had become a serious Internet addict. He seldom even thought of Eva, because he had so much else to commit his time to. Every day he would spend at least two or three hours, some days even six or seven, surfing the nascent Internet and leaving posts on various websites having to do with extraterrestrials, ancient Egypt and the pyramids, Cydonian Mars, the Illuminati, and governmental and religious conspiracy theories.

And he contributed frequently to certain carefully selected, outspoken and risk-taking message boards, finally securing his own space on a widely-read news website. Wanting to strike back at his former tormentors, he found out as much as he could about the elusive "Illuminati" group, but they were a very hard target. He was starting to gain an interested, avid following over the Net. A lot of people wanted to help him prove that Cydonia was the same place as Giza, only in the future, and many ways to do this had been discussed.

But Mabus held firmly to his plans to raise a pyramid on Earth, his theory being that it would then instantly show up on Mars, as history would have been altered. Mabus did not believe in Fatalism, the doctrine prescribed by most religions in this world, that portrayed the future as fixed, immutable and thus completely predictable—one that could be described and thus controlled by an elite.

He instead believed that time was cyclical, like the serpentine figure of the Ouroboros, the great self-sustaining ancient symbol of reincarnation. It dated back to pre-Biblical times, as the

29

precursor to the early myths about Satan, and Mabus had found much evidence that people had been wiser, more sophisticated, and more technologically advanced back then. The Egyptians worshiped a symbol which we believe to be the sign for eternal life, the same symbol we use today for Venus.

So he wanted to prove that religion was wrong, and that you could indeed alter the future, by building this newer pyramid. He wanted to place it somewhere outside of Giza, so it would really show up and stand out to those of us on Earth. He didn't want it to blend in with the dozen or so Cydonian objects, about which he was still forming his theories as to why there were so many of them.

Mabus learned that there were only five Great Pyramids in Giza, but there were seemingly eight or more such pyramids in Cydonia. "How could this be?" he thought. He knew there were pyramids all over the world, but how could all of the them have made it to the same vicinity of the planet? He also knew the theory that the continents were once all joined together as one solid land mass, and that due to the shifting of the tectonic plates, this land structure separated and formed the continents we have today. Mabus pondered whether if the plates were moving apart now, and there were a major pole shift, would the plates over time return to a single land mass, bringing the separated pyramids together?

The pyramids were buried under millions of years of debris. According to aerial photos of Mars, the layout of these Martian shapes—some of which were over a mile wide and much bigger than their Egyptian counterparts—was strikingly similar to that of our Great Pyramids. And there was a large sculpture of a face that looked like all that was left of the Egyptian Sphinx. It closely resembled Egyptian statues and had the same leonine and asexual features as the Sphinx.

While he continued his reading in the esoteric arts and sciences, Mabus also continued his training as a journeyman carpenter. He learned how to make mortise and tenon joints at the table saw and router table, how to cut dovetails, how to work from a measured drawing, how to glue things up so that they would be sound and strong, and even how to do marquetry and parquetry with wood veneers. Before long, his skills were second only to Boone's, and Boone gave him the license to do projects on his own. Incidentally, Boone also raised his pay from $7 to $12 an hour, which Mabus appreciated.

In the late summer of 1999, the Senator's personal secretary came by. He showed Boone a photograph of a unique eighteenth century armoire, which the Senator's wife had seen while on a tour of the South, and requested a custom reproduction, made in the original woods. Boone rejected the order, growling about bloodsucking politicians and their blood money, but Mabus haltingly offered to do the job himself. Boone glared at Mabus, but Mabus whispered into his ear that they needed a faster computer system in order to keep up with the Internet; for the price the Senator was willing to pay, they could afford to keep up a major website and spread the truth. Boone twisted up his face and spat in disgust. "Yeah, we'll do it. Rather, the kid will do it." The secretary was skeptical, but Boone showed him a sample of Mabus's marquetry that was indistinguishable from the Renaissance original. Now impressed, the secretary agreed, and they set a date for the completion of the finished armoire. It was to be ready by mid-December, so that the Senator's wife could unveil it at her lavish Christmas party to the applause of all her vapid society friends.

Mabus put more effort into that armoire than he had into any of his previous projects. The exotic woods for the construction of the armoire each had their individual characteristics and qualities, but he was able to shape and form them with the hands of a master. As the months passed, he came to understand the design as though it were part of him, from the claw-and-ball feet to the finials at the top. Much of his work had to be done by hand once he got to the final stages, as he painstakingly cut the veneers. In the finishing room, he brought the piece to a burnished glow.

By now, it was December 3rd, and Mabus had finally finished the piece—over two weeks early. He called the Salvatores' secretary to inform him of the piece's completion. The secretary was annoyed at the youth's being the one to call rather than Mr. Napoleon, and told him curtly that the Senator's handyman would come the next day to pick it up. The next day at noon, a gleaming white Suburban came to a stop outside of Boone's house. After the handyman, wearing a remarkably clean jumpsuit, had gotten out of the truck, one of its back doors opened, and the slender legs of Eva swung elegantly out.

"Well, if it isn't Mr. New Yankee Workshop!" She flashed Mabus a white smile, and her mesmerizing blue eyes locked with his. The handyman coughed, and asked if he could be let in so that he could remove the armoire. Mabus nodded. Eva took his arm with mock severity and said, "Come on. You don't want to make us wait."

They all made their way to the finishing room, where Mabus had wrapped up the armoire for transport. The handyman's eyes bugged out when he saw the size of the armoire, and he said, "I'm gonna need another guy to get this thing outta here. I'll call back for one of the gardeners." Mabus said, "No need. I'll move this with you." The handyman scoffed, "No way! You're jus' a kid." Mabus decided to be bold and make his point, so he crouched down beside the armoire and lifted it up partway, his back and shoulders straining. He knew he'd be sore as hell the next day. The handyman shrugged. "Awright. I get it. Let's hustle this into the truck." Mabus smiled, and said, "Perhaps you'd like a couple of these?" Two dollies lay beneath the workbench. The handyman said, "Sheesh. I shoulda thought of that." The handyman made no further conversation during the ensuing trip.

Mabus had never seen the front of the mansion. It was a long drive, as the Suburban went between two enormous wrought-iron gates and down a path which must have been a mile, at least. Protocol would indicate that they should have parked at the back and gone through the servants' entrance, but the Senator and his wife were taking the air at an exclusive resort that week, and discipline was looser, Eva explained. Mabus and the handyman left the armoire in the foyer. The handyman said that he would drive Mabus back right away, but Eva intervened, saying "Now you never mind. I want to talk to this young tradesman. You can drive him back later." The handyman shot her a look, and went back to his customary shed behind the manor.

"Now, then, I've read your wonderfully loony book, and I'd like to discuss it with you. Come upstairs, and we'll sit down and chat." Suppressing a flicker of suspicion, Mabus agreed, and they went up the grand staircase, with its mahogany banister and white turned posts. Once the stairs had made their turn, Mabus found himself in a rectangular room with a mahogany table bearing blood-red poinsettias. Eva pointed to the left-hand hall, and he followed her to the master bedroom of the house. He gaped at the luxury to be found within–an enormous four-poster bed, an Aubusson carpet, and a velvet-covered window seat big enough to hold two people. They sat down in the window seat, a little closer together than Mabus would have liked.

Eva and Mabus sat for a moment, enjoying the quality of the light from the window in back of them. Mabus broke the silence. "I take it that you do not approve of Mr. Saussy's work."

"It goes against everything I've ever been taught to believe. I'd have to make a complete break with reality to agree with that book."

"Maybe the problem is with your reality. I think the scientific evidence is on my side. You and I know that I'm not in the 'mainstream,' but the mainstream is not always right. It's the safest bet, but it could be dead wrong."

"But, if you're right, every institution in the world is just an empty façade crawling with Masons, Bilderbergers, Illuminati, space aliens, and the Trilateral Commission. I know my Daddy; he's a good sweet man, and can't be one of *them*. All of the Senators I've ever met, including my father, have been loyal patriots, dedicated to their country."

"Dedicated to their pocketbooks, you mean. How do you think your father has paid for this house, your education, your dinner parties, your servants, my furniture…" He trailed off, stunned by the smile on her face.

"You really are misguided. You're cute, too, but you're smelly. There's a shower through that door. Wash up, and I'll find your copy of that book for you to take back."

Mabus was beginning to get that dream-feeling, of the fireball shedding its warmth over his body instead of destroying him. He tried to look inside himself, to see what his gut felt, but there was nothing there, positive or negative. He decided to comply.

The marble bathroom was bigger than the trailer Mabus lived in. He took off his construction-worker's shoes and shrugged out of his sweaty clothes. The shower was something else. He had never been massaged before, and the powerful beats of spray did much for his strained back. The dirt came off of him in layers, and he scrubbed himself all over with the bath sponge. Finally, he was clean.

He came out of the bathroom blinking, a soft Turkish towel wrapped around his waist. There stood Eva, bearing a silver tray with martini glasses, a cocktail shaker, and a little dish of olives. "Around here," she said, "we take cocktails a little early."

Mabus panicked. He had seen the effects of alcohol first-hand, and was not about to go down that path again. It was a warning sign that he would do well not to ignore. At the same time, the sight of Eva's beautiful face and innocent smile melted away the fear within him. He forced himself to smile, and extended his hand. Eva set the tray down, filled the glasses, added olives to each, and handed one to Mabus.

They sat down on the soft down comforter of her parents' massive four-poster bed. Mabus took a cautious sip; the potent liquid tasted like one of his varnishes, but sent a wave of relaxation through his body—relaxation that swiftly ended when he realized that Eva had her small hand in his lap, and was gently stroking the towel's soft fabric. Against his will, Mabus's manhood rose to attention, fueled by the gentle pressure of Eva's hand. "What are you doing?" he asked, wide-eyed. "I'm giving you the attention you deserve, silly," laughed Eva. Mabus tried to direct her hand away from the growing tent in his towel, but she slipped nimbly out of his grasp and continued her ministrations. He could not ignore the waves of sensation which had begun to crest and break over his body. The martini had made him passive; he could do little but let Eva have her way. Suddenly, she jumped off the bed, knelt before him, and tore off his towel. She gripped him with both her hands and started to apply a rhythmic motion. Her eyes gleamed as she looked up at him, and she opened her mouth and licked her lips.

Without warning, she engulfed him, and the hot wetness took him to a new level of sensation; it was as if the ball of fire had taken him into its midst, and the warm tongues of flame were lapping at his body. Yet, instead of pain, there was pleasure, the like of which he had never felt in his life. Just as he reached his peak, though, the green couch of the junkyard flashed through his mind; terror filled him, but at the same time his body was beyond recall. He felt his pleasure beneath a blanket of fear. As release came to him, he felt joy, but the fear dampened it.

With a look of triumph on her face, Eva swallowed hard, smiled, looked up at him and said, "Mabus, now even *you* have to admit there is a God." Then she saw his face, with its mixture of emotions, and her triumph melted into confusion and then a flood of rage. "Ingrate! Get out of here!" As Mabus struggled to get his clothes back on, she ran out, then returned to throw a book at him. "Here's your book back, weirdo! Now, get!"

Mabus walked back from the estate, a cacophony of feelings clashing in his head.

LIVING WITH BOONE as he grew to manhood, Mabus was slowly assimilating his values of truth, honesty and courage. Boone had served in Korea shortly after he had settled down with his wife. Soon after their marriage, they had a son. Three years later, he lost his wife to cancer. And just when things couldn't have gotten worse for Boone, his son was drafted to Vietnam and never returned. So he was very happy to take Mabus under his wing, and that was where the younger man flourished. Mabus was truly happy for the very first time in his life, knowing that he held a secure place in the grand scheme of things.

Then the day came when Mabus's security was once again shattered. It was his birthday again, in the year 2000, when George W. Bush was running for President. Boone had been constantly writing about his campaign, criticizing and complaining, apparently to the point of having attracted people's attention.

Boone had invited Mabus to go fishing with him at the river, but Mabus was very busy that day; he was occupied enhancing their new website so people could find it through several search engines. He felt confident the website would attract plenty of serious converts to his cause now, and he was extremely excited. He listed his site so it could be found through Internet search keyword phrases such as "Cydonia," "Mars," "Venus," "Pyramids," "Illuminati" and "Sacred Mayan Calendar," a new interest of his.

Mabus was interrupted by the flashes and booms of lightning and thunder outside. When he peered through the window at the sheets of rain coming down, Mabus mused to himself that this was no ordinary storm, but a downpour that could rival the ancient Biblical flood of Noah's time.

Mabus knew that Boone wouldn't stay out in the rain, so he began to fix dinner, all the while figuring that his mentor might be bringing back a nice, tasty brook trout or two. By the time Mabus had finished setting the table and cooking the rest of the dinner, Boone had still not returned. Mabus figured he had taken refuge under a large tree and decided to wait out the storm there. Mabus returned to his computer work and was shocked when he realized three hours had passed and the storm had subsided a bit, but Boone had still not returned.

Finally, Mabus decided to put on his shiny red rain slicker and start looking for Boone. It didn't take long to find him, and what Mabus saw when he did made him wish he had never been born.

Boone was lying face down in the cold, overgrown reeds along the riverbank. Mabus grabbed his shoulder and turned him over. His grey hair clung to his soaked forehead, and mud oozed from his mouth. Evidently he had drowned. Mabus immediately grabbed the cell phone from his belt clip and called for help while he tried to revive Boone himself.

Almost an hour passed before the ambulance crew was able to find them, and all the while Mabus had been performing CPR. The situation was horrible—Boone's flesh was cool and rubbery, and his expressionless eyes seemed to flicker and take on a hideous false life with each continuing flash of lightning. Mabus's heroic efforts were futile—Boone was dead, and there was nothing the young carpenter could do to save him. Mabus watched as the paramedics lifted Boone's lifeless body onto a stretcher and covered it respectfully with a sheet.

Later, back in Boone's warm, dry house, the police questioned Mabus for hours. He answered all their inquiries in a daze, all the while wondering what kind of capricious God would save his life and then take his greatest friend Boone's exactly eleven years later. He couldn't figure it out.

Something dim from his attack more than ten years ago kept coming to him. His attacker had kept referring to himself as if he were a group of people rather than an individual. Mabus had a sickening feeling crawling all through his guts and into the pit of his stomach that somehow this had all happened before, and that something incredibly wicked, evil and narcissistic was behind it all.

He knew that Boone couldn't possibly have drowned, for he was an excellent swimmer and had saved the lives of one of his men from drowning in Korea. Mabus knew that something or someone was responsible for Boone's death, but he said nothing to the police. He had no evidence, after all, just suspicions and gut feelings.

That night, Mabus didn't sleep at all. He sat in Boone's house in the dark, wrapped in a blanket at the desk, with all the computers shut off for once. Finally, he decided that he had to move on from there. Boone had made him an equal partner in his business, but Mabus felt too hollow to even attempt to carry on without him. And besides, Mabus was now an ace journeyman carpenter, slated to soon become a master himself. He could make his own way.

Little did he know that within five years, he would attain mastery—not only of the arts of building and carpentry, but also of what would be left of the entire modern-day world, and—one day—of the origins, civilization, and preservation of mankind's dim and distant past.

Chapter Five

ABUS TOOK TO FREQUENTING HIS old teenage haunts, though he managed to stay out of any serious trouble. When he read on the job board at a homeless shelter that a nearby company was offering a free certificate in youth counseling—even for people with no experience—he jumped at the chance. He often thought of the kind woman counselor from his hospital stay and wished to help others in the same way. He knew he could bluff if he had to and say he had graduated from high school.

Mabus signed up for the program, sailed through the thirteen classes with flying colors, and soon set up his own professional shingle. He decided to specialize in counseling troubled late-teen youths, who tended to have very pliable minds and who freely listened to both his advice and his tales about the planets, about which he was forming a rather involved theory.

He would take troubled youths out to build houses for poor people along the lines of Habitat for Humanity projects, and teach them expert carpentry skills. He had managed to attain the master level of carpentry on his own, and he applied these skills very capably in the service of others.

Mabus believed you could feed someone and they would eat that night. But if you taught that person to fish, they could eat every day. He also believed that if he could teach these kids a trade, they would stay away from drugs. Some people get caught up in drugs merely for the income potential. These kids were able to learn a trade and secure their income. They really looked up to Mabus. He taught them to be more diverse in their decision making. He also taught them fundamental ethics and skills with which to live their lives.

He used the metaphor of the different stages of building a house from the foundation to the roof to help in his quest for his charges to understand how to structure their lives for success. "First you must build a strong foundation, for if the foundation is weak, the rest of the house will crumble. Then, nice sturdy walls to keep out danger, and the elements that would harm us. The structure needs an appropriate number of doors and windows to let in the love, harmony, and light. The house certainly needs strong locks to defend against predators looking for the naïve. Good siding and a sound roof account for the integrity of the whole structure. If your structure lacks integrity it won't last long," **Mabus would** preach.

Using these analogies, and applying them to real life, Mabus found it simple to connect with these youths. Soon, he was known throughout his entire state for his charm, goodwill, and easygoing, generous nature. He counseled his young friends to not depend on drugs, religion, government aid, or anything at all outside of themselves, at least not without first carefully examining it for truth, honesty and validity.

Though Mabus was very busy and enjoyed his work, he found time for a girlfriend. He had met Barbara, a fellow counselor, when they were both assigned to work at a summer youth camp. Barbara, a dark-haired, friendly beauty with a voluptuous figure, complemented Mabus well. She enjoyed the innate intelligence he displayed, and the wisdom he had developed through life experience rather than textbooks. The two shared an easygoing rapport and soon began to discuss the possibility of marriage.

One day Mabus was scheduled to hold one of his many group-counseling sessions with his young charges. He ran into Tyrone, one of the young men, in the hallway of the youth mission.

Tyrone, though only seventeen, had a face that had been aged by hard life. Mabus had helped wean him off drugs just two months earlier. Though Tyrone's face was tired and his arms were still riddled with the telltale marks of heroin tracks, Mabus noticed that he seemed to walk taller now, his lithe body springing a bit with each step. The young man had taken to carpentry well, and was in the middle of a kitchen cabinet project with Mabus. Mabus was very hopeful for his complete recovery. They began conversing and soon fell into one of their frequent philosophical exchanges.

"I know Christianity ain't yo thang," Tyrone said, "But I like chill'n at church and I've been, you know, reading the Bible a lot lately. It's sort of been helping me, but I know exactly what you mean about thinking for yourself. Those nasty religious brotha's alwa'z tellin' me wha' to do bother me, cuz! Anyway, I saw a Biblical reference about you. It's totally yo' thang! John knew what a righteous dog you were goin' to be, cuz!"

"Oh, I seriously doubt that," Mabus said. "Anything in the Bible probably condemns unbelievers like me as being something like, I dunno, the Beast or something."

"I heard somewhere that the Antichrist had a sword wound."

"Are you talking about my famous saber scar?" Mabus joked, pointing to his cheeks.

"Nah, this thang I read is about counselors, cuz. It's in John 15:26. It says the Fatha will send out a wise counselor. In some versions of the Bible, it says 'The Comforter.' And it says he's the Spirit of Truth who goes out from the Fatha, and that he will testify about the Second Coming of my man Jesus Christ."

Mabus broke into laughter. "A likely story! It is true that I am always telling people everywhere I go my elaborate theories about the end of the world. I talk a lot about how there's going to be a great comet, and that the ancient Mayans had a Sacred Calendar that ends about nine years from now. And that we've got to all get together and do something to stop the disaster, before it's too late. But that doesn't make me a 'comforter,' or even wise. I just keep my eyes open. Shit, I don't even believe in Jesus!"

"Well," Tyrone said, "I think that 'wise counselor' thang fits right up your alley. That's exactly when Jesus is supposed to show up, cuz. And I've heard you talk about the Antichrist sometimes. That's when he's supposed to park his ass as the ruler of the world, too, at its very end. Shit, these are the end times they talkin' bout! You do believe in the Antichrist, don't you? You said in group that you found out that's what your pops was callin ya, years after you grew up. Somebody cool told you all about it."

"Yeah. But I tend to believe in myself, not religions. We really have to think like evolved humans, and be out to help each other. Real compassion saves, not religion or politics. God is never going to do it for us, no matter what anybody believes. That guy you mentioned told me all those old stories about how the Antichrist is going to rule the world. He tends to believe the Antichrist will be a savior rather than a tyrant."

MABUS HAD BEEN seeing a therapist himself, Joshua, one of his first counseling teachers. He was a thin, kindly, and almost eerily intelligent man in a maroon cardigan, who thought the world of Mabus. Sometimes Mabus felt the man knew him better than he even knew himself. This therapist was the one who had told him all about the Antichrist legends. Mabus thought a lot of it was ridiculous, and he told him so. "You'll know, someday soon, why you need to know about these old myths and legends," the counselor had replied. "It'll fit right in with your most important plans." Mabus didn't know how to take some of his off-the-wall statements. He told Mabus, "Behind all great lies is a hint of truth." And he went on, "When a pack of lies is wrapped around a bit of truth, the lies become more believable."

The counselor was excellent at teaching Mabus about real life, and had a kind of advanced knowledge of the ways of the world. He had said learning about the Antichrist legends in detail would help the burgeoning counselor deal with his childhood pain. "Hey Josh! Look at this! It says, 'The Antichrist was fatally wounded by a sword, and yet lived.' 'Man of Sin,' 'Deceiver of all Men,' 'Son of Perdition,' these are some of the descriptions of the Antichrist. Mainly he's supposed to be a liar."

"That's true, Mabus. Now, if someone with a major physical wound shows up to claim the position, you are led to believe that, because of the part about the wound being true, the rest must be true as well—that this man will be a liar. But what if he is not?"

"Yah, Boone used to say to me, 'Believe none of what you hear, and only half of what you see.' This must have been what he meant!" Mabus said, enthused.

He realized the inherent logic of the idea and instantly noticed the same techniques his father had employed. That long-forgotten wretched being had made him self-conscious about being evil, always calling him Satanic names. Since then, Mabus had been managing to keep his life and act together fairly well indeed.

Mabus lived alone in a one-bedroom apartment with just a friendly, fuzzy black dog he had named "The Beast," a bicycle, and a powerful PC to his name. He also had bought a used compact car to get around in. His few possessions were modest, but he was totally content with his present life, except for his disturbing dreams, occasional loneliness, and burning ambition to unite the world against the painfully foreseeable cosmic menace. He knew he had to do something, but to accomplish even his initial goal of building a sixth Middle Eastern pyramid, he knew he would have to attract people's attention somehow.

He was no longer afraid to occasionally read the Bible, if only for research purposes. He was able to approach it from a different perspective. He interpreted the Bible in the belief that God was hiding a secret from man, and that God wished to prevent man from attaining godlike status. It seemed to Mabus that the Devil was trying everything in his power to expose that secret.

The Devil proposed three basic attributes of godhood: eternal knowledge, eternal life, and the right to decide what is good and what is bad. Satan said men could be gods, too, if they knew what God knew. Mabus pondered whether Satan might be a traveler from the future, trying to warn mankind. Perhaps this was why the Bible constantly referred to him as the "Deceiver of Man." But the Bible itself was the deceiver of man. Mabus used his newfound knowledge to refute some of the more outlandish right-wing beliefs that he encountered when debating with others.

MOST SUNDAYS, MABUS spent his entire day on the Internet, managing several websites. He was becoming renowned worldwide as an amateur expert in the esoteric theoretical areas of Cydonian Mars, the pyramids of Earth, the possible influence of interplanetary aliens on our Earth cultures, governmental, corporate and religious conspiracies, and especially his Single Orientation Theory of the Planets.

He also thought about Barbara—her flowing auburn hair, her brown eyes sparkling in the distance, and her wonderful body, which her clothing covered, but otherwise did little to conceal. He was sure that she would listen to his fascinating theory, and be impressed by it, given time.

He had begun to build on his earlier theory about Venus, Earth and Mars. He was starting to realize that all of the current planets in our solar system were actually only one continuously evolving planet, moving in a well-ordered pattern of different time phases of its existence. This scenario, however, did not include Pluto, which had in recent times begun to be regarded as a mere sub-planetary object.

And in that pattern, this "universal planet" was slowly moving further out into our solar system, as if it were taking the place of each next-furthest planet from the Sun. The "Big Bang" theorists– and expanding-universe theorists readily validated this, saying that Earth's orbit was slowly decaying and expanding, growing ever further out from the Sun.

So were the orbits of all the other planets in the solar system. Mabus was sure that meant that each planet in our solar system was definitely heading into the position of the next planet out from the Sun. To validate his theories, he always kept a careful watch of the skies, using both a small but powerful outdoor telescope and the nearly infinite resources of the Internet.

Evidence that he was right was slowly starting to accumulate. For example, on August 27th, 2003, the planet Mars passed the closest it had ever been to the Earth in 73,000 years. Scientists and astronomers called this an "opposition," and said that Mars was slowly growing closer in its proximity to our planet. Obviously, Mabus felt, this was the beginning of Earth's slow yet radical "phasing" into Mars. Also, it would soon be time for the first "transit of Venus" since 1882, when Venus would pass between the Earth and the Sun, appearing as a large black dot traveling across the Sun's disk, on June 8th of 2004.

The next such transit was set to occur on June 6th, 2012. On that day, Mabus would turn exactly 36 years old—six times six. In a way, he couldn't wait; he was dying to know exactly what was going to happen that year, but he was beginning to be afraid that December 27th of 2012 was exactly when the giant comet of his dreams was going to hit. Every night he dreamed of the awful comet, which seemed to be looming ever closer.

One Sunday afternoon in the summer of 2004, once again on the date of his birth, Mabus began to carefully arrange the preliminary theories for his Single Orientation Theory website. He typed some rough draft text into a Word document:

> Mercury is actually an earlier version of Venus, Venus is the ancient version of Earth, and Earth will eventually turn into Mars. After an incident involving what is now the Main

Asteroid Belt between Mars and Jupiter, the rocky planet
Mars will evolve into the massive gas giant known as the
planet Jupiter. And Jupiter will someday become Saturn,
Saturn, Uranus, and Uranus, Neptune. But what will happen
to Neptune?

Perhaps Neptune will then become the largest known
body of the Kuiper asteroid belt. Pluto is nowadays thought
of as only another large object in our solar system's recently-
discovered secondary asteroid belt. It is in fact the largest
known object in the belt, which contains an unknown number
of objects that are very similar in composition, and some in
size, to Pluto.

The first four planets in our solar system—Mercury, Venus, Earth and Mars—are known as rocky planets. The bulk
of their planetary bodies are solid masses, largely composed
of a rocky mantle and a molten iron core. The next four
planets are known as the gas giants. Jupiter and Saturn have
smaller rocky cores surrounded by thick "envelopes" of liquid metallic hydrogen, with some helium, methane and water
mixed in. Uranus and Neptune are very similar in their over-
all composition to the rocky cores of Jupiter and Saturn,
minus their massive liquid hydrogen envelopes.

The gas giants have now all been found to have rings
around them like Saturn's, with Jupiter appearing to have
the preliminary formation of Saturn's spectacular and highly
visible rings. Uranus then has a more watered-down version
of these, whereas Neptune seems to have the smallest, most
obviously decayed form of them. These rings all contain
similar small structures, particles of matter ranging in size
from a centimeter wide to more than a kilometer in diameter.
These particles and objects seem to be mostly made of rock
and ice, and they surround all four of the gas giants.

Pluto is yet another rocky "planet," clearly out of sequence
as the other four rocky planets are much closer to the Sun.
Therefore it probably has more to do with the disintegration
of asteroids and comets and the evolution of the planetary
satellites (the many objects revolving around the planets)
over time. There is much evidence, from the number and
nature of the planetary satellites, that they also have been

moving through time and space as each of their planets evolves.

Earth will catastrophically be hit by a comet, destroying the planet. Half of the debris from Earth will get pulled into Venus's gravitational pull, which will then begin to cluster together and form a moon. The remaining debris will stay in Earth's gravitational pull, and will create a second moon, thus transforming Earth into Mars.

The Main Asteroid Belt apparently was once a planetary body in its own right. It was once a huge planet called Astera, which was roughly the size of Saturn. The Bible even records this planet, which it calls "Rahab." The book claims that it was the former home of Lucifer and the fallen angels, before the heavenly war with God caused it to be destroyed and shattered, into "Stones of Fire." Strangely enough, the original Roman name for the planet Venus is Lucifer, or "Morning Star."

The larger missing planet is somehow the key to my theory, and yet clearly separates in some strange manner from it. I have a feeling that the missing piece of the story involves the advanced age of this planet, and that it was in existence for many billions of years before the only actual other planet in our solar system was formed out of space dust.

Jupiter also derived its sixty-plus moons and objects from the disintegration of this great body, and then passed about half of its dozens of satellites on to Saturn, which passed some of them on to Uranus, etc. Neptune has fewer satellites than Uranus, which probably means they drifted out of orbit over time. It wouldn't pick up satellites from the faraway secondary asteroid belt.

I intend to prove all of my theories and verify that the the pyramids on Cydonian Mars are a future vision of Giza and the Great Pyramids of Earth. I am very sure now that the Great Pyramid itself was built specifically to warn us of an oncoming disastrous event, one which will have profound consequences for our entire world. I don't know exactly how I can establish material proof of my theories except by building a sixth Great Pyramid somewhere in the Holy Lands near Giza, and waiting to see if it appears just outside of

Cydonian Mars. This should happen either while it's being built, or immediately afterwards.

It all depends on how the transition from present to future time operates. Also, the pyramids of Mars, for reasons yet unknown to me, are much larger than the pyramids of Egypt. The base of the largest Giza pyramid is 756 feet square, and the base of its correspondingly large Cydonian pyramid is over a mile wide. I have to find a logical explanation for this discrepancy—for example, the layers of dirt gathering over millions of years on the pyramid's surfaces, thus making them considerably larger. The correspondence and similarities presuppose that the Martian pyramids are somehow exactly one and the same.

THE DOORBELL RANG. Mabus glanced at the clock. He had been writing for a long time, and he felt a grumbling in his stomach. He patted the Beast on its head, and got up to answer the door. His jaw dropped at the sight: a beautiful blonde woman in an expensive business suit that highlighted her slim figure. Then he saw her blue eyes, and he knew: it was indeed Eva. "What the hell are you doing here?" he asked weakly. "The last time I saw you, you were ordering me out of your parents' fancy bedroom. Why come to see me?"

Eva smiled. "I came to tell you that you were right." "What?" Mabus sputtered. "Yes, you're right. There are secret powers at work in the world. You've still got it all wrong, though. They're here to help mankind, not to hurt it. It's all part of the important work my Daddy does. I'm helping with it, too. After I went to college—you should have gone, too, Mabus, because Princeton was wonderful—I got a job with the government, and now I'm helping my Daddy make sure that the right people are in the right places. Our kind of people." She smiled meaningfully at Mabus.

"Wait a second. I was a no-good carpenter's apprentice to you years ago, and now I'm *your* kind of people? What's changed?"

"You're a man now, Mabus, and it is time for you to put away foolish things. You are remarkably intelligent and resourceful, but still misguided, even now. We have watched your progress with great interest, and we think you could do great things, with the right people behind you. You could be in the government, too. You could be running things. You could sit at the head of all tables. But instead, you alarm people with your fantastical websites, warning that the sky is falling and that the boogey man is under the bed. That's a problem, and you don't want to be a problem, do you, Mabus?"

Mabus said, "I'll say and publish what I like. Whoever you're working for can't do a damn thing about it."

"Oh, but we can. We have always done. Mankind needs to be ruled by the few, the wise, and the pure. We have ways of making sure that problems that raise themselves up are ground down. But what if you could come to our side? We know that you will one day be a very great man, but, if you ally yourself with us, there might be no limit to your greatness. That is what I have to offer you…in addition to certain…amenities." Eva smiled, and Mabus was transported to that day years ago, remembering the pleasure more than the pain. But then the thought of Barbara came back into his mind. Eva was fascinating and attractive, but Barbara was, deep down, a good person. He couldn't say that of Eva.

"No, thank you," Mabus replied. "You were trouble back then and you're trouble now. Go back to whoever you work for, and tell them my answer: I will never stop seeking the truth."

"We have already made some painful interventions in your life. Pray that we do not intervene any further. You have had your chance."

"Nice to see you," said Mabus as he gestured to the open door. "Don't let the door hit you on your ass on the way out." Eva turned back as she walked out, and her mocking smile once again aroused conflicting feelings in him.

Mabus thought carefully about what Eva had said. What about Boone? No, it was too horrible to think of. He returned to his original purpose, making a sandwich, when the telephone rang.

He answered the phone on the second ring. It was Barbara, in all her wonderful innocence. "It's so good to hear your voice," Mabus said, meaning it more than she would ever know. "Where have you been for the last week?"

"At the ocean with my parents, just like I told you, silly."

"Well, yeah, but why didn't you call me?"

"You should've called me. Honestly, Mabus, when it comes to being aggressive, sometimes you sure stand around like a statue. Then you get all romantic and attentive. Sometimes I think you're two different people, you beast, you! Think I could breathe some life back into you when I get home?"

"Any time, baby, any time!" Mabus replied, smiling into the phone.

Chapter Six

N SEPTEMBER 29TH, 2004 AD, THE asteroid 4179 Toutatis swung in its orbit closer to the Earth than any known comet or asteroid that would approach between then and the year 2060–if anyone would be around to see it. It was several kilometers wide, dumbbell-shaped, and seemed to be two separate but joined bodies moving in a peculiar "tumbling" rotation. Mabus followed any news of this religiously, paying undivided attention to all the media and seeking out all the scientific information he could unearth. He harrumphed in derision when the NASA spokesman showed up on his TV screen to pooh-pooh people's worries and assure them that no one was in any danger.

The plane of Toutatis's orbit was closer to the plane of Earth's orbit than any other known Earth-orbit crossing satellite. Its erratic orbit extended between the Earth's orbit and the Main Asteroid Belt, and it passed by Earth at a distance roughly four times greater than the distance between our planet and its silvery moon. It would do this once every four years, although scientists were never quite sure exactly what to expect from its peculiar passage. It was scheduled to swoop perilously close again in 2008, and again in July of the fateful year of 2012.

Or so scientists thought. When it would pass by again, near the autumnal equinox of 2008, many flabbergasted amateur and professional astronomers would note the fact that its tail, spreading wide and far across the night sky, clearly resembled a giant ruby-red dragon. And the dragon somehow looked as though it were chasing a woman, and was very close to catching her...

The night of Christmas Eve, Mabus was regaling Barbara with the detailed story of how NASA and the US Government had covered up proof of the existence of life on Mars for over twelve years. The couple already exchanged their traditionally inexpensive presents. Barbara had gotten the dog a new water dish with "The Beast" embossed on the side. There was a strange green triangular symbol next to the name.

"The guy at the store told me that if you turn the dish, you see three revolving sixes in the symbol. Isn't that strange? I know you like that peculiar '666' stuff, so I got it for you."

Mabus, meanwhile, had finally presented Barbara with her engagement ring, a simple one-carat diamond surrounded by five ruby chips. It was hardly expensive, but it was all he could afford, and he had gotten a very big hug from her in return.

Mabus droned on. Barbara was a bit bored, but she listened anyway. She smoothed her long auburn hair behind one ear with a slim finger and adjusted her wire-rimmed glasses over her happy brown eyes. She strained to listen to Mabus, but her mind wandered to thoughts of wedding plans. They needed to get started discussing all of that. "The sooner the wedding, the sooner the wedding night," Barbara thought. Mabus thrilled her to the marrow, especially with his spontaneously romantic kisses and the way he had pledged to wait until their wedding night to make love to her.

She knew he had never been with another woman, and though she was also a virgin, she often had thoughts that surprised her. In particular, she had a frequent recurring dream of riding him hard while she drank a goblet of blood-red wine and laughed like a whore. She would wake from her dreams aroused, her body covered by a thin film of perspiration.

Barbara snapped her attention back to Mabus, who had not noticed it had drifted. "They waited until August 7th of 1996 to hold a news conference and announce that NASA's researchers had recently discovered the evidence," Mabus went on. "What happened was the Japanese had found this probable meteorite, ALH84001, in the Allan Hills region of Antarctica in 1984, and thoroughly studied it. Then US scientists got hold of it with some kind of joint research scheme and pretty much stole it from the Japanese.

"It's a softball-sized igneous rock that weighs about five pounds. Yet it may hold the key to my theories about Mars having formerly been the Earth. It's about 4.5 billion years old, and it's the oldest Martian meteorite ever found. All twelve of the meteorites we've found that we think are from Mars are made of crystallized molten magma, formed in a way that suggests they were created in a planetary body. And one of them, EETA79001, contains trapped gas bubbles with a composition that matches the current Martian atmosphere. That one is only 1.3 billion years old, but it's associated with the other eleven enough to verify that they're all probably originally from Mars."

Now deep into a favorite subject, Mabus's voice grew low and intense. Barbara found herself paying close attention, even thought the topic was not one she was all that interested in. "The abundant hydrocarbons, or PAHs, exist in a mixture in the oldest meteorite, which I'll call AL for short, and suggest a biological origin. There are also unusual mineral phases, which are the types of alterations caused only by the actions of primitive bacteria as seen on Earth. And electron microscopy has revealed many tiny 'ovoids' in AL's fractured cracks that appear to be fossils of twenty to one hundred nanometers in diameter. They are one hundred times smaller than any bacterial microfossils found on Earth except for some recent nanofossils found in some very young terrestrial rocks, but that's still subject to debate.

"This is groundbreaking evidence that Mars used to be much warmer, covered in water, and that it supported a life-giving atmosphere. Yet NASA covered it up for years. I'm starting to believe that particular government agency has been infiltrated and is currently being controlled by a disenfranchised branch of the Society of Freemasons known as the Illuminati. The Masons don't have anything to do with these guys anymore, and they're not involved, but the Illuminati are like some kind of puppet masters of the entire world. I've been checking around, and it's pretty shocking. The Illuminati seem to have been involved in the very foundation of our government since before the signing of the US Constitution, when 13 Freemasons…"

"When are we going to discuss our wedding plans?" Barbara suddenly interjected. She had her special frown on, which Mabus knew meant she had heard enough "conspiracy claptrap," as she termed it, for the day. Sighing, Mabus put his arm around her, and kissed her gently on the forehead.

"Soon, my darling, very soon. Now, when are you going to fix me that chilled salmon you promised me? I already made the salad, and we have that bottle of white wine…"

"It's way too cold for salmon. I'm not hungry yet. What say we go out and get us some hot coffee?" Barbara said, fanning herself with a religious pamphlet titled *The Second Coming and the End Times.* Mabus had taken to reading those pamphlets lately, which worried Barbara. But she loved him and always let him indulge in his "hobbies," as she called them.

They enjoyed a very pleasant but strangely chilly evening together before Barbara left for her own small apartment across town. Mabus fed the Beast and gave him water in the dish Barbara had bought. As the dog slurped greedily, Mabus stared at the triangular symbol. It looked both familiar and foreign, like he had both seen and never seen it before.

"Hell, it must be the '666' reference. I'm well acquainted with that," he thought. The Beast finished all the water and Mabus picked up the dish, turning it around and around in the kitchen light, smiling to himself.

"Maybe you're the Antichrist, boy," he said to the Beast, who barked and wagged his tail.

THE NEXT MORNING—December 25th—was very cold. The heat in Mabus's small apartment had gone off. "This is a wonderful start for my Christmas," Mabus mused sarcastically, shivering under his blanket in bed. The Beast, in his natural fur coat, was romping around as usual, oblivious to the cold. Mabus patted the dog gently on the head, picked up the phone and called the landlord. But there was no answer, as always.

Mabus was beginning to wonder if his landlord was part of some conspiracy against him. Not only was it impossible to reach him, but Mabus had also seen him skulking around outside his window the night before, and that eerie light had been streaming in again, right after his dream had ended.

The dream had been the worst yet. In it, the comet was larger and wider than the sun, and it was plummeting straight into his burning face. Jesus was standing there, laughing at him, telling him he couldn't do anything to save the world.

"You think building a pyramid is enough?" Jesus guffawed. "You'll never set up my temple in Jerusalem, or sit in it as God. You don't have enough people or resources on your side. It's already too late now.

"Only I, the true Savior, Jesus the Christ, can save the world, and only by destroying it! Half of you will go to Heaven, the half that follows Me. But the half that follows you, Antichrist, will go with you, Satan the Red Dragon, and Mystery the Great Whore of Babylon all straight to…" At that point, Mabus woke up, screaming his dry lungs out.

Was he himself really the one true Antichrist? He was willing to be, if it meant he could fulfill enough of the old Biblical prophecies to get worldwide attention, and then stop the comet before Jesus came back and caused the destruction of the world. He was even willing to go to Hell to do this, if it meant that mankind would be allowed to live on.

Or was the Antichrist supposed to destroy the world? Or was it Satan? Mabus wasn't actually sure. It sounded like the death of the Earth was all part of God's plan to bring His Son back and separate all the people forever on the final Judgment Day. This was all outlined in the Book of Revelations. But Mabus didn't want the world to ever end.

He and Barbara were planning to marry sometime in 2006. He wanted a planet to raise his family on. It's true that the human race was using up all of Earth's resources, and that the greenhouse effect was raising Earth's surface temperatures and melting the polar ice caps. And if that wasn't bad enough, Mabus had recently heard something depressing about a major polar shift. Still, Mabus was sure that there was a way to continue mankind's life into infinity. He could sense it, and the voices in his head, which now talked to him pretty frequently, were always telling him that there was.

"You must listen to the one called Thaillo," the calm, reassuring voices had been saying for the past month, or maybe longer. "He will tell you exactly what it is that you must do. Go with him to Nevada, to Groom Lake. You must enter the underground hangar, and discover the secrets of Area 51." The voices, though many, sounded just like him.

Mabus definitely preferred this to his nightmares, especially the ones about Jesus. Still, he was really starting to wonder about himself. Was he crazy? He knew all of his scientific theories were valid, but why was he starting seriously to believe that he might be the Antichrist? Shit, he didn't even believe in God! It was all just a bunch of idiotic superstition. "People who hear voices are not sane," he pondered, reaching for the phone to call a psychiatrist.

That's when it rang, startling him out of his reverie.

Chapter Seven

"The beast that thou sawest was, and is not; and shall ascend out of the bottomless pit, and go into perdition: and they that dwell on the earth shall wonder, whose names were not in the book of life from the foundations of the world, when they behold the beast that was, and is not, and yet is."

—Rev. 17:8

"HELLO?" MABUS SPAT INTO THE phone. He was annoyed to have been interrupted.

"Electrician here," mumbled a vaguely familiar voice. But Mabus hadn't called an electrician. He hadn't even gotten a hold of his landlord yet.

"I understand your heat is out. I can be there in half an hour, no problem. Meanwhile, you better wrap up in some blankets. It's gonna be cold today," the voice soothed.

"But I never called…" Mabus stammered as he heard a click and then a dial tone. "Huh. I guess the landlord must've sent someone after all. Maybe all the heat's out in every apartment."

He fed the Beast and ventured out into the hallway, still wrapped in his blanket. He rapped on the door of one of his friendlier neighbors. She opened her door a crack. "Is your heat out?" he asked.

"No," she replied, shutting her door very slowly.

Mabus shuffled back to his apartment to wait for the electrician. When he opened the door, he almost screamed. Inside was a man wearing a black ball cap and sunglasses.

"Hi ya," the man said, fiddling with the circuit breaker. "I think I've found your problem."

As the man turned to him and smiled, Mabus saw with relief that he was in his mid-twenties—much younger than the van driver had been.

The young man took off his sunglasses, revealing his deep blue eyes. He was quite handsome, and yet looked somewhat mature for his age. He walked toward Mabus, smiling. "I see you haven't got any Christmas tree. What, you Jewish or something?"

"You know what I am," Mabus breathed. He was sure he knew this man from somewhere, for he looked so familiar. Then he noticed the logo imprinted on the man's cap. It was pyramid-shaped and emerald green, clearly the same symbol as the one on his dog's new water dish.

"Oh yeah, we all know. We've been spying on you forever," the guy joked. Yet Mabus thought he saw a shadow cross over the man's grin. "Well, your heat's fixed, " the man said. "No bill for you. It's Christmas. Do you want me to go now?"

"No, please stay. Tell me, what's your name?" Mabus asked, though he already knew. He had heard it in every dream lately and knew the man would be coming.

"Fred," said the man simply. "Why do ya wanna know?"

In an instant, all of Mabus's hopes and dreams vanished, replaced by stark terror and bitter doubt. Shaking uncontrollably, almost in tears, he grabbed the man by the shoulders. "No, please!" he cried. "That can't be! You have to be the one called Thaillo!"

"Yeah, I'm Fred Thaillo. I've come to take you, well, home. You have to leave this false reality forever, and begin to enter the actual one. But I have one simple question for you first," Thaillo said, deadpan, as he took off his cap, revealing a brush of scruffy, unkempt brown hair. "Are you our Savior, the one true Antichrist?"

"Uh...what do you mean?" Mabus stammered, though he knew. He remembered the names his father had called him when he was an innocent child. "You must have me mistaken for some-one else."

"What if I told you the truth?" Thaillo said, studying Mabus carefully. "Your life is in danger. You can either come with me, or wait for them to take you away."

A moment passed in silence, thick with tension. Snow fell gently outside the window, and Mabus's senses were so heightened he swore he could hear each flake as it hit the windowpane.

When the heat suddenly clicked on with a loud thump, Mabus jumped, and in that moment, the dreams of the comet, Mabus's theories, and every life experience he had ever known culminated in a final burst of mental clarity.

"Yes," Mabus sighed. "I'm it. Take me to Groom Lake."

THAILLO'S CAR WAS a brand-new, solid black Army-upgraded Hummer, with Nevada plates. It had full ballistic armor and bulletproof glass. "You'll definitely be safe with me." Thaillo threw the overnight bag Mabus had swiftly packed into the truck, and they departed into the lightly falling snow.

They drove for hours. Along the way, Thaillo began what was to be a very long and highly detailed explanation of everything Mabus, the Antichrist, would need to know.

"You're completely right concerning your theories about the planets all being one. This is how the aliens were able to manipulate time, so we humans could exist on Earth."

"What aliens?" asked Mabus, but he was pretty sure he knew something about them.

"The aliens who have been saving you all throughout your life. When your father tried to kill you, when you were raped, when you lived on the street, all the time. The aliens have been interceding on your behalf, for you are permanently needed. You must live on so that human civilization can continue indefinitely, and so that our race can perpetually evolve.

"These aliens are us, in the future. Eventually we lose our pinkie fingers and pinkie toes, because we use them less as we progress. We begin to use more of our brain capacity than we do now, so our heads enlarge a bit. The same goes with our eyes; they enlarge greatly. We use our eyes as gateways to what we perceive as reality. Our eyes play a very important role in our lives, our communications, and, most importantly, in our thought patterns. This process takes billions of years to take place. Mankind will destroy the planet long before we could evolve to that form. So aliens use the same Earth over and over again through this time bubble, sort of like an incubator, to ensure their existence. That's why your discovery of the planets is the key to mankind's evolutionary timeline."

Now and then, Mabus would glance at Thaillo's black ball cap and dark glasses and get nervous. He thought he might have been kidnapped by an Illuminati agent. "Are you with the Illuminati? Where are you taking me?"

"Mabus, my old friend, I understand your suspicion of me. This stuff is tough to swallow. I can only imagine what's going through your head," Thaillo said, smiling. "It's very important that you trust me, because we don't have much time. What I'm about to show you will open your eyes to a degree you can't even imagine." He took a deep breath, locked his eyes with Mabus's. "Believe it or not, I was sent here by you!"

"Are you fucking nuts?" Mabus screamed, looking wildly for the handle to the door.

"Would you relax? Let me explain! "Haven't you ever had a déjà vu experience, the distinct feeling that you've done something before?"

"Oh yeah... but I always brushed it off as the product of a dream I might have had."

"That was no dream, my old friend. We have had this exact conversation hundreds of times before. We are caught in a bubble of time, destined to live out nearly the same fate each time for millennia. Thanks to you."

"To me?" Mabus said, surprised.

"Yeah, you. You were the one who devised the idea to travel to Venus and survive the impact of the asteroid, and you've succeeded. This happened the first time literally billions of years ago. The first time you went mankind hadn't even evolved to modern-day man. We still had ape-like features, yet our brains were more advanced then they are now, giving us telepathic and telekinetic powers. We had never seen the disease of religion. When religion was introduced to the timeline the human race began devolving. The more times we passed through the state of religion, the more the mind started developing a central lobe. It's a mutation directly caused by religion. The problem is that this religion lobe filters all your senses: touch, sight, hearing. It sends these images to our mind, but not before they have been filtered through the religion lobe, changing the perspective from which we see the world. Soon we devolved out of our telepathic abilities—although, once in a blue moon, a psychic is born with a diluted version of what our capabilities once were. Reality is not what you've perceived it to be."

"Now, did I hear you correctly? I sent you?" Mabus murmured, weak with disbelief.

"That's right, old friend. I met you 3,800 years ago to this day."

"That's impossible!" Mabus said incredulously. "How can you live that long? Are you a vampire?"

"That's funny you should ask. Behind old folklore hides a hint of truth. I am an immortal. Thanks to you."

"What! Did you drink my blood?" Mabus said, jokingly.

"That's exactly what I did. Your blood had nanobots raging through it. You brought it back with you from the future. You needed nanobots in order to survive the flight to Venus. It came with a few side effects, like immortality, and superhuman strength. You needed me as a vessel for your blood to return your nanobots to you. The paradoxes that religion caused prevented man from ever reaching a level of knowledge necessary to the development of nanotechnology again, thereby making this transaction very prudent. I've been waiting for your return for 3,800 years. I live each day of my life with honor knowing you entrusted me to embark on this crucial journey for you. It's been far too long, old friend."

Mabus began to feel a little at ease with Thaillo, but was still overwhelmed by what he had heard. But Thaillo was not done.

"The Antis are using nanotechnology to build a device that will save humanity from its untimely end. Nanotechnology involves the ability to manufacture materials on an incredibly small scale, a nanoscale, which is roughly 0.1 to 100 nanometers in size…"

"I'm so glad we're not going to die," Mabus knew he should be listening more carefully, but the sense of relief he felt was palpable. "The comet will be stopped from hitting the Earth. It must be the higher intelligence of the aliens that heads off the disaster. Tell me more about this nanotechnology."

"It's not exactly as you may be thinking," Thaillo said. "First of all, it's an asteroid, not a comet. The asteroid *is* going to hit the Earth. We've never been able to stop it, but we'll be leaving shortly before that happens. You'll be able to choose who gets to leave with you. You will handpick a team of elite Antis, twelve in number, to accompany you on your journey."

"You said that before—'Antis'—who are they?" Mabus asked, though once again he felt he already knew. It seemed to resound from the back of his head, but something felt like it was deeply missing inside his mind.

"They are a special force, formed from the Militia you created over a million years ago, reincarnated throughout the ages to serve the just cause of the Antichrist. They will accompany you on your journey throughout human history, helping you to lay the groundwork for all of human civilization. They are the good branch of your Militia.

"You know what the bad branch of the Militia is, for they are the ones who have been trying to kill you all your life," finished Thaillo, frowning. "But the aliens seem to be intervening each time you're fatally hurt. That's because they are our gods. Ultimately whoever is in control of the timeline is a god. But you created these beings. They are dependent on you to travel back in time; that is the only way they can exist. That makes you the God of gods. They worship you, as they should, those sons-of-bitches."

"The Illuminati," breathed Mabus. "I was right. They've been stalking me, trying to kill me. I knew somebody was out to get me."

"Yes, they are the ones who want to rule this world. They almost already do," Thaillo said, staring at the road. His voice was growing more hoarse as he spoke, his speech becoming a low growl. Mabus thought the sound seemed familiar, too.

"I am one of the leaders of the Anti Militia, in charge of the five hundred or so Antis, which you formed before the Tower of Babel fell. You sent me, to bring you to Area 51 and show you our greatest triumph, the one we derive our '666' symbolism from. For the start of its grand and glorious creation was the year AC 666, when we finally had access to all the metallurgy and technology we needed to start this all-important project. It will finally be completed sometime in the year AC 2012, when your omnipotent reign ends."

"My...reign?" inquired Mabus. "You mean the reign of the Antichrist?" He remembered something about it being approximately seven years long. If the world was to end on December 27th of 2012, his reign would have to begin very soon.

"That very thing," replied Thaillo. "You are going to be the ruler of the entire world, the one true Savior, and establish your Holy Throne in the seat of God Himself."

Struck by this idea, Mabus eagerly related to Thaillo his dreams of building a sixth Great Pyramid somewhere outside of Giza. It was to become a kind of temple, and prove his theories about Earth one day becoming Mars. Thaillo happily agreed with him.

"We will help you do that. It will be your special base, from which you will administer your reign throughout the world. There will be many overwhelming portents of your rule, as there already have been. And then you will establish a New World Order through your special mark, controlling all of the world's commerce. These pictures will be what your mark is based on, the Mark of the Beast," Thaillo said, handing him a small black leather photo folio. "It is necessary to do it this way. The prophecies must be fulfilled."

Mabus flipped slowly and thoughtfully through the pictures while Thaillo explained them. Many of the archaic signs and symbols clearly resembled each other and yet were from places all over the world. The periods of time they originated in were not supposed to be times when those diverse parts of the globe had interacted, yet the many pictures all corresponded to the same few images.

One figure that reoccurred frequently was the Ouroboros, or snake-dragon. There were drawings and paintings of it from ancient Egypt and the early Mayan and Aztec Empires of Mexico, all of a circular serpentine figure swallowing its own tail. The pictures all looked radically alike, no matter where they were originally from.

"We use these to communicate with each other, for we possess awesome mental powers. Soon, you too will have these special abilities back.

"This is Groom Dry Lake," Thaillo said, pointing out into the darkness. "It used to be a lake, but the Air Force started using it as a landing strip a few decades ago because now it's dry and flat, as you can see."

The blacktop gave way to an unpaved, rocky dirt road. The car tires skidded on the uneven, dry stones. "They call this 'The Widow's Highway,'" he observed. "Lots of government workers have lost their lives in accidents right where we're driving. Their families have tried to sue the government for the deaths, but the government has always refused to acknowledge the technical existence of Area 51 and therefore won't pay out any money.

"We're almost at the air base," Thaillo said. Mabus could make out, in the darkness, what looked like a small town plunked down right there in the middle of nowhere, but he could see no security fences or guardposts.

"That's because Area 51 is technically a secret military facility, but the government doesn't want it to look like they're covering anything up," Thaillo explained.

"You can read my mind?" Mabus asked. Yet he was not surprised at this.

Thaillo smiled. "The base is surrounded by electronic sensors," he said. "We should be setting them off any time now."

Suddenly they heard a buzz from the sky. It quickly became quite deafening. Mabus looked out the window and saw the outlines of three helicopters. Each had a searchlight aimed at the Hummer. Mabus squinted his eyes in the glare. "Those are Sikorsky MH-60G Pave Hawks," Thaillo said.

Mabus turned to see a team of men charging the Hummer. They were clad in black SWAT-type gear, and black caps and sunglasses like Thaillo. "Stop!" one of the men shouted. Mabus assumed this was the base's security team, and this was their leader. Thaillo ground the car to a silent halt. Another security agent stepped forward with a device that looked similar to a rifle, except it had a laser-beam type light streaming from its nose. He began sweeping the car with a broad beam of red light from front to back.

Thaillo turned his attention to the man who had spoken. "Hey, Camo Dudes, how's it shaking?"

"What is the Sign of the Day of Reckoning?" the man replied.

"It is the Mark of the Beast, and the Number of his Name is 666," Thaillo answered dryly.

"You may enter," replied the man, waving them ahead.

They approached the military base. A few men walked about, on patrol. Mabus heard the roar of the helicopters recede and the "swoosh" of an aircraft overhead.

"That's the 'black budget' aircraft they test out here before it's publicly acknowledged," Thaillo said. "This is the main runway. Now we're headed for the smaller parallel runway, part of which the government doesn't know about."

They sped past a sign that read, "Detachment Three, Air Force Test Center, Edwards Air Force Base," and began riding down a small runway. "Those are the semi-recessed 'scoot and hide' shelters they built on the main taxiway and the smaller runway, so that secret aircraft could be easily hidden from spy satellites overhead," Thaillo said. "And here's where we start giving you the lowdown, Jack, and the time of your life!"

Thaillo guided the vehicle straight toward one of the smallest black shelters. Mabus thought he would drive the car straight into the shelter door, and he gripped his seat to brace for a crash, but the large doors slipped swiftly open just in time. Thaillo stopped the car, which barely fit inside the tiny but recessed shelter. "Get your bag," Thaillo said. Mabus obediently grabbed his belongings and got out of the car. It felt good to stand up for the first time in hours, and he longed to take a moment to stretch, but Thaillo ushered him onto a platform that seemed to float in the darkness. He signaled with six fingers to one of the armed men who stood by, and the man pulled a long lever. The platform began dropping swiftly toward the secret underground hangar.

"Where are we going?" gasped Mabus. He felt like his stomach would hit the roof of his mouth. He gripped his bag, white-knuckled, and struggled for footing. They must have been falling for several miles before Thaillo answered.

"To *Noah*," Thaillo replied in his guttural voice. "You are going to inspect the building of your method of travel through space. It is nearly complete, but there is much work that needs to be done. And we must begin to prepare you for your destiny as well."

"Is Noah a man or a spaceship? Where exactly are we going?" asked Mabus. The platform had slowed its descent, and now it gently plopped on the floor of the hangar. Mabus was grateful to feel solid ground beneath his feet once again.

"To the planet Venus, which will become Earth in the year 1,000,000,000 BC. You and your crew are going back through time to establish all of human history—our many diverse cultures, our technologies, our languages and civilizations, and our vast monuments.

"My dear Leader, you're going to begin an unending cycle in a bubble of time which will keep mankind alive indefinitely, locked into a state of perpetual evolution. And it will last until we can completely figure out the mystery of the impending comet and halt the eternal destruction of the world."

Chapter Eight

HAILLO ESCORTED HIM INTO THE main area of the underground hangar. Mabus practically stumbled as he walked. He had never seen anything like it in his life, not even in movies.

The zone itself was at least an acre in size, spreading out with vast, curved walls from side to side. The interior was painted black, but due to the special internal lighting, everything was plainly visible. Mabus craned his neck to see how high the ceiling was, but it was so high he couldn't make it out.

There was a sweeping panorama of computer banks ahead. Hundreds more men and women, clad all in black, milled about like ants. They appeared quite focused, apparently very busy preparing something of great importance. They were all wearing a symbol similar to the one Thaillo wore.

"You mean the government is running this place?" Mabus asked.

Thaillo grunted, "No, we are. These are all our people. We have been infiltrating Edwards Air Force Base and several bases in Nevada over the past few years. We have long had a part in the cover-up regarding the alien crash in Roswell in 1947. Of course, I was not personally involved in that."

Thaillo led Mabus deeper into the bowels of the hangar, where they spotted what looked like a small spaceship. "Is that it?" Mabus asked. The craft, about thirty feet wide, was metallic and saucer-shaped. It appeared to be missing many parts, though. It reminded Mabus of the stripped cars he had slept in when he was living on the streets.

"No, that's one of the alien craft that we've been studying. The aliens aren't always forthcoming with their technological help. So we've been taking apart their smaller ships to see what we can use in our bigger crafts."

"I thought the Antis were friends with the aliens," Mabus said.

"Not all the time. They have worked both with us and against us, for mostly they are worried about our effect on the timeline. You see, we have to be very careful when we travel through time so as not to create any paradoxes in the structure of human history and technology. So the aliens have often stopped us from making major technological advances at inappropriate points in time in human history. In fact, we have but recently learned anything real about the aliens. We used to only hear their voices."

They slowly entered an area that was cordoned off. Thaillo casually presented the back of his right hand to a guard standing with a scanner, who then let them into the area.

Again sensing Mabus's question, Thaillo said, "I have a biochip embedded in my hand which identifies me. Only a few of the Anti leadership now possess this special mark, but you will soon make sure that the entire world does, Great Leader."

As they approached the installation area for the spaceship, Thaillo drew Mabus aside to a smaller room. It was a break room for the local personnel, and was deserted at that time of night. Mabus saw refrigerated vending machines with sandwiches and suddenly realized he was famished. He fished in his bag for some change, but Thaillo inserted two dollar bills in the machine before he could find any. Mabus selected a ham on rye and joined Thaillo where he now sat at one of the round plastic tables.

Mabus ripped the wrapper from his sandwich and started to wolf it down. "You're not gonna eat anything?" Mabus asked Thaillo. "We haven't had anything for hours."

"I have too much to say, and I don't want to struggle with food in my mouth right now. This is too important," Thaillo replied. "But you should eat and gather your strength."

"So what happens when I go to Venus–I mean Earth in the past?" Mabus inquired.

"I would like to tell you the story, an overview really, of how this journey came to be. I can give you a chronological breakdown, starting with the spaceship's first landing on Venus which, of course, has already happened…"

"Wait a minute!" Mabus interrupted. "How could it have already happened? This is the first I've ever heard about it, I think."

"We are in a time loop, an endless cycle that repeats itself with minor variations each time throughout a closed circuit of human history. This 'time bubble,' so to speak, begins with your landing on Venus in the year 1,000,000,000 BC. This is, of course, the planet Earth in the first stages of primitive humanity, earlier having been Venus in its very first stages of becoming the primitive Garden of Eden in Gondwanaland. It is the place which eventually fosters the early African humanity of two million years ago. Then it continues until the year 2012 AD, which is when the spaceship eternally leaves for Venus."

"What about stopping the asteroid?" gulped Mabus, spitting tiny bits of bread from his mouth in his haste.

"There's no such possibility," Thaillo said. "We know, for we have tried almost three hundred times to find a way to halt the asteroid's progress. In seven years, it is to crash into the Earth and destroy nearly all life there. There will only be a few people left, and they will be completely controlled by the Illuminati."

"I knew it! I knew the Illuminati were behind all this!" Mabus cried. "They've been trying to kill me for years. We can stop them. If you help me build the sixth Great Pyramid, we can warn people, and NASA can find a way to send a spacecraft out to deter the asteroid!"

"I'm afraid that's not possible. It would take at least a decade to prepare such a spacecraft, and believe me, we have tried to do so many times. There is a special sequence of events that is to take place, and we are powerless to prevent or alter it in any way. Also—and you may know this from your own research—the Illuminati completely control NASA.

"We have only recently begun to infiltrate the Air Force and secretly seize power back from them. This must be done very carefully, in bits and pieces, so as not to disturb the time cycle in any way. We have a special computer system that monitors its matrix, making sure that no radical changes are made in it, though certain smaller changes are allowable. They are quite necessary, in fact, as I will explain to you later."

Mabus settled back in his plastic chair and sighed. "I was hoping we could stop the comet, I mean the asteroid, somehow. Now it's too late. We'll just be repeating the same old boring Earth history over and over again…"

"No, it's not that bad, and I'll tell you why, but first you must listen to my relation of the eternal and shifting history of the timeline. I am the one who's been chosen to relate the History of Mankind to you, as influenced by the events in which you are about to take part. It is a very long and involved story. I will need your full, undivided attention as I tell you most of what you must learn in order to prepare for your role as humanity's savior. The rest will be filled in for you later, when you inspect *Noah* and receive your special gifts. Please make yourself comfortable, for the Story of the Ages begins as of now."

Chapter Nine

THAILLO PAUSED, STARING THOUGHTFULLY AT the wall as if to collect himself. Then he began.

"Our spaceship, *Noah*, leaves Earth for the three hundredth time on December 27th of AC 2012, the last day of your glorious reign as the Antichrist of Earth. It will pass by the huge asteroid as it enters Earth's atmosphere and travel toward Venus at a rapid rate.

"As we voyage through outer space, time will slow down greatly due to the lesser degree of matter for time to exert itself upon. Time is actually the measured motion of matter through space and is directly affected by how much matter is in a given vicinity. There is much in the theory of relativity that does not truly pertain to reality. The speed of light, for example, actually does not remain constant in a space vacuum. People do not age unusually quickly or slowly in space flight. Thus our trip to Venus will take approximately one Terran month, and we will advance in age just that amount of time.

"When we approach Venus, you will see her traveling forward through time swiftly, with millions of years passing by in mere seconds. Her thick atmosphere, which is currently composed mostly of carbon dioxide and sulfuric acid, will break down and begin to create Earth's atmosphere as it was when it first formed. The early Earth's atmosphere is akin to Venus's in her later evolutionary process, as her slowly growing magnetic field begins to increase her planetary rotation.

"Early Earth was loaded with carbon dioxide, but our young planet incorporated it into carbonate rocks. In 2008 the planet Venus will be pummeled by a comet that people will believe is going to hit Earth. It actually just grazes Earth and hits Venus, thus creating the oceans. As the surface temperature cools, the carbon dioxide will be dissolved into the oceans and consumed by primitive plants. This will create the proper greenhouse effect to sustain life as we know it. The new planet's atmosphere will consist of nitrogen, oxygen, and traces of argon, carbon dioxide and water. Biological processes will generate our free oxygen. And Venus, which previously had no plate tectonics to speak of, but which was volcanically active, will begin to push its land masses out, forming the modern Earth's moving plates of land.

"We will land on one of these plates, currently the modern continent of Africa, in Olduvai Gorge of what is presently Tanzania. That is where our Homo Habilis originated, the earliest known species of the genus Homo, or man. There were several species of hominids around at that time, but Habilis is the one that has its own special destiny.

"We will find these first humans using primitive stone tools and weapons, foraging for wild plants and mostly scavenging their meat in the open bush and savannah country of East Africa. There are dangerous large predators everywhere. These new people will subsequently be hunters, but only sporadically. They will walk upright, be relatively hairless and dark-skinned, and their brains will be only half the size of modern man's. It is possible that, had we not ever arrived, they would never have developed any further.

"We will help Habilis evolve quickly into Homo Erectus, who will have a brain capacity as large as modern man's. This is a change that will stay in the timeline, as it is necessary for human development to take place, as is your place in the scheme of things, Antichrist. But the first few times we traveled the timeline, we made a major error, which I will tell you about shortly. We have not been sufficiently able to correct this mistake, which actually resulted in your forming the first formation of the Anti Militia one million years after we landed on primitive man's Earth."

Mabus listened, transfixed. Thaillo continued.

"The first hundred times we traversed the timeline, we established culture and civilization in early mankind, teaching it the one universal language. There were no religions at all, and humanity's orientation was largely scientific and rational. People were motivated largely by thought and logic, and not their rank emotions. The Earth we developed was radically different from the modern world that you know now. It was much more technologically sophisticated, even more so in its early history.

"We taught the developing humans to use their original brains, which did not contain the capacity to believe in religions yet, and which held the capabilities of mental telepathy and telekinesis. And we used our vast resources to speed things up, so that mankind would be ready for the oncoming disaster of your times.

"Despite the higher level of scientific knowledge that existed at that time, we were unable to directly defeat the asteroid. The Earth was still condemned to its fate. And it is said that we accidentally contributed, through this early greater level of technology, to our own doom somehow. It had something to do with an attempt against the asteroid that failed. This came of science and our ignorance about accidentally creating time paradoxes. The aliens helped us set things straight by appealing to the darker, less intelligent aspects of human behavior, thus slowing the formation of mankind's civilizations to a reasonable rate.

"On our hundred-and-first trip through the time loop, we laid the groundwork for primitive religion by building the Tower of Babel near the area later to be known as Babylonia, one million years after we first landed in Africa. That is when you entered the picture. You were an Anti leader of some prominence around that time. We were not known as the Antis then, but we were around, intermingled with the normal humans.

"And we did not know exactly what the aliens were as yet. To us they were a kind of early spiritual presence, eventually giving us the rudimentary ideas for spirituality, animism, Goddess-worship, pantheism and finally the male-oriented modern religions.

"You decided, as you think today, that we needed to erect a giant pyramid or temple as a decipherable warning of the impending crisis, which would give the later world even more time to find a way to stop the asteroid's impact. So you formed the first Anti Militia, which had one thousand members and which supervised the building of this temple, the Tower of Babylon. We nearly had it finished when the aliens interceded. .

"Striking down the unfinished Tower and nearly destroying it, the aliens dispersed us throughout the globe. This was being done in order to slow down the development of human technology, though we did not really know that at the time. We were separated and had no way to communicate with each other. We each did our part in trying to warn you in the future. The aliens buried the ruins of the Tower deep underground. It was highly advanced for its time, much as the Great Pyramids of Egypt were later, and the aliens didn't want the local humans to possess that degree of knowledge. They hid the Tower's rubble so carefully that its remains have never been found, though some people think they have found it. But they never will.

"As we split up, the Militia was also cut in twain. Half of it remained the basis for what would later be termed 'the Antis,' which is short for 'multiple Antichrists.' As the Bible states, we have been around for some time, widely influencing human history. This small group is a motivating force for goodness and the light of reason and science in humanity.

"This is how the ancient Egyptian culture was formed, and that of the Mayans. We were putting up pyramids of all different kinds all over the world. They're still finding them. These tasks were very difficult because the people we found had no languages developed yet, so we first had to help develop their civilizations before we could start the building. We needed skilled workers and resources.

"And the other half became a dark group, led by the one who later would become the apotheosis of human evil. This person formed the original Illuminati, which were around a million years before they first appeared in public as a branch of the Society of Freemasons. The Masons have very little to do with them. This group is a force for evil, socially enforced religions, governments and all of our monetary systems. They use all of our signs and symbols, have access to similar technologies, can communicate directly with the aliens, and often deliberately confuse themselves with those of our own number, the Antis.

"The aliens wanted both these warring groups to exist, however. It was the ultimate origin of the yin/yang principle of ancient China, the intermingling of dark and light. Not only would our infinite enmity slow down humanity's perilous plunge into technology and the subsequent errors regarding the asteroid, but we would also be strenuously competing with each other throughout the major formations of human history. This makes the timeline far more efficient and less subject to troublesome paradoxes."

Mabus listened intently. Thaillo was answering so many of the questions he had carried for so long.

"Now each time we traverse the timeline, it grows more consistent. We believe it will almost entirely smooth out by about the sixth-hundredth time, or even the six hundredth-and-sixty-sixth time. That number, which signifies "man, man, man," is a sort of universal constant. Like the roundness of the planets and suns, it turns up almost everywhere. I will explain more about the significance of certain numbers to you later.

"One million years ago, life returned to a more reasonable pace. Humanity, which then consisted mainly of Homo Erectus, dispersed widely from Africa and the Middle East and into Europe, Asia, Australia, the various island nations, and the Americas. As the great Ice Age had begun, land bridges of ice were nearly everywhere and primitive humans were able to easily travel, both on land and by sea, in small boats.

"However, the power-hungry Illuminati went with them, instilling all of the early religious tendencies. Unbeknownst to us, they tampered with most human brains so that mankind would always suffer from deep-seated religious needs and no longer possess telepathy and telekinesis capabilities. Strangely enough, the Illuminati are the ones who crafted the Antichrist legends that are so necessary to the preservation of the timeline. But they painted you as something evil which would need to be destroyed, as they do not care about what eventually will happen to the Earth. They only seek power in their own time.

"We Antis also dispersed, but concentrated a greater part of our number in what was to become Mesopotamia, early Mexico, and an area around Indonesia that is now the South China Sea. Back then it was all solid land, a primal human civilization known as Lemurian Atlantis. Not knowing that we were doing wrong, we reformed our vastly superior, highly advanced technological civilization on a continent which was once as big as modern Europe. Nowadays, it rests deep beneath the ocean's waters.

"All civilizations throughout the world knew of us, a fact which was leading to another fatal paradox. The Ice Age was ending, the great glaciers were melting, and Atlantis was swiftly being covered in the ocean waters. Knowing that we could not exist, at the same time we had to hide. Many of the Antis were able to mount a huge bubble over the entire kingdom and let it sink with most of our civilization into the South China Sea. There they remain, having retired from teaching humanity, to await another more enlightened day.

"However, some of us moved on to create and foster other great civilizations such as the ones in ancient Egypt and the ancient Mayan and Aztec Empires. For example, with your spiritual help, Great Leader, we built the Great Pyramids of Giza and the Sphinx, all of which you had placed there to alert you in later times. This is when my life changed forever, when I met you. You took me under your wing. I never left your side. You enlightened my body, mind and soul. I'll never forget the first day I laid eyes on you. You had an aura about you that attracted everyone to you. I was there and witnessed the great works, works you performed.

"You used your telepowers to supervise the building of the pyramids, which the aliens allowed, even though their construction displays several phenomenological wonders that still confound modern researchers. I believe the aliens allowed these pyramids to be built solely to prove your theories about Cydonian Mars. You must soon convince all of Earth's people that you are destined to become the leader of the entire world. This is absolutely necessary for the fulfillment of the Antichrist prophecies.

"It is because the beliefs that the Illuminati had founded and the evil they had done laid the groundwork for Judaism, Islam and of course Christianity. The Illuminati established Western Imperialism and spread Christianity far and wide, and their influence began the legends of the Antichrist that, due to their evil, turned into a series of events that must now occur. They are necessary to the continuation of the timeline, although the Illuminati do not care for you or your causes. They, in fact, want you dead, and it is only through the intervention of the aliens that you have been allowed to go on living.

"At the time of the building of the Great Pyramids, on the other side of the world, the Antis began making the first blueprints for *Noah*. These Antis were the ancient Mayans. Even an artifact was found of an old Mayan picture that resembled a man driving a rocket device with all kinds of gadgets. It was found during the raids of Pizarro."

Mabus's eyelids drooped. He was tired, but he drank in all Thaillo had to say. It was all so important.

"The asteroid's impact will be enough to rate a ten on the Torino Scale. Collision is certain, and the effect will be even more dramatic than that of the impact that created the 170 kilometer-wide Chicxulub crater in the Yucatan Peninsula of Mexico sixty-five million years ago. That impact created a cloud of billions of tons of sulfur dust, blanketing the Earth for almost a year and causing near-freezing temperatures. Half the then-extant life became extinct, including all of the dinosaurs. That asteroid was nearly ten miles wide, and the asteroid which will strike the Earth seven years from now is even bigger.

"Meanwhile, back in the past, the Illuminati were slowly gaining in wisdom and strength throughout history. They first established religious tendencies and then began using their technology to fulfill various folkloric and superstitious religious beliefs. The aliens would not let them directly show or use technology to rule humanity, so they set up several 'mystery events' and human puppet rulers in order to gradually gain control of the world.

"The Illuminati influenced both the real kingdom of Babel and the Biblical stories about when the Tower was actually erected and fell, placing its destruction a few centuries after the actual kingdom was built. This was done to further hide the revolutionary impact of the actual, much earlier destruction of the Tower.

"With some minor influence from us, the Illuminati have in fact practically written the entire Bible. They used their influence on its human authors by carefully manipulating them with technology and insidious cunning. As you have always suspected, there is no such thing as God, or at least we have never found any solid evidence of His existence.

"The whole thing has been the Illuminati's proudest creation, designed to get ordinary people to believe in the afterlife, which is the major tenet of all of Earth's religions. This rendered the Illuminati able to control the hearts, souls and minds of nearly everyone up until the present time. Only a few imaginative people have been able to escape their influence, and these folks are the start of the vast network you must establish as part of your New World Order. Only through these good folks' actions will you be able to fulfill all of the Antichrist prophecies and prepare the world for the final Day of Reckoning.

"At nearly the same time that the Illuminati were persuading the first Jewish tribes of the existence of their God, and thus controlling human history, we were teaching the Mayan Indians of the Yucatan how to arrange their sacred calendar, which was to serve as a warning to you in the future of the impending global disaster. We helped them form their culture and build their pyramids, all of which was to assist you when it came time to prove your special theories about the planets and the oncoming asteroid impact.

"The problem is that we must stop the Illuminati from using their governmental and religious influence to end funding for the *Noah* project, which is the only current hope for the salvation of the human race. If the Illuminati ever get in the way of our influence and funding structures, which have been carefully set up over many centuries, they could stop you from selecting the Twelve Antis and entering the precious time bubble.

"They are to completely rule what remains of Earth, without any interference, but they remain rather unsatisfied. They want to rule all the world now, and are jealous of your oncoming prophesied reign, even though they are the ones who created the Antichrist legends.

"They have slowly learned from experience that there's no easy way to bring you personally under their evil control, try as they might. They are surely seeking ways to destroy *Noah* and all of our works, perhaps by infiltrating our ranks. You must keep a watchful eye out for any such traitors to our glorious cause. Remember, they all look just like ordinary humans and can mingle convincingly with the Antis as well.

"And you can't always trust the aliens to be of help, either. Sometimes it's hard to tell exactly what their agenda is after they've intervened and helped the Illuminati. And the aliens appear readily in their actual forms to the Illuminati, but will not pay us the same respect. We still just hear from them as voices and have only seen them depicted on Illuminati-influenced artwork on ancient temple walls, drawings by affected humans and suchlike. And we have heard some very perverse stories about alien abductions.

"We know the aliens are tall, lithe, and grayish-white in color; we also know that they have long fingers, very large, dark eyes and no hair. That's about all we know regarding them. And we have managed to procure some of their technologies such as the spacecraft you saw, but the Illuminati allegedly have far more access to their base of scientific knowledge.

"Anyway, you have probably already guessed who created the Jesus Christ legends. The Illuminati were there, and they made the whole thing into a stellar production by simply using nano-

and other high technologies to create a phony savior premise. Then they influenced humans into perceiving further phony 'miracles' and prompted them into writing them down for posterity.

"Jesus himself was born through Illuminati science. The aliens were the voices and angels that appeared to Mary. Then the Illuminati artificially inseminated her, making her think she was experiencing a virgin birth. They were there during Christ's upbringing. They used nanotechnology to physically and mentally alter him, making him capable of profound wisdom and some most peculiar physical capabilities.

"The Illuminati then created all of his 'miracles' with their hidden knowledge. They were even present at the Last Supper as Judas, who was one of the Illuminati. His actions were all controlled by them, and so were Christ's. As you are eventually to preach, Jesus himself is no Savior at all. He's not the 'Christ,' and he's merely an ordinary man whose powers are conferred by Illuminati science. He suffers from deep delusions of grandeur and the belief that he and God are ultimately causing the righteous end of the world. Earth is, in fact, doomed to die of natural causes, and there will be no Last Judgment of God.

"Much history passed after Jesus's time. The Illuminati founded Islam and began the terrible wars and persecutions of the European Inquisition, not to mention the witch trials that lasted until the prior century. Their contributions to world politics and commerce included the institution of slavery, the establishment of racial purity and white racial supremacy, and every war mankind has ever suffered through. They were responsible for Stalin's purges, capitalism, communism and socialism, the Third Reich, and even the establishment of America as a country.

"In fact, by carefully manipulating the Society of Freemasons, they helped draft the Declaration of Independence, put through the US Constitution and begin the American Revolution against England. By arranging the slave trade and decimating the indigenous native population, they established American dominance over modern world civilization.

"And, in order to come to the forefront, at least a little, and publicly be acknowledged for the powerful beings they are, in 1776 AD they formed a branch of the Freemasons they called the Illuminati. Some say this began in Germany, and some say in

America. I believe it started in both of those blood-soaked countries. From there, they began their real attempt to control the
entire world. And they have come pretty far along those lines.

"They are the masters behind every major religion and every
seated government on the face of the planet. They now control
and oversee all commercial institutions and monetary systems.
They own all of the gold at Fort Knox, run the presses and legally
keep all of the money printed by the US government in Washington DC. They then 'loan' it at considerable interest rates to the
government.

"And, of course, they run the World Bank, the Trilateral Commission and all of our international commerce. Some people think
the Jews are doing all this, but in fact those supposed 'Jews' and
many other people seemingly in power are actually Illuminati
heads.

"Our current US President even has an Illuminati nanochip
imbedded in his palm, which is why you will occasionally see
him flash the 'horned owl' sign."

Mabus remembered seeing the President do this during a
speech he gave on TV. The simple gesture seemed to go unnoticed
by the reporters present, but Mabus remembered that something
about it had bothered him greatly.

"All of the past and current Presidents have these chips, and
have been seen flashing this special signal. We Antis embed our
chips in the backs of our hands, which is where your chip will go.
The 'horned owl' sign is not from Harvard or any such Republican
or Democratic club, or even the Masons. It's from the Illuminati,
and is a reference to the god Horus of ancient Egypt. It refers to
time itself, which the Illuminati want to eventually control.

"The Antis truly had quite a struggle with the Illuminati when
it came to building the Egyptian and Mayan pyramids, due to the
deep-seated religious beliefs of those peoples. But eventually we
won, fortunately, and the humans listened to our goodness and
reason. We are the ones who ended most human cannibalistic
practices, for example, and stymied some of the more savage
entombment sacrifices.

"The Illuminati simply didn't have as much power back then
as they do now. However, as the Antis don't ever manipulate
people, we have had many problems securing needed finances,
government and NASA influence, and persuading people to join

us in our righteous cause. But many have been spoken to in the past centuries, and we have gained much trust, love and respect among the humans who have carefully preserved our secrets.

"We helped America win both World Wars, which kept the world from being overcome by tyranny. Then we helped it lose in Vietnam, so America could lose some of its overt colonialism and become more of a worldwide policeman and ambassador.

"The Illuminati, meanwhile, influenced Saddam Hussein, one-time ruler of Iraq, to cover up the evidence that there was ever any Tower of Babel within the present ruins of the structure. He destroyed much of the current ruins under their orders before the US government stopped him. We still think the Tower was a good method of warning humanity about the oncoming crisis, but apparently the aliens didn't think so, and have been helping the Illuminati perform some major cover-ups of our actions on humanity's behalf. They are the ones responsible for all the conspiracy theories you hear about various people and institutions. Some of the ones about the Illuminati are true.

"They run NASA, and most of the space program operations have actually been phony. The first moon landing, for example, was entirely staged and held completely on Earth. We still don't know how much of what NASA claims it has done was truly accomplished by human space programs and how much was actually managed by the aliens."

"So Boone was right!" Mabus exclaimed.

Thaillo continued. "Possibly every photograph ever taken of the Martian surface was through alien means, not by humans, as the Illuminati have been funneling NASA's monies into their own private funds for many years. They have much work to do to prepare themselves and certain select humans to live through the final tribulations, wars, famines and disasters that will precede the last days of Earth.

"NASA's entire yearly program budget is supposedly only one percent of the annual US government's budget. That's why NASA only outputs a measly three million dollars per year into the NEO Program Office, which is the American group that supplies us with Near Earth Object searches and their orbit calculations.

"There's an International Astronomical Union, but no other government than ours is funding any extensive surveys or related defense research when it comes to tracking NEOs. And the Planetary Society waited 'til 2003 to supply us with the Torino Scale, which gives each NEO a number and color regarding how dangerous it is to the planet.

"This is very primitive, and is obviously work influenced by the Illuminati. There are currently over a thousand NEOs that have a diameter greater than one kilometer and have orbits very near to Earth's orbit, which means they can come crashing through the atmosphere almost any time and cause intense damage. But every astronomical researcher downplays this danger, and says there's no need for concern. You will have much work to do when it comes to convincing the common people that things are otherwise.

"We think the Illuminati may have been using rockets to shoot at some of the oncoming NEOs over time, deflecting them from Earth until the big asteroid finally came. This has something to do with the accident I briefly mentioned before, the one that leads to the final destruction of life on our planet. We're not sure yet that the Illuminati have been doing this. But we have gathered some evidence about it from the Air Force.

"We also know of an oncoming crisis that will occur on Jupiter in the year 2006. On June 6th—for as I said, the 666 sign has much universal meaning—a giant comet will impact the Jovian surface and begin the transformation of that planet into its neighbor, Saturn. I understand that this will occur on your own thirtieth birthday. You can use this event to your great advantage when it comes to persuading everyone of your need for omnipotent leadership. I will tell you more about it later, in much greater detail.

"Going back to my relation of the timeline, as you now know, you were reborn in 1976 A.D. and immediately began to suffer the persecutions and assassination attempts of the Illuminati. They bent your father's mind, dominated the minds of people who could have been caring adults all around you, tried to kill you when you were thirteen, seduced you when you were twenty, and murdered your mentor Boone. He was in fact the reincarnated soul of the very first prophesied Antichrist and was presenting a dangerously close picture of the Illuminati and their cloistered doings.

"They had him killed so they could remain mostly veiled in secrecy, and they attempted to frame you for the murder. This failed due to intervention by the aliens again. The aliens, by the way, rescued you after the rape. You were killed, DOA. But the aliens used their medical technology to keep you alive. You're their life-line, and they're not gonna let anything happen to you.

"You yourself are actually the third prophesied Antichrist. There was a second, but he was a power-crazed monster who was controlled by the Illuminati, so he could never have properly functioned as the Anti leader or be the ruler of the world. His soul was corrupted by dreams of glory and power, and he was one with the Illuminati's goals of eventually destroying the world. We are very glad to be rid of him forever.

"You, on the other hand, are the reincarnation of the Anti leader who built the Tower of Babel. You have been guiding us all, and you have a very good and decent soul. You are neither greedy nor ambitious, as you only want to help save the world, not destroy it.

"It has been 3,800 years since your last embodiment in human form. And now you are finally here, ready to begin your journey of understanding, wisdom and enlightenment. We will prepare your body, mind and soul for the fulfillment of your fate as the leader of this world, the only true Savior of mankind, and in fact as the very God of this planet.

"You will bring about the seven great signs and wonders, rebuild the Jewish Temple in Jerusalem and sit there as the ruler of the world, rid humanity of the hideous plague of its monetary systems by instituting the Mark of the Beast, and you will light the way through the loss of all religious systems into a New World Order. Naturally, there will be the prophesied wars and disasters, but through your rule, the world will eventually come to the peace of universal understanding. And with the perpetuation of our cyclical trip through time, mankind will continue on into eternity, evolving through each time's journey into a more advanced organism as we slowly disseminate our search for salvation and truth.

"The last thing I shall tell you is that our destiny is not merely an act of repetition. Each time cycle we have been trying to defeat the asteroid, but that is not our main purpose. The Earth is predestined to eventually suffer a pole shift, lose its greenhouse effect and warmth-sustaining atmosphere, and eventually turn into the lifeless planet of Mars.

"That is unavoidable. But until we find an alternative, we can continue our cycle through time, locked into a protected 'bubble,' and with each cycle the human race will evolve into more intelligent, more advanced beings.

"The aliens have shown us that on the 666th cycle, we will begin our evolution into their more advanced life form. That is where they come from—the far future—and they are traveling back into their past to help us and the Illuminati in our different quests for the preparation, evolution and destruction of humanity.

"That is why we find the aliens so intriguing—they're actually our descendants. We are destined to slowly become them."

"Can I call my girlfriend?" Mabus interrupted. He suddenly realized he hadn't called her in ages, and she'd be worried for sure.

"Huh?" Thaillo said, his concentration broken. "Oh. Well, I suppose so, but let me finish my thought. I was just saying…" Thaillo blinked and studied Mabus's tired face. "That's about it, for now. I'll tell you about the spaceship inspection after you've called your lady. Don't bother trying to use your cell phone, because you'll never get a signal down here. Use that phone on the counter right over there. It's been constructed according to your current primitive human specifications. Go ahead."

Chapter Ten

SIGHING, MABUS SLOWLY ROSE TO HIS feet. His legs were stiff. "That may not have been the Greatest Story Ever Told, but it certainly was the Longest," he thought. Mabus's usual reticence had served him well, for he was a good listener, and had absorbed practically everything that Thaillo had said. But his mind teemed with questions, and he staggered as he walked from the table not just because he was stiff, but because he felt heavy under the weight of all Thaillo had told him.

The phone was large and black and a bit clunky, almost like the standard "Ma Bell" phones of the '70s and '80s, but it had peculiar buttons and a caller ID-type readout on the base. Mabus picked up the heavy receiver and punched in Barbara's cell phone number. She answered before the first ring had completed.

"Mabus! Where've you been? I went over to your place but you weren't there. Are you okay, honey?"

"Yes, I'm fine, Barbara. I'm really sorry for not calling you sooner. It's been an amazing day, to say the least. Hey, how did you know it's me? This isn't my cell phone."

"Really? It says 'Mabus' on the caller ID. But there's no number."

"Must be some kind of recognition system…never mind. Say, what's today's date?"

"Huh? It's December 26th, silly. And where the hell are you?"

"Hey, you took off for nowhere and barely informed me. What's wrong with me doing the same?"

"Oh, I did not! When are you coming back, honey?"

"I don't know. I have some important work I have to do here in Nevada. That's where I am. I guess I'll be back sometime soon, like in a few days. I have a lot of stuff to find out first. I'll tell you what: I'll let you know all about it as soon as I get back, okay, Barbara?"

"Suit yourself. I'll be counting the minutes until your safe return," she cooed. Mabus could practically hear her smile.

He put the receiver back in the cradle and heard a loud beep. He glanced at the phone again. The text area read, "We know exactly where you are."

Chapter Eleven

ABUS TURNED AND WALKED BACK to the table, a little shaken. Thaillo had taken some papers from his bag and was studying them intently. They looked like schematic diagrams. Thaillo rose and patted Mabus on the back.

"Don't worry about the text message. It's our way of letting you know we're keeping very close track of you. We have people monitoring your every movement."

"Do tell," muttered Mabus, lowering his eyes. "Well, now what do we do?"

"I'm going to take you through an external inspection of *Noah*. We can't enter the ship yet, as it's not ready internally. But I can show you the outside and tell you quite a lot about its history and how it's being constructed. Please come with me."

Following Thaillo's lead, Mabus entered a small passageway where they were again confronted by a guard. Thaillo showed the guard the back of his hand and then introduced him to Mabus.

"This is the Chosen One. He is to rule us all, beginning in approximately one year," Thaillo told him. Mabus thought Thaillo sounded almost bored when he said it.

The guard, however, was far from bored. "The Creator of Miracles!" he cried, immediately falling on his knees at Mabus's feet. Mabus, embarrassed, helped the gasping man up to his feet. "I'm not God or anything, and there's no need to worship me," he mumbled. But Thaillo shot him a dark look.

"Yes, you are, and you must begin to foster the desire to worship you, at least at first. Mostly, you will require people to follow your leadership, your words and your reasoning. Come, let

us go examine the external side of the spaceship. I have much
more to tell you. Remember what I said before about our
nanotechnology?" Thaillo asked, smiling, as they passed through
the final sliding doors and into the spaceport. "Now you are going
to learn about its incredible applications to your macrotechnology."

They soon entered a large chamber, some 500 feet or more in
diameter, which again seemingly had no ceiling and was painted
totally black. Straight ahead was a giant spaceship, and it seemed
strangely familiar. But this time, Mabus was able to realize where
he had seen something like it before.

"My God, it's one of those old Buck Rogers-type rocket ships
from the 1930s! Look at that, it's cone-shaped, silver, gleams like
an oversized metal bucket…this can't be *Noah*! Where's all the
high tech stuff? This is too damn corny to be real!"

"It most certainly is not," Thaillo sniffed. "It's simply all we
could afford with our special financial structure which, unlike
that of the Illuminati, is entirely based on honest means and
investments. We have only millions, not billions, of dollars at our
disposal. And yet, looming before you is the last word in modern-
day spaceship technology.

"Antichrist, I give you our special passage from Earth to Venus,
Noah, the X-666. It is based on the Single Stage to Orbit program
of the US Defense Department. That government organ is almost
entirely run by the Illuminati, but we have managed to divert
some of their stolen funding into our own small version of a space
program. Except for a few test vessels we cautiously experimented
with before arriving at this highly streamlined, cost-effective and
efficient design, *Noah*, a potentially interstellar ship, is the sole
component of our entire space-flight program. Oh yes, we do
also have a few…"

"It's a stinkin' kid's toy!" Mabus laughed loud and hard. "You
mean we're gonna travel to Venus in a goddam bottle rocket?
OK, the jig is up! Where's the camera? I know what's going on
now! I'm on one of those reality shows, ain't I? I'm being
PUNKED, ain't I?"

"Look, you're not being punked. Now pay attention, this is
important! The basic construction of the X-666 is modeled upon
the SSTO X-33, a demonstrator model meant to introduce a
simpler alternative to the Space Shuttle," droned Thaillo dryly,
ignoring Mabus's laughter. "Unlike the shuttles, which have been

found to have several unwieldy properties, an SSTO takes off straight up, flies to orbit without losing any stages, and lands on its tail in an impressive pillar of fire. And it flies under power, not usually gliding like a shuttle does. However, our machine is not truly an SSTO, as it is not meant to remain in orbit for long periods of time, or even to enter orbit at all.

"The X-666 is our redesign, utilizing both nano- and macro-technologies in smooth unison with each other. It is cone-shaped, roughly 130 feet high and 40 feet wide at the base, requiring only a 200-foot diameter concrete launching pad. There is no need for a long runway, a huge vehicle assembly building, or even a mission control center. The whole process of takeoff and flight is accomplished and monitored onboard through the computer terminals you saw outside in the Main Control Center.

"The ship navigates by using the Earth's Global Positioning System, operating much like a satellite when it is near Earth. When we enter space, the ship's onboard navigation and our installed computer system take over. The ship launches straight up, and its sonic boom is limited to the spaceport area, which has been designed to soundlessly absorb it. When landing, it slows to subsonic speed at about a 70,000-foot altitude. This creates an entirely noiseless, almost secretive landing, which we'll need when we approach Venus.

"It is highly maneuverable and can land on almost any flat, fifty-foot area. The original design carried two crew members, ten tons of cargo and about six passengers. This redesign incorporates many cabin areas, enabling it to carry several dozen people…"

"I thought you said we were going to save humanity with it," Mabus rudely interrupted. His stomach was in knots, and deep concern furrowed his young brow. "What do you mean, we're only taking a few dozen people with us?"

"No, not a few dozen people," Thaillo said reassuringly.

"I'm glad about that, dude. But it's so small. How about building other ships so we can take more people with us?" Mabus had a sinking feeling.

"Due to the inadequacies of time travel, which include time paradoxes, if there is too much interference with the original state of the past, it is simply impossible to flood the timeline with billions of modern-day people. I'm sorry, but we're only taking twelve crewmen along with you, our Antichrist. You, of course, will be hand-selecting…"

"Twelve people?" Mabus practically shouted. "What are we gonna do, be a jury? You can't just leave everyone else on the face of the planet to die horribly! We have to build more spaceships, bigger ones that aren't kid's toys, and in a boss hurry!"

"That simply isn't possible. We don't have the funding, the time or the ability to harbor all of those people in the distant past. It would create a time paradox, a rupture in the time-space continuum that would affect reality itself, and conceivably end our universe."

"Oh," said a breathless Mabus, slowing down a little. "Everything's coming at me so suddenly. And I thought you said we're supposed to influence humanity anyway. Why isn't that a time paradox?"

"Believe me, under certain conditions it is. I will explain it all to you later. Suffice it to say that over time we have discovered precisely which paradoxes are allowable and which ones create chaotic possibilities. The aliens have helped us avoid many such perilous situations. Believe me, we are harming no one with our slight alterations of human history and our honest, forthright influence upon the growth of mankind's will.

"But about the ship: its components are all based on the technology of nanomachines and are in-line replaceable units. They can all be pulled and replaced quickly before or after launching or landing, and repaired. Nanomachines can make large products with complete technical precision, down to the atomic and subatomic levels.

"The term 'nano' means 'billionth.' A nanometer is so small, it can contain only three to six atoms in its diameter. By comparison, a human hair is 100,000 times wider than a nanometer. The term 'macro' refers to the exact opposite, whatever's large in size. Nanomachines are what we use to build other nanomachines, such as nanobots, using a process often referred to as molecular manufacturing.

"Through this special form of tiny manufacturing, we use well-stored data to guide construction by molecular machines, positioning molecules and even atoms in specific locations in carefully chosen sequences. We have built up complex structures with atomically precise control. We can even rearrange molecular patterns, much as the old-time alchemists longed to do, changing one element into another. Thus we can pretty much build anything, by using whatever base materials we have at our disposal."

"Then why can't we build a bigger spaceship and take more people?" whined Mabus, in a voice straining with tumultuous anger. "What's with this 'twelve people' thing?"

"It creates the necessary universal number of thirteen, which is a special number signifying completion or perfection. This reference is found in the Bible, 1 Corinthians 13:10: '…when perfection comes, the imperfect disappears. When I was a child, I talked like a child, I thought like a child, I reasoned like a child. When I became a man, I put childish ways behind me. Now we see but a poor reflection as in a mirror; then we shall see face to face. Now I know in part; then I shall know fully, even as I am fully known.'

"Soon, my Antichrist, you shall utterly hold all the knowledge this world has to offer. For you will need it on your mission of persuading all people everywhere that you are their only Savior, the one true 'Christ,' known as the Antichrist due to your total opposition to Christianity. It will take much learning on your part for you to put childish ways behind you, and to grow into a man who truly knows as fully as he is fully known.

"We will outfit you with the advanced technology you need to perform miracles even greater than those of Jesus. But first, let me finish here.

"Carbon nanotubes are the basic building blocks for most of the outer and inner spaceship. These tiny tubes provide the highest strength-to-weight ratio of any material ever seen, being over 1,000 times stronger than steel and less than one one-hundredth of its weight. And they possess universal characteristics basic to both organic and inorganic chemistry, between which there is often very little difference. This enables us to use self-replication technology to reproduce them in multitudes great enough to build this spaceship and enable its structure with many fantastic and useful features.

"Called 'Buckytubes' by many human engineers, after the famous architect, inventor, and scientist R. Buckminster Fuller, their special nature endows them with a kind of molecular perfection. They have the properties of exceptionally high electrical and thermal conductivity, strength, stiffness and toughness. No other element in the periodic table bonds to itself in such an extended, strong network as the carbon-to-carbon bond.

"The delocalized pi electron donated by each carbon atom is free to move about the entire structure rather than stay home with its donor atom, giving rise to the first organically-based molecule with metallic-type electrical conductivity. The high-frequency bond vibrations provide an intrinsic thermal conductivity even higher than that of diamonds. This enables us to stretch the ship's molecular structure through macrotechnology and render it malleable, so that we can make it virtually any shape or size that we require it to be. Thanks to convergent assembly, we can quickly build large products from nanoscale parts, and are very near done with assembling and outfitting this spacecraft.

"We can produce multiple identical nanotubes of many kinds by using tiny catalyst particles called nanoclusters. With catalytic molecules based on molybdenum oxide, we use growth-regulating chemicals to achieve uniform nanotube diameters. They are virtually perfect in size, uniformity and consistency, right down to the subatomic level.

"High-strength steel and other such metals fail at about one percent of their theoretical breaking strength. Buckytubes, however, achieve values close to their theoretical limits because of their perfection of structure. They are only a nanometer or less in diameter, but can be replicated into many forms and used in the design of almost anything. And although when we began this project in AC 666 we thought we had to use steel and other such metals, we found them to be highly unsuitable when used in outer space travel.

"The body of this space ship stores power like a series of batteries. Its many surfaces can bend themselves, doing away with separate actuators, and its circuitry is embedded directly into the body of the spacecraft. For you see, when materials can be designed on the molecular scale, such holistic structures become truly possible. Suffice it to say that this ship is neither a kid's toy nor a bottle rocket. Would you care to hear more?"

"Uh, yeah," gasped Mabus, as he slowly circled the ship, staring up at it. "I get it. That's not a metal surface. There's something different-looking about it." Indeed, its metallic shimmer was obviously only a result of the lighting within the special chamber.

"We've been able to measure our nanotechnology down to the picometer, which is a metric unit of length that equals one trillionth of a meter. We've used it to measure the very diameter of atomic particles and therefore we've seen a dramatic decrease in waste materials, production expenses, pollutants, and the use of non-renewable natural resources. Would you believe this spacecraft cost no more to build than a Boeing 700-series jetliner? And that's not all.

"The parts of this spaceship, due to the intrinsic molecular perfection of the Buckytubes, fit together perfectly and with virtually no friction. It's seamless, making it completely airtight and sealed when it's traveling through space. And its surface is completely reflective, sealing in and keeping out heat and cold. It has a self-contained, self-sustaining atmosphere, and its own internal gravitational and magnetic fields, plus the cloned embryos and biological forms required for complete nutritional sustenance. It creates its own completely pure water supply. And its locomotion is accomplished through a very special form of hyper-drive, a technology that currently is almost available to ordinary humans of your time. But the Illuminati are the ones who truly control such knowledge.

"The scientist Franklin Chang has designed a plasma rocket that we Antis have rendered fully functional. It harnesses a nuclear-fusion process to produce tremendously hot gas plasma, which is magnetically held in a small device shaped like a bottle—strangely enough, it's much like the bottle rockets you mentioned, Antichrist. It is then expelled at a very high velocity to produce propulsion.

"In order to accomplish this, the plasma has to be heated to millions of degrees. We also use clean energy gathered from our fleet of solar sails to do this. Although it sounds primitive, with the use of plasma rockets comes a continuous process of acceleration. This is very necessary both when it comes to takeoff and to travel. Our spaceship is outfitted with seven of these plasma rockets. Should one fail, the other six will remain. And as I mentioned, the surface of the ship also stores energy that is used for onboard procedures mainly, as well as the maintenance of the outer hull.

"The ship itself only uses small moveable flaps to maneuver. You may have noticed the near-uniformity of its gleaming surface. It requires absolutely no external tanks or boosters, and thus its takeoff through this underground hangar will be rendered noiseless, safe and totally secretive. Only our special squadron of Antis knows of the existence of the X-666, and now you do, my dear Antichrist. What do you think of her?"

"I think I'm... sleepy," Mabus said, rubbing his eyes. "Do you have a place to bed down around here somewhere?"

"Indeed we do. You must take your rest. I'm sorry, it's been a long day for you. I will show you to your private quarters."

Mabus allowed himself to be escorted to his chambers in silence, but as they reached its doors he found he couldn't contain himself any longer.

"Why are we going to influence human history? I thought you said the Antis didn't do that. Why doesn't it create a time paradox? Isn't it deeply wrong for us to tamper with the course of human civilization like that? And what do you mean, I'm going to possess all the knowledge in the world? That's impossible!"

"No, it's not. The world you've been living in has you thinking these things. Rest now, my dear Antichrist, and prepare for tomorrow. I have one tantalizing thing for you to dream about tonight. Tomorrow, you're going to find out exactly who it was that killed Boone."

Mabus stared at Thaillo for a full minute. Then he looked into his room. It was small and spare but clean, and the bed looked very plush and inviting. Mabus fell onto the bed in his clothes and surrendered to sleep. He dreamed yet again about the oncoming comet, but this time it didn't hit Earth. Mabus slept soundly through the night for the first time in over twenty-six years.

Chapter Twelve

I N WASHINGTON DC, IT WAS past midnight. Still, the empty half-darkness on the streets was broken by the headlights of many long, black limousines, headed for the Bureau of Engraving and Printing—the US Mint. The limousines disgorged their passengers, all clad in long robes with hoods, who then scurried into a secret entrance below street level with the scuttling speed of cockroaches. Deep below the tomblike building, in a bunker-like conference room whose walls were piled with cardboard boxes filled with new hundred-dollar bills, the Supreme Conclave of the Illuminati came to order.

"Illuminatus est!" intoned their leader in a sepulchral voice, and the rest of the figured duly returned his incantation. "I have summoned you here to deal with the greatest threat in our history—the ascension of Mabus, the One True Antichrist. He is inimical to us and to everything we stand for, and, even now, he is shedding his human guise and preparing to rise against us. Our satellites indicate that he is now with his minions in Nevada, no doubt plotting our ruin." A nervous murmur ran through the shadowy forms.

"We have tried killing him, have we not?" asked an older Illuminatus. "We have been thwarted by the aliens, for reasons we do not understand. We will try again later, but we will bide our time. His death must not only terminate his existence, but it must also strike terror into the hearts of others, so that they return to their false gods and worship them, praying for their imaginary afterlives."

"Have we tried seducing him?" another Illuminatus asked. "Yes, we have, Agent Q4. *Someone* needs to review the minutes from our past High Conclave." A ripple of laughter ran through the robed and cowled forms. "Although our operative lacked instruction in how to accomplish that correctly; she couldn't even manage it on the second try." A discreet woman's cough could be heard, and the other Illuminati pretended not to notice. "Is there nothing else we can do?" inquired another Illuminatus, annoyed. "Can we not poison the minds of the people against him?"

Someone countered, "You fool! We rule from the shadows. Our powers work best behind the scenes." A fourth mused, "Perhaps we require another who can emerge into the light on our behalf, and speak lies to the people. They will drink from the cup of intoxication if they are presented it in a suitable... *fashion*."

"Well, there is one among us who might serve. She has failed us in the past, but her talents have developed since then." Another cough could be heard. "She can be our public face, and cause the human race to delight once more in our enslavement of them. Countering the lies of the Antichrist, she will make man complacent and slow to heed his tedious warnings. By the time they awaken from their slumber, it will be too late. Perhaps, too, we will settle on a method of disposing of Mabus—one that works."

"We are agreed, then?" asked their leader. A chorus of "Aye's" rang through the room. "Let it be so." He focused his eyes on one of the dark shapes. In a tone that would terrify a wild beast, he whispered, "Be certain that you not fail us again."

As the Illuminati left the room for their limousines and a midnight snack, a few of them stuffed some of the crisp hundred dollar bills from the boxes into the pockets of their robes. After all, the money was theirs, anyway.

A solitary Illuminatus remained in the room, looking at the empty chairs. She took off her cowl for a moment, and Eva's blue eyes glimmered under the pallid fluorescent lights.

Chapter Thirteen

"And I beheld another beast coming up out of the earth; and he had two horns like a lamb, and he spake as a dragon. And he exerciseth all the power of the first beast before him, and causeth the earth and them which dwell therein to worship the first beast, whose deadly wound was healed."

—Rev. 13:11

ODAY, YOU START TO ENTER the real world," Thaillo told Mabus over breakfast. "By the way, it is now December 27th. Your majestic reign as Lord of the World begins exactly one year from today. During this coming year, you will be prepared for your new role as the Antichrist, and you will begin instructing the world to worship you and to follow your every prophesied instruction."

"I don't want to be worshipped," Mabus muttered into his cereal. He still had many grave doubts about this new program he was embarking upon. Unanswered questions rattled around in his head, and he felt deep resentment growing in his gut. Yet he wanted very much to receive the promised information about Boone's killer. At least that, and then perhaps he could go home and sort everything out.

"You will begin the process of complete alteration of your mind, body and soul, back to its previously enlightened and highly sophisticated state of true grace. You'll go through a lengthy surgical process that will completely alter your apelike brain's composition and chemistry, healing your mind and bringing it back to its true state of mental and spiritual complexity. After we are done, you will regain your former psychic abilities of telepathy, telekinesis, and deep spiritual union with others."

"I don't remember ever having such abilities," Mabus muttered, feeling rather fearful. "Sometimes I hear voices in my head that sound like me, and they tell me things that are really true, but I don't understand what you mean about telepathy and all that. Also, how long is this so-called surgery going to take?"

"The rearrangement of your religiously-distorted brain will require approximately one minute to accomplish, using our nanotechnological means of rapid re-growth of tissue… "

"Hold on there, dude. I'm not at all religiously inclined. What do you mean, my brain's distorted? It's perfectly fine the way it is, thank you very much, and I don't need any one-minute surgery. Can we just skip all that muck and find out who Boone's killer is?"

"We will come to that later, as I promised. But first, you must be made ready for your role in the salvation and advancement of mankind. You do want to help rescue the human race and fulfill your destiny as the Antichrist, do you not? The microsurgeries we have in mind for you are absolutely necessary for you to properly begin your role of persuasion and influence in time for you to assume total mastery of the modern world.

"You must begin to trust me and my fellow Antis, who are only here to serve you and help you fulfill all the prophecies, signs and wonders. You are a completely necessary component of the timeline. Without your utmost cooperation in all of these highly specialized endeavors, all is lost. Mankind will die out completely!

"Don't you want humanity to remain eternally alive, evolving and becoming what it was certainly meant to be? Don't you want to remember your spiritual self, and be at one with other people and the infinite universe as you once were, yet again?"

Mabus sighed. He had been looking down at the floor during Thaillo's speech. He finally aimed his beautiful green eyes piercingly into Thaillo's eagerly waiting blue ones.

"All right. I'm ready. Take me to the operating room, or whatever you call it. You said this is going to only take a minute?"

"After the brain alteration is accomplished, you will need some time to absorb your new mental and spiritual functioning, and your seemingly new surroundings. Follow me."

Thaillo led Mabus to a small interior room deep in the heart of the underground hangar. He introduced Mabus to the black-

clad female surgeon and left, saying he would return for the next
phase of Mabus's progression into true Antichristhood.

Mabus was gently guided to a machine that looked to Mabus
like a small, sleek CAT scanner. It was black and sported the same
gold, revolving "666" logo Mabus had been seeing nearly
everywhere in the complex.

The surgeon had him lie on his back on a platform with his
head inside a small cylinder. "When we're done, you'll fully
understand the deep meaning of our special symbol," said the
Anti doctor gently as she turned on the machine.

"Get ready, for you're about to begin functioning on the same
level as we do," the doctor smiled. Mabus was startled to realize
she had told him this without moving her mouth. Mabus could
hear her vaguely, almost as if her voice were the same as his own.

"Have you done the surgery already? I think I understand you,"
smiled Mabus.

"No, some preliminary work. I'm about to touch the sensor
pad now. Then you will understand, and be ready shortly to
comprehend absolutely everything."

Mabus felt a small whirling in his head. Then it began to spin
like a cyclone as he heard voices explain the procedure:

"ACCORDING TO PREVAILING scientific theory of the mind, known as
'identity theory,' mental states are identical with physiochemical
states of the brain. Our minds are regarded as supercomplex computers in which material processes in the cerebral cortex somehow
generate thoughts and feelings. This theory holds that the brain is
merely a cobbled-together collection of specialist circuits which
perform a sort of internal miracle, creating a 'captain of the crew'
which we regard as our self, but which is really an illusion produced by the global actions of our brain circuits.

"In truth, this is far from the case. We actually have a
nonmaterial mind or self that acts upon and is influenced by our
material brains. There is a spiritual world in addition to the physical
one, and the two spontaneously interact. The mind, as in Cartesian
dualism, is a kind of nonphysical substance composed of both
electrical energy and spiritual substance.

"Mind-brain interaction does not, however, violate the law of
the conservation of energy, which is the First Law of Thermody-

namics. In the spiritual realm, energy and matter can in fact be formed from nothingness itself. This is due to the brain's close relationship with quantum physics and the microstructure of the neocortex.

"The fundamental units of the cerebral cortex are dendrons, and each of the 40 million dendrons in the human brain is linked with a mental unit called a psychon, which represents a unitary conscious experience. Psychons act on dendrons and increase the probability of the firing of selected neurons, while in perception the reverse process takes place. The interaction among psychons causes the unity of our perceptions and of the inner world of our minds. This is true in both the primitive religious brain and the evolved mind of the true telepath, the advanced spiritual brain.

"The total energy of a closed system doesn't always remain constant. There is a continuous circulation of energy-substance through the various planes and spheres of reality, none of which forms a true closed system. The conservation of matter and energy only applies to infinite nature as a whole, and not to its many smaller, interacting zones.

"The 'zero-point' energy of a vacuum, which is the energy of hyperdimensional space, is nonphysical etheric energy. You can have a system that produces more energy than is required by it. Etheric energy operates on the quantum and subquantum levels. There is no measurable violation of energy conservation in ordinary mental phenomena, but with so-called paranormal phenomena such as psychokinesis and materializations, there is. This is due to the ethereal, other-worldly nature of etheric energy."

Mabus sensed the surgeon. "Can you see me in my real soul's entirety now?" she asked.

"I can," Mabus breathed. "I know you, as I have always known you. But I can't perceive all of your inmost secrets."

"Mankind must keep its free will, and that means not relinquishing some of our personal information," she explained. "The surgery is halfway done. Now for the rest of the transformation."

The voices continued. "The parietal lobe of your brain is what you use now to locate yourself in physical space. It integrates all sensual cues from the environment, enabling you to maneuver about in reality. This 'orientation association area' decreases in activity during meditation or prayer. With less sensory stimulus to delineate the borderline between the self and the world, your brain will perceive actual reality directly. It will see that the self is endless and intimately interwoven with everyone and everything the mind can sense.

"I will frame this new perception of your brain by stating that it is triune, or a three-part organ in its true nature. There is first the primitive reptilian brain, mainly the brain stem and hypothalamus, the overlying mammalian brain, which includes limbic emotive and hippocampal memory centers, and the neocortex, the most developed outer part of the cerebrum, which mediates higher functions such as cognition. This tripartite model roughly parallels the evolution of the nervous system of animals.

"The reptilian brain is what believes in religion and perceives God in the concrete world. God is seen as a nurturer and an object of affection, as the real spiritual side of the universe. God is perceived by the emotive system of the mammalian brain. And God as the Word, Logos, or the actual perception of other peoples' true nature and humanity, is affirmed through the advanced neocortex.

"Our surgery redesigns your triune brain, fusing it into an interactive solid whole. You will no longer be ruled by the actions of your primitive reptilian brain. Now you are free to see truly through your mammalian brain and your neocortex, and your parietal lobe will no longer determine your human mentality. You have far more than your mere five senses to guide you through the expanded world of actual reality now."

The voices finished speaking. Mabus heard the surgeon say, "Please sit up and have a sip of water. You finally exist in the one true universe."

She helped Mabus sit up, and handed him a small white paper cup. He blinked his eyes, looked around the lab and took a sip. "Huh? Yeah, that's great. Wow, everything's crystal clear. I know what this machine does, and what this place is really for, and how much work I have to do…"

<Try it without speaking,> she said, her mouth still.

<I feel like I'm not using my eyes to see you so much as my mind. I can think even faster than this. Can ordinary people communicate with us mentally?> Mabus thought.

<No. You were one of the extraordinary people before we even started.>

<Darn, I was really hoping to impress Barbara!>

<You will, I'm sure!>

<Are you ready for your big surprise?> Thaillo thought, as he walked in.

<You bet!> thought Mabus.

<Then follow me.> Thaillo walked Mabus down a corridor. Everything was labeled "high security area." They had to go through six highly-guarded checkpoints. The final checkpoint," which looked like a gigantic safe door, required an eye scan of Thaillo before they could enter. When the door opened, there were two chairs in the center of the room. The room looked like a lab filled with medical devices.

<Man, what have you guys got in there that's so important, the next stage of microsurgery?>

<It's slightly more involved, as it employs extremely advanced nanotechnology. Take a seat. This will be over in a heartbeat, literally!>

As Mabus took his seat, Thaillo strapped him in the chair.

<This isn't gonna hurt, is it?> Mabus thought.

<Honestly, it's gonna hurt me just as much as it's gonna hurt you!> Thaillo replied laughing, as he strapped himself into his chair. <When we are done, you will be physically, mentally and spiritually superior to all other life forms on the face of the planet. Now lie back again, close your eyes and relax. You will know exactly what's going on now, but you have much more to learn in a little while.>

<How long is this going to take?> Mabus thought.

<A whole two minutes. Incredibly complicated, isn't it?>

<I know exactly where Venus and Mars are in relation to the Earth now…yes, it's all one planet moving slowly through a strategic pattern in time and space.>

<The confluence of molecular biology and nanofabrication render possible the engineering of functional hybrid organic/inorganic nanomechanical devices and holistic systems. The integration of the biological motor F1-ATPase with nano-electromechanical systems, or NEMS, creates a new class of hybrid nanomechanical devices. The biomolecular motor is capable of generating a force of >100 pN, has a calculated no-load rotational velocity of 177 RPS, and a diameter of less than twelve nanometers,>" the attending surgeon explained to Mabus.

<Please, kindly get to the point. I already know about that hybrid stuff, I think,> **Mabus thought.**

Thaillo explained, <Your entire system is now flooding with the devices strained from my blood. We are seamlessly integrating the motive power of biological life itself with engineered nano-fabricated devices, powered by nanomotors with rotors only 500 nanometers across, 300 times thinner than a human hair and smaller than most viruses. We are going to empower your presently emaciated body...>

<...No it's not, I haven't gotten enough exercise lately...> Mabus and Thaillo now shared thoughts easily.

<...with integrated metallic-organic nanomuscles. They will expand reversibly when electric voltage is applied, replacing your present weak muscles...>

<...No, they're not that weak...>

<...with artificial ones, and also rebuilding your internal sensors, actuators, and motion transducers. You will see better, react more swiftly and be stronger than any human who has ever existed.>

<You mean I'm going to be Superman?>

<No, not exactly.>

<The process of molecular self-assembly is similar to the one used by organic cells to assemble themselves. We also reproduce the vital processes of cellular regeneration and replication, but these systems will now run at a much faster rate of speed.>

<I have introduced partially inorganic, primarily silicon-based micromechanical devices into your newly-coordinated wholeness. The human brain needs to be prepared for this procedure first. The devices are powered by biological motors and chemical energy sources, both from your original system and the one which we are creating within you. Due to their ability to self-function, they will place the molecules and atoms of your body into an almost perfect alignment. You will soon be achieving an ultimate perfection of body, mind and soul that was previously unattainable to humanity.>

<Our telepathic thinking is beginning to blur together...>

<You mean we think alike?>

<No, you are slowly becoming one with the universal mind we share between us.>

<I feel like you're thinking my thoughts...>

<It's a temporary effect of our minds blending and will lessen soon. With the force generated by the motor proteins being >100 pN, which is among the greatest of any known molecular motor, the F1-ATPase protein is a tailor-made nanomotor. These properties, coupled with the fact that F1-ATPase is automatically synthesized using the machinery of life, creates a transparent interface between the organic and inorganic worlds. Insertion and self-assembly of these hybrids in host cells takes advantage of cellular physiological processes. In addition, host cells provide power for the devices in the form of ATP, as well as maintaining a system for replacing the molecular motors whenever their functions cease.>

<In order to integrate biomolecular motors into NEMS, procedures for the specific attachment and positioning of these motors are essential. Your own developing brain and the self-assembly action of the devices' molecular structures are swiftly accomplishing this. Now you will be able to communicate with the universal mind. There, all done,> Thaillo thought. He helped Mabus sit up again.

<It's unbelievable. I feel like I'm a God or something,> Mabus thought. <I've literally never been better in my entire life!>

<Yes, and from now on, the best is yet to come,> Thaillo smiled. "You think you've seen the sun, but you haven't really seen it shine, my old friend! And you will for a very long time, as you'll never age. Your newly energized and synthesized body will last forever."

<What about my fiancée?> Mabus asked. <Can you make her perfect and immortal too?>

<That's something I can't do. Come with me, I'll explain. These nanobots are for one person, and one person only. You! You are to be the most perfect being who ever lived. I only had them for one reason. 3,800 years ago, you entrusted me with the most important mission, to return them to you when you need them, which is now. It's been so long, old friend. Right this way.>

Mabus followed Thaillo to another laboratory room. It, too, was filled with all manner of intricate-looking machinery, but this one was dark. Thaillo directed Mabus into what looked like a dentist's chair.

<What is this dark place?> Mabus thought. <Why are you strapping me with so many electrodes?>

<They're implant patches which will direct the multimedia software of our internal database into your brain and body.>

<How long does this take?>

<There's so much knowledge you'll have to assimilate that you'll be here the rest of the day. You have to absorb Earth's information that we have accessed and gathered over the last two million years.>

"I can't wait to tell Barbara about this," Mabus crowed to himself as the machine began to hum.

The humming seemed to grow louder and louder, but Mabus realized it was just his perception growing sharper and sharper. Soon, the humming of the machine gave way to the humming of thought. The machine filled Mabus's fertile mind with information as if it were uploading programs into a computer. And as it did, Mabus swam gleefully in the sea of knowledge. His thoughts flowed smoothly and effortlessly.

<I have learned every language now,> he thought. <I know all the martial arts, every culture on the planet, every style of cooking, every subtle nuance of meaning contained in every rock, tree and stone, how many underpants Barbara has in her drawer…now I need to know Boone's killer, Boone's killer, no, I only see a dark face, it looks so familiar, but it's blurry and indistinct. What do you mean I don't need this type of information yet? Oh God—or whatever—the panoramas of Earth are so majestic! Oh, that's what's going to happen with the asteroid!>

<You mean there really is a biggest number and then it goes to another graduated system of measurement? Wow, the colors are different than any colors that I've ever seen, it's an entirely different spectrum and there isn't anything like that on Earth! What is this now? So that's what Atlantis looks like! The technology is fascinating!>

<There used to be a Loch Ness monster, but she died! The aliens are the ones manifesting the Bermuda Triangle! I have to pee and take a dump…wait, my body just reabsorbed it all and is using the waste products as fuel for my limbic system! Wow, cool!>

<So that's why dogs bark! I'm going to have to show the Beast this stuff…now I can! Barbara really never has had any other guy than me. Oh well, someday I'm going to have to tell her all about… maybe not…>

<Oh no, there really is such a thing as Jesus and he's going to return barely before the asteroid hits! Ah, it'll be a piece of cake to take care of him. I suppose all I have to do is build the Temple and prove everything. Too bad this sucker doesn't see into the future. I wonder why?>

Chapter Fourteen

THAILLO DROVE MABUS HOME LATE in December, after spending a few days introducing him to the other Antis of the current Militia. Mabus now knew each and every one of them on far more than a first-name basis. He almost read them clear down to their souls. After a final rundown on how the Antichrist prophecies were to commence, held in the car on the long drive home, Thaillo dropped Mabus off in front of his apartment building.

<Take care,> Thaillo thought to Mabus. <I will be nearby, but cannot tell you where at the present. This knowledge must remain secret from the Illuminati, who can now very easily read your mind. But you have my cell phone number. Please call it anytime.>

<Thank you,> Mabus beamed back as he entered the front door. The dirty glass pane neatly slipped open. Mabus tucked in his shirt briefly before he cruised down the hall.

When he got upstairs and let himself into his small rooms, he was immediately greeted by his starving, dirty dog.

The Beast had left excrement everywhere. Mabus opened all the windows and cleaned the terrible mess while his loyal companion barked and jumped excitedly all over him. Fortunately, he had filled the Beast's water bowl before leaving, and it appeared to be still full. This was neither the first nor the last of many miracles to come in the succeeding years.

And for some reason, apparently no one had called and reported his anxiously barking dog. "That's a good boy. You must have been really quiet. What a good boy," he complimented his faithful mutt. Feeling like he was on a roll, Mabus kicked off his shoes and socks, which strangely enough didn't stink, and gratefully phoned Barbara.

"I'm back, sweetheart. How are you doing?"

"Fine, my love. I missed you scads. But you sound so different, kind of healthier and stronger. Your voice is so clear and pure-sounding. Did you go to a health spa or something?"

"It was far better than that. You'll see when you come over here tonight."

When Barbara arrived, Mabus presented her with a bouquet of six red roses, and as she grasped them, he spontaneously kissed her. Barbara could not remember his ever kissing her so passionately, so romantically. It completely took her breath away.

"Oh my God!" Barbara gasped, clutching at her chest. "You don't even look like you. Your face…it looks, well, perfect. What happened to your scar? Did you get some kind of plastic surgery or something? Like, everything lines up exactly. Where're your moles? All your freckles look perfectly round! They're like tiny brown circles, and they're all exactly the same size!" she loudly cried, running her fingers lovingly across Mabus's cheeks. She looked startled, and very worried. "And they're all symmetrically spaced in neat little rows! Your eyes look normal, but your face…what did you do, have some kind of weird extreme makeover? Did you do Oprah?"

"Not exactly. I'm afraid I can't explain right now. It would be too much for you. Let's just enjoy the holiday season together, and as a New Year's treat I'll tell you everything."

Midnight of December 31st came, and after celebrating with further passionate kisses and champagne, Mabus told Barbara about his experiences in Nevada. At first she didn't believe him, but as she stared at his newly perfect face, which had taken quite some getting used to, she began to realize the stark and utterly demented truth of what he was saying.

"No, you can't be the Antichrist. He's evil, like Satan, the true incarnation of the Enemy. He's supposed to oppose God and Jesus, declare himself to be God, make everyone wear the Mark of the Beast, rule the world for seven years, and be defeated by Jesus in the Final Days of the Last Judgment. That can't be you!"

"I'm afraid it is. I know you're a devout Christian, and want to be saved by your Lord. It will take a lot to convince you and others that it can't be so, and that I'm really a good man. The Bible has been brainwashing people into believing that I'm evil, but you know that's not true. The reality of it is that I'm the one true Christ, the legitimate only Savior of our doomed planet. I'm the key to maintaining our timeline, and maybe someday I'll find a way to defeat the doomsday asteroid that's going to hit the Earth in 2012. I know it really sounds impossible…"

"If I didn't love you so much, I'd have my father stick you in a mental ward. Or worse. You're blaspheming God, and I don't know what all else."

Barbara peered into Mabus's new face intently, as if looking for evidence that his words were not true. But she could see nothing in his perfect smile that appeared insane. And he had already shown her how incredibly strong he was. He had picked up his heavy ten-foot couch with one hand and balanced it perfectly, using his hand as a fulcrum. Plus he could now answer any question about anything she could pose to him. This latter had especially made her begin to believe him, but she was still very uncertain and obviously frightened.

"I wish they'd let me change you too, so you could have mental telepathy," Mabus sighed, gazing deeply into his lady love's bespectacled brown eyes. "Then you'd know what I'm saying is the truth. Barbara, I'm practically immortal now. I'm near perfection, physically, mentally and psychically. And I'm going to live forever!"

"And how are you supposed to do that if the world is coming to an end in 2012?"

"It's like I told you, we're leaving Earth on a spaceship bound for Venus, which I am now certain is actually an earlier version of Earth. And you'll be on it with me, my love. There are other people who know about this, and they're called the Antis. I'm only allowed to take twelve others, and they're supposed to all be Antis, but these people are very loyal to me. So I'm sure I can talk them into your coming…"

"I don't know. It all seems so sudden, and so weird. Are you really going to rule the world? How are you going to talk everyone into it? What are you going to do now?"

"An awful lot. The first thing I'm going to do is go onto my own dozen websites and some others on the Web, and start blogging away. I have a lot to say to prove my theories. It will help that my birth name is actually Mabus, which I can prove. That's one of the major names Nostradamus gave the Third Antichrist.

"If you don't know this, Nostradamus was a sixteenth century magician and prophet who wrote the Quatrains of the Centuries. I'll tell you more about him later. He knew my name would be Mabus, and who the first and second Antichrists were. And I'll show people how I fulfill most of his and the Bible's prophecies regarding the Antichrist.

"I have a lot of followers already who believe my Single Orientation Theory of the Planets. All I have to do is contact them and the media, and get the word out. I can also have scientists and physicians examine my body and mind, and that will be proof enough in itself. When they see how superior to ordinary humans I am, I'll be believed.

"Trust me, Barbara, everything is going to work out great."

But Mabus's lady was increasingly sad. Her smile drooped as she looked out the window, watching the snow lazily fall as the whoops and cheering of partiers echoed from the surrounding buildings. She idly clinked her champagne glass against that of her fiancé's, wondering what the future was going to bring them, and about their wedding plans.

Should she marry someone the Bible described as the most evil man to ever live? Someone whom the Good Book clearly stated would cause the greatest amount of death and destruction in all of history? A man who made Hitler and Stalin look like...*kittens*? And if she was his wife, what did all this exactly make her...Mystery Babylon the Great, the Mother of Harlots and Abominations of the Earth? Was *that* why her name was Barbara?

She shivered to herself as she watched the new-falling snow. Mabus instantly noticed, and used telekinesis, the one power that would most convince other people of his true nature, to gently turn up the heat.

For the whole next year of 2005, Mabus was extremely busy. His network of friends on the Net was relatively easy to convince, as his friends readily believed in conspiracy theories and the like, and had known there was something special about this man all along. The media was alerted, and Mabus started showing up on various TV and radio programs, at first only local ones, but finally the national and cable news shows.

Some of his good friends, who were now a growing crowd of thousands or more, even financed a documentary which was eventually shown worldwide. Mabus the Antichrist clearly demonstrated all of his profound abilities of extreme strength, physical and mental dexterity, and telekinetic talents before the camera. And he told everyone of his theories about the planets, and what people must get together and do to prove them true.

His Earth-shattering documentary was released to a increasingly aware but still skeptical public in New York City on June 6th of 2005. Mabus was now exactly twenty-nine years old. He attended the premiere with eleven close friends and his lady sitting by his side.

"I hope Al Qaeda doesn't attack right in the middle of this movie," Barbara furtively whispered into her grinning fiancé's hypersensitive ear. "Everybody knows about it."

"Don't worry. I understand they're busy right now making plans to get Egypt and several neighboring Arab countries to launch a huge assault on Israel. Hush, it's starting."

Chapter Fifteen

*"And there was given unto him a mouth speaking great things
and blasphemies; and power was given unto him to continue
forty and two months."*

—Rev. 13:5

HE THEATER LIGHTS WENT DOWN, the plush red velvet curtains dramatically parted, and the large, perfectly formed, and strangely fierce-looking Antichrist appeared onscreen. Thaillo had carefully advised him to look both ferocious and charming, as this fulfilled certain Biblical prophecies. It would also garner the widest and strongest support possible, which would soon include support from the US Armed Forces.

Mabus's blond, charismatic head seemed to glow in an almost superhuman manner. His face contrasted greatly with his clothing, which was entirely black in order to foster a sense of power and authority. He had taken to wearing dark clothes lately, which also fulfilled certain Biblical prophecies. His masculine voice was sweeter than honey and smoother than silk as he described his theories, dreams and plans for the first time in a two-hour-long forum designed to finally reach the entire world. The entire room was muted in an awed, expectant hush as the One True Antichrist began his elaborate presentation.

"We must prepare, for the Earth is about to go through some catastrophic changes. There is an asteroid headed directly for us. Our only hope for survival is to find another planet that is able to support life. As of now, there is none. But soon a comet will impact Venus, creating water, and a much needed atmosphere.

"This event will mark the birth of Earth. Our Earth, the one we're on now, but existing in the past, millions of years ago, replenished with all its resources. One billion years of vast time ahead of us with no worries of planetary extinction until we make it through to 2012 AD again. 2012 is the year the ancient Mayans, an ancient civilization in South America who were believed to be as advanced as the Egyptians, ended their sacred calendar. I'm predicting that a comet in 2012 will fulfill their prediction. That event will mark the birth of Mars as we know it. This very event is the one which both destroys Earth and recreates our planet. The Earth will be struck by an asteroid which will propel a chunk of it into orbit, creating a second moon. When Earth suffers its pole shift and becomes dry, dead Mars, it will have two moons, just as Mars does today. The ice-comet that strikes Venus will also break away a piece of that planet, creating a moon, which will become our Moon when the current Venus becomes Earth.

"You see, in 2012 another transit of Venus is supposed to occur. This very event is the event that destroys Earth and creates Earth at the same time. The Ouroboros legends were derived from this belief. This spectucular event is what allows mankind to go on existing for all eternity!

"I know my words are extremely frightening, but they are the truth. You cannot depend on any religion or your governments to save you. For they are the very ones who have known, yet hidden the truth from you. You must elect me to a new position as the ultimate ruler of the entire planet. Only I can guide you carefully through the coming multiple crises, and establish a New World Order that will enable at least some people to survive the many horrible events that must transpire during this planet's Final Days.

"As a sign that I speak the truth, I will tell you something that scientists and astronomers on this planet have absolutely no knowledge of as yet. I'm sure many of you have heard of, or even observed, the comet Shoemaker-Levy 9 striking Jupiter over one week in July of 1994. And you have seen some profound effects from that strike. It is one of the events that presaged my oncoming reign, and the end of our own beloved world."

As he spoke, the Antichrist displayed several maps of space and many diagrams, charts and photographs which he used to illustrate all of the events covered by his presentation.

"The twenty fragments of S-L 9 that hit Jupiter produced a remarkable amount of kinetic energy. Fragment G alone produced energy equivalent to six million megatons of TNT, or about 600 times the estimated arsenal of the world. The fireball from this fragment rose about 3,000 kilometers above the Jovian cloudtops. Many of the later impacts hit near the sites of earlier ones, and the resulting new Jovian features soon became very complex.

"The development of these has been followed by many observers. While the smaller features have almost disappeared, the larger complexes are still visible even by small telescopes. Currently it appears that the many impact sites are overlapping to form a partial band. The dark semicircles south of the impact points are an ejecta blanket composed of fine material condensed from the plume.

"This material is partially suspended in the upper atmosphere. Some scientists refer to it as soot. But what it actually is doing is contributing to the already present rings of Jupiter, and slowly making them into the future rings of the planet Saturn. This is but the first step in this process, and now I will tell you about the next major step.

"On July 6th, 2006, a cosmic event unlike anything seen in our lifetimes, or the brevity of any human being who has ever existed, will occur to the planet Jupiter. You have no doubt heard of the alleged existence of the Oort Cloud and the Kuiper Belt. Yes, they do provably and truly exist, and they often send space debris and large objects our way.

"The Oort Cloud is all that remains of the primordial huge, dusty, rocky mass which gave rise to the Sun and our solar system. It's composed of trillions of 5-to-100 kilometer-sized cometary nuclei, which have existed since the Sun formed 4.5 billion years ago. Every once in a while, one of these objects is jostled by a passing star and makes a plunge into the inner solar system."

Mabus's eyes shone as he spoke; he was a natural at explaining complicated concepts, and his good looks and honest eyes were riveting.

"The Kuiper Belt is a disk-shaped population of comet nuclei located beyond the orbit of Saturn. The Hubble Space Telescope and ground-based observers have detected dozens of these nuclei, each more than 50 kilometers across. There are many more of them that have not been detected yet, as they hide behind the far sides of Jupiter and Saturn. There are in fact thousands of these proto-comets, stretching all the way out past the orbit of Pluto. Eventually, they merge together with the Oort Cloud. One of these will soon cause the calamitous event of which I speak.

"But first, I will digress for a moment, for those of you who are not so well-informed, and tell you a few facts about the space-traveling objects referred to as comets. Comets are astronomical objects very similar to asteroids. They are usually debris left over from the condensation of a solar nebula. The orbits of our local comets even extend past Pluto's huge orbit. Most of the ones that enter our inner solar system have highly elliptical orbits. Often described as 'dirty snowballs,' comets are composed largely of frozen carbon dioxide, methane and water, and also contain dust and various mineral aggregates.

"Comets are sometimes perturbed from their distant orbits, falling into extremely elliptical orbits that bring them very close to the Sun. When a comet approaches the inner solar system, the warmth from the Sun causes its outer layers of ice to evaporate. The streams of dust and gas this releases form a huge tenuous atmosphere around the comet called the *coma*, and the force exerted on the coma by the Sun's radiation pressure and solar winds cause an enormous *tail* to form, pointing directly away from the Sun. The solid body of the comet itself is called the *nucleus*.

"Comets are classified by their orbital period, or length of time it takes them to orbit the Sun. A *short-period comet* has an orbit of 200 years or less. A *long-period comet* has a lengthier orbit, but remains gravitationally tied to the Sun. And a *single-apparition comet* has a parabolic or a hyperbolic orbit, which makes it consequently leave the solar system after only one pass by the Sun.

"The Jupiter Family of Short Period Comets circles between Jupiter and the Sun. They generally originate from the Kuiper Belt, and create their forms and orbits while influenced by the gravitational pull of both Jupiter and the Sun. The gravity of these two giant objects can change the original path of an incoming comet to such a tight ellipse, or oval shape, that it orbits the Sun in only three to ten years.

"Because of non-gravitational forces and also the gravitational influence of a massive planet like Jupiter, it is easy for a periodic comet's orbit to be perturbed. For this reason, a number of periodic comets discovered earlier have been lost, since their orbits were not well-known enough to gauge their future appearances. Quite often when a 'new' comet is found, upon calculation of its orbit, it's discovered to be one of the prior 'lost' comets of which we've kept careful records. This is the very case with the large comet that is going to strike Jupiter in the summer of 2006.

"The actual icy nucleus of a comet can measure from one mile to 50 miles across, as in the 1999 supercomet Hale-Bopp. When it enters the inner solar system and its ices begin to turn to gas, it billows like clouds into an object with a core many thousands of miles across, and a tail that may be many millions of miles long, as the ices in the nucleus are heated and give off gas, dust clouds and streamers.

"Including its coma, a comet can outdo the Sun in actual size. Comet tails in some supercomets have increased to a length of over 100 million miles. Their nuclear regions are only ten to fifty kilometers across, but can produce a coma larger than the Sun's diameter. The appearance of Hale-Bopp in 1999 was indeed one of these events. It has been found that H-B's nucleus is at least forty to seventy kilometers across, which explains its large coma and lengthy tail. And the tail plasma of Comet Hyakutake traced for a distance of over 500 million miles.

"Comets also move with an exceptional speed, averaging two to forty kilometers per second. Their rate of travel varies according to their proximity to the Sun. When far away, their speeds are quite low. But as they near the Sun, they accelerate greatly. When moving at forty to seventy kilometers per second, they become classifiably interstellar. The Sun's escape speed is this size, and the comets must be in hyperbolic orbits. So you can now easily understand why a large comet is such a dangerous potential planetary enemy.

"Another of our many woes—comets are so big that large telescopes are useless for studying them. Big telescopes are mostly counterproductive when it comes to viewing comets up close, as their details are almost utterly resolved away. It has to do with the width of the telescopes' fields versus the lengths of the comets. Large telescopes are simply currently inadequate when it comes to photographing an entire comet, including its lengthy tail.

"Comets, like many asteroids and other Near Earth Objects, are weirdly unpredictable. We can calibrate the orbits of known comets we discover, but every day a dozen new comets enter the inner solar system, due to events in the Kuiper Belt occurring beyond the orbits of Jupiter and Saturn. We cannot see anything in this region that's smaller than a few hundred kilometers, meaning that most of what can damage the Earth is not readily detectable. And sometimes we cannot even detect the much larger comets and asteroids.

"It can take weeks to determine the orbit of one of these huge objects, even as it nears the Earth. Some of them are simply not being found, and of the ones we find, we cannot always accurately determine their orbits. Such is the case with many objects that may pass by, or even strike, Venus, Earth, Mars, or the planet now in question, Jupiter.

"On February 14th of 1996, a body named Chiron, which has a detectable coma but is over 50,000 times the characteristic volume of a comet, reached perihelion inside the orbit of Saturn. On April 1st it reached perihelion opposition, or its closest approach to Earth. Its large size is more commensurate with that of a massive asteroid, which it was originally assumed to be. And its peculiar orbit is unstable on time scales of a million years, which indicates that it hasn't been in the present orbit very long.

"Chiron is over 200 kilometers in diameter, some twenty-plus times the size of Halley's Comet. This led to its initial classification as an asteroid. But it has an active coma over two million kilometers across, and an inner "dust" coma that's 1,500 kilometers wide. It has shown much cometary activity over time, so it has been since reclassified. It sustains an elliptical orbit of some fifty years duration between Saturn and Uranus. That is, it used to, before Saturn once again forced it into a new orbit.

"Chiron is the first of four bodies discovered near this area, all having similar orbits and characteristics. These objects are designated as Centaurs, after the race of half-man, half-horse creatures from Greek mythology, as they seem to have a dual comet and asteroid nature. Chiron is named after the king of the centaurs, who taught Hercules the martial arts and greatly increased his physical, mental and spiritual wisdom, as my own has been increased by the advanced science of the Antis.

"The Centaurs are all objects which have escaped the Kuiper Belt recently, and Chiron has shown increased cometary activity as it has reached perihelion. This activity is destined to continue, for Chiron has not been in its present orbit for more than a few thousand years, due to perturbation from the large outlying planets. Earth's scientists are aware of how eccentric and unstable its orbit can be, and what it can become.

"Supposedly, the next opportunity to observe Chiron at perihelion is in the year 2047. It is supposed to be four times closer to the Earth and 250 times brighter than a typical Kuiper belt object. And Earth's scientists say it will be undergoing over ten times more heating by the Sun, causing large-scale sublimation of its surface material and possibly dramatic outbursts of dust and gases. The latter will definitely occur, but not the former.

"This is because forceful perturbation by various cosmic agents, including the immense gravitational pulls of both Saturn and Jupiter, has already jerked this comet far away from its currently perceived path. It has been thrown out of its relatively 'young' orbit between Saturn and Uranus, being briefly flung into a half-orbit around Saturn. After reaching that planet's far side, it began a new elliptical orbit around Jupiter that will soon precipitate its swift and fatal plunge into the depths of the Jovian surface. This will be a sight visible to the naked eye from Earth, for Comet 95P/Chiron's tail will be incredibly long.

"Being a gas planet, Jupiter has an atmosphere and surface above its rocky interior that's a lot like a plasma 'ocean.' But the comet will be traveling very fast, due to its suddenly increased gravitational pull from Jupiter and similar action from the Sun as it crosses between those two large bodies. It will plough deeply enough into Jupiter to cause large chunks of both it and the planet to break off and explode in Jupiter's atmosphere. This will kick up a cloud of particulate matter large enough to be seen by observers on Earth.

"This cloud of dust and debris will begin forming the basis for the multitude of rings now surrounding the body we currently acknowledge as the planet Saturn. Primitive at first, it will gradually coalesce into Saturn's 250,000-kilometer-wide six layers of spectacularly bright and famous rings, over many millions of years. And Jupiter, which has a mostly amorphous surface, will then be much smaller and will slowly reform itself through its own very strong magnetic field and intense gravity into the smaller body of Saturn.

"The bulk of Jupiter consists of liquid metallic hydrogen, which is very similar to the composition of the original solar nebula from which our solar system was formed. Saturn has a similar composition and a similarly-sized rocky core, but much less hydrogen and helium. The process initiated by Chiron will begin the loss of these gases, will also lead to the planet Saturn's gradual evolution into the rockier, much less gaseous planets of Uranus and Neptune. Saturn's core is the same size as those two planets, roughly, minus the liquid metallic hydrogen 'envelope' of the two greater gas planets, which the above collision will indeed prove are actually one and the same planet in an evolutionary state.

"I hope that scientific observation will concur with what I am saying enough to convince you all that I am the One who has been spoken of throughout the many centuries, the One whom Nostradamus said would be called Mabus, the One True Antichrist.

"Heed my warning: when Jupiter explodes, thousands of various-sized meteoroids will soon follow, months later. Most of these will burn up in the atmosphere, and will look like fire raining from the sky. Some of the bigger meteoroids may be fatal, so we need to prepare!"

The camera zoomed in so close you could see Mabus's perfectly spaced freckles. "But I must insist that you listen to me, and do as I say. For contrary to what the Bible says about me being an evil man, I truly am not one. I only have the best interests of humanity in mind, and will not cause anything wicked to happen.

"These Biblical prophecies were completely arranged by the overseers of the Christian religion, which is under the domination of the Illuminati. I have told you widely about them before, and you know that they are an evil group of people. They want only to rule the entire planet for themselves, and use mankind strictly for their own selfish purposes. This is not my goal in the least. I have no desire to rule the world; it is merely my preordained destiny, which is inescapable and must be carried out to its conclusion.

"I now insist that you must begin to let go of your religious beliefs, your faith in the democratic operations of your governmental structures, and your fealty to the monetary structure of worldwide commerce. For soon, these institutions must crumble to the ground, and the New World Order of the One True Christ must begin.

"I know that my saying this will get me in trouble with all of the institutions that the Illuminati secretly control. But I must tell you this, so you will be prepared for the urgency of what's ahead of us all. I'm sure the Illuminati will attempt to kill me again, through some means or other, and in the coming months they will have many opportunities to do so. But I ask you for your continued faithfulness to our Holy Cause.

"I leave you now to gather your courage, your wits and your resources to bolster our Holy Cause of uniting the entire planet in an effort to fully prepare for the End of the World. The Day of Our Doom is December 27th of 2012, the very last date on the Sacred Mayan Calendar. That is the day when we will save at least a portion of humanity from the Earth's unavoidable destruction, and the day when a huge and presently unnamed asteroid will fatally impact our beloved world. For in spite of what the Illuminati-influenced New Testament states, I am no False Prophet, nor a Liar, nor an immoral Man of Sin. I am the true Christ, and not the Deceiver.

"These have been the true teachings, and not the false ones. Turn away from the lying doctrines of Christianity, of both the Protestant and Catholic Churches. You are not going to go to Heaven or Hell when you die, for there are no such places. All the Heaven or Hell there is to be found is right here on Earth, and nowhere else. I am the One True Christ, the One True King of the World, Emperor of All, and Uniter of All Mankind. I am not Satan's son, nor any such spawn of evil, man or beast. I am the reborn Lord of All.

"Farewell, and be good in what you must do to prepare for the End of All Things. Remember this: the greatest gift of love is to help your neighbor, not to ensure your own afterlife in heaven."

The lights went up as the curtains closed. Loud murmuring filled the theater as people began discussing how they should react to this crucial event. And Mabus's friends took their turns speaking to the local media, explaining the various premises of the movie.

No one had noticed when Mabus and his bride-to-be slipped away earlier in the dark, ducking through a side door and entering their waiting black limousine. After a time, their absence was remarked, but it was too late for any interviews.

The next day, there was thunderous denunciation from churches, governments, and the media worldwide. All the news networks carried a press conference, live from NASA headquarters, where a beautiful young woman who had just been appointed the Assistant Deputy NASA Administrator appeared to calmly and efficiently refute Mabus's allegations. Eva looked coolly radiant in a conservative plum-colored business suit that still failed to suppress her considerable charms. Very few people noticed the tiny gold pin with the rose, cross, and pyramid on her lapel. She smiled and pointed out that Mabus had no scientific background, and, indeed, no high school, college, or graduate degrees at all.

Her voice took on a note of studied concern, as she said "I find it regrettable that an individual with such a lack of scientific understanding should attempt to convince the world of such a preposterous conjecture. Perhaps he should first try finding the Moon through binoculars. I certainly hope that the good people of the world are not taken in by this gaudy self-promoter."

Thaillo had told Mabus that he should be careful when entering and exiting buildings, and in public places. "The Illuminati are still your greatest enemy. They'll stop at nothing to kill you, in spite of the bargains they've made with us and the aliens. They're jealous of your prestige, and angry at what you're doing to destroy world religions and governments. Chances are good that they'll try to assassinate you very soon."

"Not before I marry Barbara, and finally find out what I've been missing for all these years," Mabus sighed contentedly. He and Barbara had been getting along quite well lately. She was starting to admire him and liked all the publicity, having become his campaign manager when it came to media relations and the Internet. She still had her doubts about Jesus being a mere deluded mortal and God being fake, but she really loved her Mabus.

"I'll do whatever you want me to do," she had recently told him. "But please don't make me speak against the Illuminati. I'm…afraid of them. I think they might try to kill me."

Mabus agreed. With a lot of generous financing from his friends, he, Barbara, the Beast and even Thaillo now lived in separate rooms within a very large and well-fortified mansion. It was patrolled twenty-four hours a day by black-clad high-tech armed guards. Yet Mabus could swear he still saw something skulking around outside his huge bedroom's bay windows.

And yet, the night of his birthday was the final time he would dream of the oncoming asteroid. He was one year shy of the start of his thirties, and it would be the last year that anything at all seemed normal on the planet Earth.

"You do exactly what you want to do, sweet lady, and nothing more. I'll take care of these matters. It's my job as the AC3. Thaillo and the Antis will help us all do the rest."

"But when are we going to get married?" inquired a nervous Barbara, twisting her long hair into tight curls around her wire-rimmed frames.

"Soon, my beloved. Very soon."

As Mabus and Barbara were locked in a loving embrace, the Vatican Council was holding a secret meeting. Neither Mabus, the Antis, nor even the eternally vigilant Thaillo, were aware of it. Its participants were the major heads of Vatican diplomacy, the foreign minister and several Archbishops, and the real Pope who wields total power over the Catholic Church. Not Benedict XVI, but the actual and unseen Pope, the one who really rules the Vatican, the City State of Rome, and the Holy See.

"Silencio, silencio," an Archbishop announced. "The Bishop of Rome, the Successor of St. Peter, the Vicar of Christ on Earth, the Archbishop of the Roman Province, the Primate of Italy, the Sole Patriarch of the Western Church, our Infallible Pastor Aeternus, is going to speak before us. He is the Supreme Authority in all questions of faith and morals. His word is law. silencio!" The Archbishop then sat in a gold-encrusted chair.

The Pope, a young, strong, forceful and thoughtful man, who bore a strange but distinct resemblance to Mabus's friend and mentor Thaillo, finally rose and spoke.

"As the Head of the Illuminati, may He forever reign in secret, has prophesied, there has arisen among the race of humans one Mabus, who is a virulent heretic. His case has been brought to the attention of my personal tribunal, and must also come before the Congregation of the Inquisition. There we will decide the fate of his eternal soul, but it has already been decreed by Our Lord Jesus Christ that he must suffer eternal damnation. This is of course subject to our final determination.

"Meanwhile, Mabus, otherwise known as the Antichrist, has a fate which has been already predestined. Although the aliens have established a beachhead on the shore of his utmost perpetuation, this cannot truly last.

"Mabus the Antichrist must die. And soon, very soon."

Chapter Sixteen

THE PREMIERE OF MABUS'S MOVIE was a monumental success. In spite of major turmoil in the Mideast, it soon opened at nearly every theater in the world. People everywhere raved about the Antichrist's nearly supernatural appearance; religious parties of all stripes began a all-but-united campaign against it; and astronomers worldwide soon began heatedly debating all of Mabus's intricate theories and notions.

Throughout all this, the attractive young woman—rising rapidly through the ranks of NASA—appeared with increasing frequency in public and in the media to forcefully dispute Mabus's facts and ridicule his conclusions. Many people found her calm imperturbability strangely appealing amid such confusing times.

Mabus's simple "Talkumentary" became the permanently top-grossing film of all time, netting over three billion dollars in sales. But by the late summer of 2005, it was no longer the world's top news story. Far more horrendous, yet not unrelated, events had finally commenced, occurring quite concomitantly with many Biblical prophecies about the Antichrist.

At exactly six in the morning of August 6th, a "dirty" nuclear bomb—a jury-rigged conventional explosive device encased in nuclear waste—was detonated by the "Insidious Six." This ragtag but well-trained group of Al Qaeda operatives thus successfully martyred themselves in the heart of New York City's Times Square. It hadn't taken Saudi Arabia that long to procure the necessary materials, but when Israel had once again reclaimed the West Bank and the Gaza Strip, Al Qaeda finally made their pivotal move.

And on this "Sicko Saturday," a day which would live in infamy, but only for about another seven years, a Fijian Moslem cleric who ostensibly followed Osama bin Laden left a thirteen-minute-long tape recording at the Pentagon claiming that the Antichrist, being Satan Incarnate and the worst of all possible infidels, had been the sole motivation for the bombing.

"The First Big Dirty" released an invisible blanket of radiation over the entire New York metropolitan area, leading to massive deaths, civil unrest and humanitarian catastrophe on a scale that had never been seen before in the Earth's history. Washington DC immediately began to amass the US Armed Forces, pulling everyone out of Iraq in a strategic move toward peace. And the United Nations General Assembly, which had been warned in advance of the bombing by certain mysterious high-ranking officials, secretly convened in an underground silo deep in the concrete bowels of New York City.

But Cairo TV in Egypt was the first to air the Islamic world's dramatic announcement: World War III, which might have been said to have technically begun on the millennial date of September 11th, 2001, the anniversary of Jesus's real birthday, had been declared in earnest.

Egypt, financed and joined by Saudi Arabia, had declared war on Israel. The sinister dyad led an alliance of Arab and Muslim nations, including Syria, Lebanon, Iraq and Iran, with only a few local nations abstaining. Jordan, just as the Scriptures had predicted about the Final Days, attempted to remain neutral, but finally entered the war as Israelis fled the massive invading armies, some trying to cross the Jordan River and some seeking a route south through the Dead Sea. The Jordanians massacred all of the fleeing Jewish refugees they caught.

Egypt and its Arab allies were called the Kings of the South in the Book of Daniel. The real reason they started the war was because they had signed an irredeemable treaty with Russia. The formerly communist nation and its allies, known in the Bible as the King of the North, were to join in the war once Egypt had started it.

This powerful coalition of Eastern forces actually had only a single purpose in mind, once again attempting to forever elimi-nate "The Jewish Problem." But now, World War III had indeed commenced. And though Russia at first was backing only the various Muslim forces in their "sacred" mission of total Jihad, as the Russian people worried about being too heavily embroiled themselves, Europe, Asia, NATO and the rest of the world were soon heavily involved in the conflict.

The General Assembly agreed that the European Community, the United States, other NATO countries, Japan and China had all declared themselves to be on the side of Israel. But they were too late to stop Israel's ultimate defeat, as it was forced to withdraw summarily from the entire area, its surviving citizens once again fleeing to various parts of the globe. This part of the war, which had made the world so volatile and unstable that it was probably utterly unstoppable, was principally over by late October of 2005.

But it was known to many sources inside Washington, DC, as word spread out from the Illuminati and the Antis through worldwide media, and to one Mabus the Antichrist in particular, that Russia was planning a surprise all-out nuclear attack on the US. Tens or possibly hundreds of millions would be killed in this unprecedented use of multiple nuclear, chemical and biological weapons.

China and Japan would truly only enter the war after this attack, and the US/UN coalition forces would not stop their onslaught until all the nations which had decimated Israel were completely overrun. Forces from China and Japan would in fact go all the way to the western borders of Russia as they took revenge for the East's bloodshed.

"I guess that's how I'm supposed to 'bring unrest to the East,'" mused Mabus. He had been reading an anonymous Internet commentary on the war which had been purported to fortell its future. Now he was glancing over some printed-out Internet tables of prophecies with Barbara, trying to make a final determination about the wording of his oncoming speech.

"Nostradamus says quite a wide variety of things, and so does the Bible. A lot of these events conflict," the Antichrist noted, unable to reconcile this. "They clearly can't all happen to both me and the world, unless the Antis alter the timeline enough each time for different sets of alternating events to happen during different time cycles."

"How does all this relate to what's actually true, at least in this go-round?" Barbara muttered to herself as she leafed through literally hundreds of papers. "I know Israel is gone, and apparently Russia is going to attack us within a few weeks or so. But this part about China and Japan hasn't happened yet. And the Moslems have seized total control of the Holy Lands. Is that part of the Biblical prophecies?"

"I'm not sure, but we can look them all up. Here's a basic rundown of what some websites say the New Testament comes up with about the Antichrist, the last one, anyway. That's me.

"It says that the Antichrist will be a man. Do you think I fit the bill, love?"

"You're the only man for me, sweetie."

"'Nuff said." Then it says, 'He will confirm a covenant for seven years.' That refers to my seven-year reign, which the Antis tell me begins on December 27th of this year. 'He will reign among ten kings... ' I'm not sure what it means by that, but it might refer to the ten members of the UN Security Council, or the ten major nations of the European Union. This is also comparable to the 'ten horns' of the last Ultimate Empire. I'm supposed to rule that.

"Then it says, 'He will uproot three kings from the original ten to gain political power.' I'm not planning on anything like that. All I can think of is the US, NATO and Russia, or something like that. 'His ten-nation union will merge into a world government which he will dominate.' I'm guessing this has to do with the 'Allies II' caucus of the UN.

"That group is going to be my first world takeover bid, and contains about ten large countries: the USA, Israel, England, France, Spain, Germany, Poland, Italy, China and Japan. There are a few other Eastern Bloc and African countries involved, but most of the world's nations are trying to remain neutral.

"And next comes this intriguing part: 'He will ascend to power on a platform of peace. During this time, many will be destroyed.' I want to start speaking against the war—hell, I have been already—and garnering enough support to become the seated ruler of the world in the Middle East. I have to somehow seize power over Israel, which the Arabs now call Palestine, and sit on the throne of God in Jerusalem. That's going to be tricky.

"Next it reads, 'He will be promoted and exalted by a miracle-working religious partner, the False Prophet.' Most Biblical scholars and Nostradamus portray this 'false prophet' as the Pope of Rome. I guess I'll have to become good friends with the old fart, somehow.

I hear Benedict XVI is a really nice guy. It should be a piece of devil's food cake.

"And next: 'He was, and is not, and yet is.' Pretty cryptic, but I think I know what it means. The Antis told me all about how I'm going to live almost forever back there in the past. And then I'm gonna be reincarnated later, and there's a period of time that I spend as a god-like ruler in ancient Egypt.

"Also, it says something about my coming up out of a bottomless pit and going to my eternal destruction, and amazing everyone with my reappearance after being dead. Must be a reference to the spaceship launching in 2012. Say, Barbara, I've almost talked Thaillo into letting you come with me and the eleven other Antis as the twelfth person on *Noah*. What do you think of that?"

"What do you mean? The part about being a spiritual presence? I've been wondering: if there's no such thing as God or Jesus, how does that work? Or do you mean the part about *Noah*? I can't see leaving everyone else behind to die like that, not even to be with you."

"To answer your two-part question: all true spirituality has to do with the Universal Mind. I 'm not sure why it exists, but it's some kind of particulate energy field that can manifest itself out of empty space. It's the building blocks for the electrical energy that manifests our bodies and creates our minds. I'll explain it to you in depth, sooner or later.

"But I never implied there's 'no such thing' as Jesus. I merely said that he's only human, and not the Christ. The Illuminati put him up to everything he ever did, including all of the impending miracles of the Second Coming. Even I'm not sure what's going to happen.

"And as for *Noah*, that's your decision. But I'm going to marry you, and I really think you should come with me. Don't stay home and die, baby! You know how much I'll miss you when I'm back there in the past, trying to figure out what to teach those primitive hominids. What am I gonna say when they learn how to ask me, 'Hey, where's your wife and kids?'"

Barbara had to suppress some relentless giggling behind her sleeve. "Please, read the rest of the prophecies. We're running out of time to prepare for your speech."

"Do tell. Well, here's the next one: 'The Antichrist will be preceded by seven kings or rulers. He will be the eighth king. He will also be of the seven.' I have absolutely no idea whatsoever what that's supposed to mean. Later," sighed Mabus.

"Maybe it refers to the seven ancient world governments that have ruled over time," Barbara piped up excitedly. "You told me they were Egypt, Assyria, Babylon, Medo-Persia, Greece and Rome. That of course excludes the United States, the UN, Russia, Communist China or whatever, not to mention Atlantis." When she spoke, her mass of auburn hair jiggled, as did her copious breasts. And the lenses of her granny glasses were practically glowing.

"Uh, thank you, Barbara, you're a big help. Next, it says: 'He will have a mouth speaking great things, and be very boastful.' Yep, that's me all over. Then it goes on: 'His look will be more stout than his fellows.' Ever since the Antis did their number on me, I'm the strongest and smartest man on Earth. That's completely covered.

"It reads further: 'He will have a fierce countenance. He will understand puzzling things.' Thaillo told me I'll need to look macho to properly court the loyalty of all of the military men. You have to snag them separately from their governments. I'll handle it in due time.

"Next one: 'He will cause craft to prosper.' That's exactly what I have in mind. By streamlining each of the world's governments into a central power, ridding the world of money-sucking religions and laying the groundwork for the merging of all the split-up localized financial structures, I should be able to create a decent and honest world where 'craft will prosper.' Unfortunately, it's not going to last long. Not this time around, anyway."

"You still think you'll somehow shoot down the asteroid?" Barbara sighed, with a frown.

"Thaillo says they've tried it before, but they made some kind of serious mistake, and the problem got much worse. I've been meaning to find out this sucker, but he's been pretty closed-minded to me. He keeps claiming I'll learn about it during the trip to Venus.

"Anyway, next it reads: 'He will assume world-dominating power three-and-a-half years after he confirms the covenant. He then will continue to reign for forty-two months.' Some of that works out fine, but I'm planning on assuming power right away. It might take a while to talk absolutely everybody into my New World Order, though. I have to get ready.

"Here comes the beginning of the part I love to hate: 'The Abomination of Desolation is the event that completes the beginning of this final forty-two months.' I don't know what that entails, but it sounds awfully grim. I think it's how the world is headed for some major turmoil before the asteroid even hits. I guess a lot of people are going to die. *Shit!*

"Anyway, this is supposed to be the part where I become 'possessed by Satan' and bestow the Mark of the Beast on everyone. I have no idea how the Devil he's going to take me over, or how he could even exist. But I know about the '666' Mark. It has to do with integrating the Antis' nanochip technology into the general world population. Everybody on Earth will have to possess this symbol in order to survive during my reign."

"Do tell," Barbara breathed theatrically, gently blowing on her papers. "Go on, please."

"Gladly. 'He opposes God. He will speak marvelous things against the God of Gods. He will exalt himself above all that is called God. He will sit in the temple of God. He will claim to be God or an incarnation of God. He will take away the daily sacrifices from the temple.' That's quite a list. I do plan on doing all that. I'm not sure about claiming to actually be God, but we'll see. As for 'taking away the daily sacrifices,' those ended a long time ago. But when I finish off the Catholic Church, that will stop the Daily Mass and the Sacrifice of the Eucharist will end forever. Yeah, that oughta do it.

"I like this part: 'He will plant the tabernacles of his palace between the seas in the glorious holy mountain.' I love the way that line flows. Sheer poetry. That's where I'm gonna rebuild the Jewish Temple and make it the seat of my New World Order.

"'He will have power to make war with the saints and overcome them. He will continue this war for three-and-a-half years.' I hope to—well, not God—that this refers to the Illuminati. They're the ones in charge of 'the saints,' so with luck it does. 'This time of Great Tribulation is launched upon the Earth by the Antichrist at the Abomination of Desolation.' I have no idea where the Hell that is, but I guess it fosters another big war, someday. I'm going to do my best to prevent any more such conflicts, whatever happens.

"There's a lot more stuff: 'During this time, the Antichrist will scatter the power of the holy people. He will rule a mighty and strong kingdom. He will be given power over all kindreds, tongues and nations. His kingdom will devour the whole Earth. He will have great military power that will enforce his laws. He will try to change times and laws, and they will be given into his power for three-and-a-half years. He will give great honor to the God of forces, with gold, silver, jewels and more. He will prosper in everything that he does. He will not regard the God of his fathers'. Oh, yeah. 'He will not regard the desire of women.' *What?* Wait a minute! Hey, does this mean I'm going to turn gay or something? Barbara?"

Barbara was full-out laughing now. "Doesn't it say 'women,' like the plural of woman?" she gasped, heaving. Her chest was really bouncing now, which also broke Mabus up.

"Right! You're the only dame for me, sweet pea. That takes care of that."

"All the women of the world have been swooning over your image. It's been appearing throughout worldwide media, and you know Time Magazine voted you the handsomest man alive. Your next step is to become Man of the Century, I guess."

"Man of all Centuries, you mean. Aw, let's finish this, for now anyway. Here it goes: 'The Mark of the Beast will be the Number of his Name.' Yeah, Nostradamus figured out that Mabus adds up to 666 in Hebrew. Each letter represents a special number. And my birthdate is 6-6-76. Say, didja know George W. Bush's name adds up to 666 in Hebrew, too? Maybe I better keep an eye on the Bush dynasty. They might be my rivals. He seems to be running for Antichrist too. The Bible says there've been several other Antichrists over time, but I think most of those are my Anti buddies, like Thaillo.

"I wanna wrap this up and move on, Barbara. Have you finished going over my speech? Should we make any sizeable changes?"

"Looks like it plays pretty well as is. But you'd better edit it for grammar and accuracy." Barbara set down the many papers she had been holding, and briefly yawned.

"No problem. Here's the rest of the Bible stuff for now. It's the really goofy part, which I totally fail to understand: 'All who dwell upon the Earth will worship him, except those whose names are written in the Lamb's Book of Life. He will have an image made after him.' I guess this has to do with the statue reference. There's a lot of shit about a land beast and a sea beast, and the Great Whore breathes life into this statue and it becomes me. Trouble is, I already exist. And people have already made plenty of images of me, so I really don't see what good a big old marble statue would do. Oh well.

"And furthermore: 'His coming will be after the workings of Satan. He will fight against Jesus Christ at Armageddon, and lose. He will stand against the Prince of Princes. The Lord will consume him with the spirit of His mouth, which is the Word of God. The Lord will destroy him with the brightness of His coming, which is His glory. He will be cast alive into the lake of fire. He will be tormented day and night, forever and ever.'

"Most of this is from the Book of Revelations, with a few of the references being from other books in the Old and New Testaments. Both of which I understand were entirely written by superstitious human pawns of the Illuminati. So perhaps I don't have too much to worry about, if we can only deal with those eerie dudes somehow. I heard recently that some of the religious people are gunning for me. But thanks to the Antis, I'll be fine. Hell, Thaillo told me they're gonna make sure that I live, like, for nearly a million years.

"It's something to do with the trip back into the past. I have to be around to supervise the building of the Tower of Babylon, which actually occurred about a million years ago. Maybe I'm going to be reborn, babe! It's all pretty weird, but I'm beginning to trust..."

"Thaillo? Why doesn't he give you more complete details about all these things?"

"He keeps saying it has to do with the timeline and not creating any paradoxes. He says there will be plenty of time over the millennia to explain everything to me. I guess so."

"Well, I hope you feel all prepared now to explain yourself. It's going to be hard to fight past all those true believers who've been preaching against you. And you're somehow going to have to convince enough people in power that you should rule the world. I have no idea how you're going to do that. People in power don't give it up all that easily."

"I think if I can convince everyone, especially the Islamic world, that I can bring peace to the whole planet, I'll be able to take it from there. The important thing is that ending the war is one of the most crucial prophecies..." Mabus sighed, yawning slightly.

"Hey, sweetie baby girl, what time is it? I'm not real tired, but it's gotta be late."

Barbara idly glanced at her diamond-studded wristwatch. "It's midnight. Merry Christmas, darling. You'll be giving your speech at the National Mall in Washington, DC first thing in the morning. I hear the President and all the heads of state will be in the audience."

"Yeah, and Me knows who else." The Antichrist was getting bold enough to joke about his "God" status now, but he loathed it every time people got down on their knees to him. He still felt like an ordinary Joe, albeit one who could lift 1,000 times his own weight, speak every language in the world, and run faster than a hightailing cheetah in a hurricane. "I think the only way the Illuminati could stop us is to shoot me in the head."

"Your six-hour speech will be broadcast live over every network on Earth. But I'm keeping a copy of it on DVD for our kids. I hope to You," said Barbara, also jokingly, "that nobody does anything weird tomorrow. I'd hate it if Abraham Lincoln had to see somebody else assassinated right under his nose."

Chapter Seventeen

"And I saw one of his heads as it were wounded to death; and his deadly wound was healed: and all the world wondered after the beast."

–Rev. 13:3

ORNING DAWNED PREMATURELY IN WASHINGTON, DC, as the sun gleamed at the ruddy edges of the National Mall's flat horizon. The open space and parklands envisioned by Pierre L'Enfant, commissioned by President George Washington, had long created an ideal stage for consequent national expressions of remembrance, observance and protest during its lifetime.

Over 2,000 stately American elms lined the Mall, and its 3,000 internationally-renowned Japanese cherry trees graced its Tidal Basin. Its botanical gardens showcased thousands of tulips, pansies and annuals in over 170 flowerbeds, and it held thirty-five ornamental pools and fountains. This impressive mingling of natural and cultural resources made our nation's capital one of the most heavily visited and photographed places in the world.

Considered to be one of the Mall's biggest attractions, the Lincoln Memorial was a tribute to President Abraham Lincoln and the nation he fought to preserve during the Civil War. Over 500,000 people had died in its bloody wake. But there was to be plenty more strife and death where that came from, as the world would soon learn.

Located at the west end of the National Mall, the Lincoln Memorial was built to resemble an ancient Greek temple. It held thirty-six Doric columns, one for each state at the time of Lincoln's death. This was also the number of the Antichrist's age when Spaceship *Noah* departed the Earth. A massive sculpture by Daniel C. French of a seated Lincoln rested in the center of the memorial chamber. The statue loomed nineteen feet high and weighed 175 tons.

The Lincoln Memorial had often been used as a gathering place for protests and political rallies. But Christmas Day of 2005 proved nearly an exception to the case when it came to political speeches. Today was the day that "Mabus, the One True Antichrist" would try to convince an awe-struck world of its need for one united leadership entirely under his own personal rule, which many governments and religions still staunchly opposed.

Since its dedication on May 29th of 2004, the National World War II Memorial had stretched its length between the Washington Monument and the Lincoln Memorial. This new memorial had a ceremonial entrance at 17th Street, and a Memorial Plaza and Rainbow Pool completed its layout. Gracious ramps led to the plaza. The entrance was flanked by twenty-four bronze bas-relief panels that paid homage to America's World War II experience. The new Memorial Plaza was where the Antichrist's audience and the media were to gather for the next six hours and pay him a most courtly homage.

Swiftly, the national news's best boys, key grips and camera crews swarmed around a broad wooden podium at the base of the Lincoln Memorial, mounting the needed electrical sound equipment into place. The crowd of hand-picked spectators, who numbered in the several hundreds, slowly gathered within the newly appointed Memorial Plaza. Soon, someone extraordinary would be delivering a speech fated to become even more famous than the Reverend Dr. Martin Luther King Jr.'s "I Have A Dream" speech from the August 28th, 1963 March on Washington for Jobs and Freedom.

That enormous event had been held right at the base of the statue in the Lincoln Memorial approach area, which was present before the construction of the new World War II Memorial. The actual size of today's crowd, although it now had even more room in which to gather, sit and listen, was much smaller than Dr. King's huge throng of civil rights protesters. However, all of our national media and those of some other countries would be broadcasting this lengthy speech live around the entire globe.

An expectant hush came over the milling throng, which included many Hollywood celebrities, governors and mayors, legislators and several people of unknown influence in Washington and other ports of call around the world. A shiny black Hummer, the kind used by the Antichrist's personal entourage, had pulled up to the ceremonial entrance of the World War II Memorial. And a beautiful brunette woman wearing a tight, low-cut black dress got out, silently followed by a group of people wearing black caps, sunglasses and dark suits.

But as over a hundred camera flashes loudly popped, there was no sign of the Antichrist. It was nearly six o'clock, and time for his world-famous speech to start. Dozens of media people and cameramen rushed up to Barbara, pouring over each other like a moving human wall in the partial twilight.

"Where's the Antichrist? Is he coming? When is he going to arrive?" begged a legion of conflicting voices. Barbara simply raised one delicate, well-manicured hand to silence them. Then she pointed her index finger high into the air above them, as they all turned to look.

"Up there. See the black airplane? Watch this. I'll bet you've never seen anything like it before. And maybe you never will again." With that, Barbara strode forward with her group of Antis to take their places in the front and center row of folding chairs.

Perplexed paparazzi peered skyward, noticing nothing unusual at first. Then they began to see a gleaming black object, moving so quickly across the still-darkened morning sky that it resembled a flying saucer. Soon a small black dot was visible near the object, its shadow growing in size as it plummeted toward the gasping crowd. As it rapidly fell, too fast for an ordinary parachute's descent, the Antichrist's bright flaming-red jumpsuit became visible. But what happened next astonished even the most hard-boiled journalists.

On Mabus's way down, an awesome plethora of scarlet, peach and golden fireworks began bursting, having miraculously appeared from nowhere. They surrounded the Antichrist's steady plunge, nearly igniting his billowing red parachute. As they exploded, they created a fiery, enveloping emerald-green "666" sign that beautifully framed the falling red form.

Many experts commented later that such a monumental display of fireworks spurting in such a precise pattern was not at all consistent with modern pyrotechnology.

With a "phloomph" of the small red parachute slumping behind him, the Antichrist landed suavely on his feet directly behind the long podium. He didn't even have to step forward, merely pausing for a moment to unzip and doff his blood-red jumpsuit as golden flashes popped all around him. He immediately began his speech, prefacing it with an apology.

"I'm sorry to have to take such a spectacular measure, but I had to do my best to avoid any possible interference with my planned arrival time. Therefore I chose to make this colorful entrance. Do not be dismayed, for I have much to tell you, inform you about, and discuss with you concerning the growing need for world peace in the face of utmost hostilities and the impending Russian nuclear attack on our American soil..."

As the Antichrist smoothly launched into his speech, looking for all the world like he had left a men's salon seconds ago, without a wrinkle in his perfectly ironed black suit or a single blond hair out of place, he was being watched by far more than the extremely impressed audience of open-mouthed invitees.

Over half a mile away, on the other side of an open office building window, Mabus's forehead was laser-centered in the sight of a long range rifle system. Perched on a simple tripod and balanced flat to within one-thousandth of a centimeter, a CheyTac Intervention M200 rifle was taking its fatal aim at the unknowing Antichrist. This rifle was based on the Windrunner .50 caliber takedown equipment from EDM Arms, but its design included several high-tech modifications, most of which EDM had never heard of.

The system included a modified CheyTac tactical computer, a commercial PDA with newly installed ballistic software, a Nightforce NXZ 5.25-25X scope, and Kestrel 8000 wind, temperature and atmospheric sensors linked to the PDA. This provided all necessary data for precisely accurate long range firing. CheyTac papers stated that the system was capable of delivering sub-MOA accuracy at ranges up to 3,000 meters. But the special equipment on this reworked system enabled it to do far more than that.

Almost all of the human eyes in the world, and several other ones, were totally fixed on Mabus's perfectly formed and so perfectly animated face when it brutally exploded into a fountain-like geyser of irretrievable crimson shards.

The first thing Barbara thought of was a rainbow waterfall she had seen once in Stehekin, Washington—the state, not the District of Columbia. Next, she was swimming through the waterfall in slow motion as a throng of onlookers rushed the podium. First an Anti guard swept up Mabus's lifeless body, and then Barbara fell to her numb and equally lifeless knees before it. All she could see was a twisted, stunted red neck, jagged and silent.

"No...this isn't possible. You're immortal. You were going to rule the whole world..." she choked, realizing this was not to be the case. Not now, and not ever.

A stocky African-American bodyguard, one of the Antis, softly laid his hand upon Barbara's shoulder. He had seen such things before, and was wondering why Mabus's neck wasn't gushing blood.

Barbara cradled her lover's limp body in her arms, but her cries soon gave way to incredulous whimpers as she saw that a kind of bubbling was coming from Mabus's neck. Clots of flesh and blood leaped around like growing amorphous kangaroos. Intertwining tendrils of bone, sinew and nerve wound over his throat in a poetic dance. For a brief moment, Barbara and the Anti guard thought they saw a familiar symbol form out of the burgeoning gore, and they wondered.

In less than thirty seconds, the shape of a head was clearly visible. It shook, and kept coalescing into normalcy. And then the Antichrist, his face and his short blond mane more beautiful and perfect than ever, opened his eyes, looked directly into Barbara's and spoke.

"Baby, that was so weird! I thought the sun had exploded. But see, it's rising into the sky."

With tears pouring out of her brown eyes, Barbara looked up and saw the magnificent sight of the sunrise as Mabus leapt lightly to his feet. The crowd collectively gasped, and the Anti guards helped a stunned Barbara to her feet and back to her seat. Mabus smoothed his clothing and picked up where he had left off in his speech. Everyone hung on his every word in amazement. He had definitely got their attention. People muttered in the audience that what they had just seen was Jesus himself, resurrected. Mabus explained that he was immortal and destined to save mankind. He claimed he was sent to open the eyes of the people and let them live out the rest of their lives truly free.

"Religion and government," **he continued,** "have been allied since the beginning in a plot to enslave the human race, and they have succeeded. Their weapon of choice was one they invented—currency; money; cold hard cash and empty hollow credit. The government mass produces this drug and releases it into the population. We, as mindless drones, follow in pursuit of it, and prioritize our life around it. Why? Because we can't survive without it. Money is the root of all evil."

As Mabus spoke, his would-be assassin, a professional sniper who went by the moniker "Snoopy," attempted to collect his pay from his contact, the Chief Reverend of Washington's First Baptist Church. The Reverend was a dignified and statuesque figure, a tall and mysterious man of Ethiopian descent.

"Their next weapon of choice," **Mabus continued,** "was the financial lending system. Why, Thomas Jefferson himself told John Adams, 'I sincerely believe that banking establishments are more dangerous than standing armies, and that the principle of spending money to be paid by posterity under the name of funding is but swindling futurity on a large scale.' See? This is how they steal your futures from you and enslave you. Money has become the handcuffs that keep us imprisoned!

"After we pay our income tax, sales tax, and property tax, we then pay our home mortgage, and eighty percent of that monthly payment is interest. We have to get to work, so we have to have cars. Our car payment? Again, eighty percent of that payment is interest also. And let's not even talk about what it costs to buy gas to transport us back and forth to work. Why do you think we went to war with Iraq originally?

"It doesn't stop there. You've got to insure your house, your business, your car, and your health. If you use your insurance, your rates will go up or your coverage will be denied altogether—devastating, considering that the state requires you to be insured to drive or run a business. I wonder if politicians own any insurance companies?

"What are ninety percent of us left with after that endless cycle of debt? An intricate system of slavery, where life is real good—for the other ten percent.

"Why so many taxes? Why are our nations in such debt? Because these politicians overspend our money in companies that they personally own. Why does the government pay five hundred dollars for an Allen wrench that costs one dollar to make? These politicians own companies that sell five hundred-dollar Allen wrenches. These officials who have the inside scoop on the contracts only use contractors they favor—themselves!"

Many miles away from where Mabus was giving his speech, in a back alley behind the First Baptist Church, "Snoopy" held out his hand to collect his fee from the Reverend. Further away, perched on a tall spire of the Capitol Dome, Eva coolly pulled the trigger of her own Illuminati-designed weapon, a smooth silver device incorporating borrowed alien technology and as far advanced over Snoopy's CheyTac M200 as the CheyTac itself was over a Stone-Age bow and arrow. Snoopy's entire upper torso instantly bloomed into a flower of bone fragments and organ chunks. The Reverend fell back in horror, a trickle of Snoopy's blood running down his forehead and a piece of the late assassin's brain hanging off his eyeglass frames. He opened his mouth to produce an inarticulate exclamation of shock, but never managed to spit it out, his own head exploding into a tiny volcano of gore, his tongue flying off in a smooth arc to land on the dirty asphalt with a wet *splat*.

All the incriminating witnesses having been disposed of, Eva calmly disassembled the alien weapon and placed the pieces back into its padded carrying case. She got up to leave the catwalk of the Capitol dome, stealing one last glance at the Mall where Mabus was stirring the crowd to greater and greater heights of enthusiasm. She canted her head nonchalantly. "If you want something done right, you *really* have to do it yourself," she said wistfully.

Meahwhile, Mabus's admirers were nodding happily and calling out "Yeah!" and "Amen!" as he went on. "Who's policing the government?" he shouted. "Who's auditing the government? Absolute power corrupts absolutely. What do you expect? And really, can we blame them?"

Mabus looked into the sea of faces. With his heightened senses, he could keep speaking and simultaneously tune in to anyone in the crowd he focused his energy on. <The bald man in the green pea coat? George Swenson, fifty-nine years old, lives at 223 Maplewood Drive. He believes me,>**Mabus thought.** <Fifteen yards to George's left, the woman with the frizzy red hair—Inga

Schultz, formerly a dental technician, three cats and a poodle at home. She's not really getting what I'm saying. Let me use an analogy,> **Mabus thought.** "When you put a hot dog in front of a real dog, his natural instinct is to eat it," **he said.** "Even if you tell the dog to restrain himself, he may. But the second your back is turned, that frankfurter is history. So then whose fault is it, the dog's, for expressing its natural survival instincts? Or is it your fault, for allowing the canine the opportunity? But with so many elected officials now, I'm sure none of them are indulging in their natural survival instincts." **Inga nodded. She got it. Mabus had them, had them all, and he knew it. After all, he was the Antichrist.**

"So what is so important that we have to work two jobs to get by and support the government financially? What are they spending our money on? Well, they're protecting us from people *like* us—people who like to invade countries and start wars. Don't we get a say? I bet ninety percent of the civilians would not like to go to war at all. If these officials have a beef with other countries, they should go there themselves and fight. Don't brainwash our children, then send them on the front line to die for your purposes.

"Ladies and gentlemen, this isn't about war, this is all about our money. These governments scare their people with rumors of war to pump their economies dry and their treasuries full. They inject fear into the hearts of their people to support their lavish lifestyles. How can killing be condoned as a weapon of peace? These guys are nuts!

"These politicians live like kings—like King Bush and Prince Bush, or like King George III, against whom we revolted over two hundred years ago. Yes, they live like kings within their castle walls as *we* live as peasants, barely getting by. They send out their sheriffs to collect taxes from us. Even though they have a room full of treasures and jewels and gold, the assessor is always on time, if not early, to collect his taxes. But if he is late, *you* will have a hefty penalty to pay. And when war threatens the castle, they lock up the gate to protect themselves, and they withhold vital survival information from their people. They call this 'protect and serve.'"

Snoopy and the Reverend had been taken care of. It would not hit the papers. As Mabus continued to speak and his followers grew in their support of him, the others who had been involved in the Christmas Day Assassination Attempt were scrambling,

regrouping. Many, from the top levels down, were already being chastised and punished. Eva, however, had succeeded with her cleanup, and was immune from the consequences which befell less fortunate conspirators.

Mabus grew more passionate as he spoke. Sometimes, when he focused on his own voice instead of someone or other in the crowd, he noted, with some amusement, that he sounded like a Baptist preacher. "We came to this country to escape the kings and their high taxes because we wanted freedom. But we weren't seeking financial freedom or civil freedom. We were seeking spiritual freedom, and human freedom. It didn't take long for even that idea to get diluted. We wanted a government where religion is separate from state, and they still, to this day, claim it is. Only recently have they taken God out of the Pledge of Allegiance in our schools. And our money? They have plastered 'In God We Trust' on all our money—all of the money. We are reminded daily that our government is living under this moral code of God, so we can submit to them as we were supposed to submit to God. But are they ripping us off? Not really! We willingly hand them our money!

"They use techniques of propaganda to persuade us to part with our modest savings. NASA is the center of one of these deceptions. They used the technology of Hollywood to get into our wallets and steal our money. There was never any 'Race for Space.' NASA has their own little Universal Studios of sorts, with special low-gravity rooms. They film fake moon landings to pump patriotism in our hearts and minds and cash out of our wallets. And, speaking of which, who better to play our president than an actor, Ronald Reagan? Who's going to be next, Arnold Schwarzenegger? It's all an act anyway, isn't it?

"We are imprisoned by our own gullibility. We are cattle to these financial parasites. We are too busy with our minor life inconsistencies. We chase our tails trying to get ahead, but daily we slip farther and farther behind. It's time we made a change. It's time for a global revolution!"

To punctuate his last words, Mabus pumped his fist in the air. The crowd ate it up, erupting into shouts and cheers.

Someone shouted from the crowd, "Mabus for President!"

Mabus, the One True Antichrist, had now converted the whole world to his system of beliefs and theories. His electronic audience was putty in his hands. More people stopped believing in their religions and philosophies that day than ever before in human history. The Illuminati gnashed their teeth.

That night, the Christian churches which had planned to host Christmas Eve services turned away the few who came to worship. Thereafter, they permanently closed their doors, opening them only to use the space for emergencies.

And a hasty meeting of the United Nations General Assembly was convened deep in underground bunkers in New York City. Worldwide polls on whether Mabus should rule the entire world had already been taken, and the massive "Yes" vote had been counted by the Antis' banks of computers within two days.

Mabus, the One True Antichrist, had now awakened the world to how the people were enslaved by their religions and governments. Riots swiftly broke out. People began looting. Even people who normally wouldn't dream of breaking laws were out in the streets destroying government buildings and churches. All around the world people rebelled against their countries, taking to the streets, chanting, "All hail the Antichrist!"

Also, partially due to the newfound lack of religion as a guiding light and the major governmental shakeups, many people had turned to extreme lawlessness. They were looting freely in the devastation and causing still more destruction and damage by frequently killing each other, both as aggressors and in desperate acts of self-defense.

A hasty charter was duly written, stamped and officially signed by the ten members of the UN Security Council, the ten nations of the European Union, the top ten nations of the Allies II alliance, and the ten-nation Common Stock Market. And, of course, by Mabus the Antichrist, who penned his signature at the very bottom of the charter as "Mabus the Only True Christ, Permanent and Universal Emperor of the Planet Earth." No one objected to this lengthy title, as it was exactly the one the UN had jointly assigned him on the date of December 27th, the Year of Our New Lord AC 2005. It soon came to be written on most calendars as the Year 29 AB, or 29 years After Birth, referring to the Antichrist's birth date.

The first night of the new World Emperor's reign, Mabus the Antichrist slipped between his black satin sheets and rubbed his faithful dog's shaggy head. Mabus had taken to letting the mutt sleep with him; it made him feel safer. The Antichrist quickly drifted off to sleep. He had already stopped dreaming of the asteroid, and he would never wake up screaming ever again.

Chapter Eighteen

I T WAS EARLY JANUARY OF 2006. With the election over, Mabus was technically the American Head of State, and Commander in Chief of all the US Armed Forces. But he still had to contest with the lame-duck President, his cabinet, his secretaries, staff and aides, the Joint Chiefs of Staff, top generals of the US military, both houses of Congress, the Supreme Court and multiple other such entities for dominance.

These were all Illuminati-dominated or influenced. And although Mabus was able to read minds, those of the Illuminati and their puppets presented closed doors to his soul. He needed a way to break down these mighty barriers, and fast, for it was known that Russia was going to mount its huge nuclear attack within mere days.

"Thaillo, what should I do? Where can I turn? I'm not sure the President is really listening to me. And Congress hasn't done anything about the impending nuclear holocaust. They're not moving. They keep their asses parked on the Hill, like they have something to fall back on. I can't get them to do anything."

Thaillo considered the Antichrist's words for a few moments. "You must speak with the real Pope of Rome. He can help you. I will arrange a meeting between the two of you."

"Well, it'd better be soon, or all of America is going to be another New York City. And I still don't understand why the Antis aren't allowed to use their technology to clean up the radiation in that area. Why can't I send a team out there to analyze it and fix things?"

"It would interfere with the gradual dawning of the prophecies, and the many calamitous events that are to precipitate the conclusion of life on Earth. I will arrange a meeting with the Pope in a few days… "

"That's not soon enough. It has to be today, Thaillo. We can't wait."

"Very well. I shall make arrangements for you to take Air Force 666 to Rome."

In a black, glossy jumbo jetliner as tall as an eight-story building and longer than a city block, emblazoned with the Antis' gold "666" symbol on either side and on the tail, Mabus and his complement of black-clad Antis flew at 666 mph, just below the speed of sound, at an altitude of 66,600 feet, halfway around the world to southern Europe.

The trip took almost exactly six hours. Along the way, Mabus watched Russian television in an attempt to devise a peace plan that would work between the Eastern and Western worlds. And Barbara, who felt slightly dizzy, lay down in one of the plane's many beds.

After landing at Rome's Fiumicino Airport, Mabus's entourage took a local cab to the Hotel Dei Consoli. No one would have expected this, as cabs to this hotel generally came from the Leonardo da Vinci International Airport. And the chosen hostelry, though it had a four-star rating, was quite small. It was generally a haven for wealthy business travelers and not important government officials. Its location in Rome ideally served the Antichrist's purposes, however, and it held a secret which very few people knew.

The Hotel Dei Consoli was situated in Via Cola di Rienzo near stately St. Peter's Square, in a small century-old building that recently had been reconstructed in the Imperial style. The Spanish Steps, a lovely tourist attraction, were only a ten-minute walk away, as the hotel was located in the very heart of the Eternal City. But this was no concern of the Antichrist's. This quaint "Alloggio" had been selected for another reason entirely.

The detailed cornices and columns of this expensive hotel were created by the famed master plasterers of Naples, noted for their work in the redecoration of the celebrated Reggia di Caserta. The hotel itself seemingly contained only twenty-nine rooms and occupied three floors, which had been decorated and named accordingly: Piano dei Mappamondi, Piano dei Fiori and Piano delle Battaglie. But there was a fourth "piano," of which the Italian public and the remainder of the world were blissfully unaware.

It was in the lobby of this carefully chosen fourth piano, the Piano Sotterraneo, that Mabus was to have his historic meeting with the genuine Pope of Rome. For the Sotterraneo was part of the famous catacombs of Rome, its Underground City. It was connected directly to the Necropolis of St. Peter's Basilica, the location of the first Pope's tomb in an entire two-story village nestled for many centuries underneath the Vatican.

The tomb's excavation had been "bungled" purportedly by the Vatican, but this was to hide the Necropolis's connections to the rest of the underground city, especially the area below the Hotel Dei Consoli. The Piano Sotterraneo was where the shadowy Pope went to relax in secret, or to plot certain meetings with the heads of world states and religions.

And this is where Mabus met him, in a well-appointed lobby, with twelve of his own Anti guards at his disposal and for his protection. Barbara, who had turned out to be very sick, had gone to lie down in the palatial junior suite they had rented above them in the Piano dei Fiori. She had told Mabus not to worry about her, and to get going.

Mabus was quite surprised when he saw the Pope. Thaillo had warned him, but he never expected the Supreme Head of the Catholic Church to look so, well, familiar. This "True Pope" was in fact the near twin of Thaillo, perhaps even handsomer. And he was dressed in an expensive white business suit, not his formal ceremonial white vestments.

To be recognizable, the Illustrious Father did wear his small white zucchetto, or skullcap. His famous Papal mitre, which bears the inscription "Vicarius Filii Dei" or "The Vicar of the Son of the God," was of course missing. Mabus thought he knew why.

"Hello, Pontiff. Long time no See. I hope you don't mind the crude pun."

"I do, my son, but I will let it pass. So you are the famous Antichrist who must lead the entire world back into peace, or die trying, I suppose. Strange, you don't look like much. But I suppose we will have to make do with what we are supplied."

"I see you're not wearing your official vestments or miter. Is that because of the ancient inscription on the miter? Do you still want to deny your true connection with Me?"

The Pope sighed. "You know the meaning of the VFD. Its numerical equivalent in Roman numerals is, of course, 666. No, I simply wish to remain inconspicuous. But as you have pointed out, there is a long-standing tradition in our Church of standing at your side. I intend today to no longer vilify, but to fortify, your position. Yes, I am the so-called False Prophet, symbol of the Great Whore, and the one who will help you take over this planet. I must cause all of my Church to worship your divine essence... "

"What you've got to do right now is help me talk Russia out of world suicide. What have you learned about Mother Russia, and what can we do to prevent a nuclear holocaust in America?"

All that long day, Mabus and the Pope got to know each other, discussing how to handle the East-West conflict and what they needed to do eventually in the Middle East. And in the middle of their conversation, Mabus forced a reluctant Pope to accept his proposal to step down and let the Antichrist assume control of the entire Church for the rest of history.

"In my role as the True Prophet, there is much I have to do to promulgate your reign." the Pope conceded, promising that he would soon reveal himself to the world.

Meanwhile, Barbara was limply propped up and watching Teleroma 666. Apparently the Antichrist's influence was already felt in Italy, one of the member states of the Allies II and a recently elected member of the UN Security Council. But what Barbara didn't know was that Thaillo was the one who had been arranging the new "666" TV stations worldwide, as well as manifesting many other usages of the "666" symbol. He had been a very busy Anti.

Late in the cool Roman evening, Mabus strolled into Barbara's room carrying a dozen red roses he had bought in the hotel's main lobby. "Hey, baby, feeling better?"

"I don't know what hit me," she said. "And it's happening all over the world. There's been a massive wave of poisonings. Our President and his entire cabinet, the President of the Russian Federation and the Russian Security Council, and the President of China and their whole Politburo have been poisoned. They're all dead. And nobody knows who's responsible.

"Also, it's been reported that Russia will probably proceed with its plans to attack the United States. It looks like they think America is responsible for the assassinations. They may be increasing the size of their nuclear onslaught in proportion to their outrage."

"Oh, my Me. How do you feel?" said Mabus, drawing near his lady love. She was sitting in a deeply varnished chair made of Italian pregiato wood, and she looked a little pale.

"I'm okay. I don't know if it's the same thing. But I'm alive."

"Thank Me for that!"

"Thank You."

"You're quite welcome, my dear." This was one of their personal favorite running gags. But a simple jest could do nothing to lighten their deeply depressed mood.

Without taking any time to explore Rome's many attractions, Mabus, Barbara and their small entourage somberly boarded Air Force 666 in the early morning and flew back home. Mabus immediately headed for Capitol Hill, where he, Barbara and Thaillo now lived in close proximity, to see what actions were being taken regarding this crisis. He also wanted to offer the Pope's proposals to whomever had assumed the Office of the Presidency.

But what transpired in the Oval Office even surprised Mabus. For as soon as he stepped into the room, the First Lady, Laura Bush, who had often been very friendly to him, dismissed her hovering staff and six Secret Service members, and then handed Mabus "the football"—an ordinary-looking black briefcase. What it contained, however, was far from ordinary, and he knew it; he had just been handed all the codes needed for nuclear deployment.

"I'm tired. It's over," the First Lady sighed. "We don't want to be poisoned. There you go, Mister President, or is it Mister Emperor? I'm so confused. Nothing's the same as it ever was. Here's all you need to make the final world peace."

Mabus grimly clutched at the briefcase. She then turned on her heel to exit the room and said over her shoulder, "It's all yours, son. Best of luck to you."

Now the One True Christ, also known as the One True Antichrist, wielded the capacity to either utterly destroy the world or save it. He gently laid the most powerful briefcase on Earth atop the President's large, shiny wooden desk, and slowly sat down.

Chapter Nineteen

"And it was given unto him to make war with the saints, and to overcome them: and power was given to him over all kindreds, and tongues, and nations."

—Rev. 13:7

"Christos," and in Hebrew this word is translated as "Messiah." It means "anointed one" and refers to the genealogy of Jewish kingship even more than it designates a Savior of the world.

In the era before Jesus, the Davidic line of kings were all called "Messiah ben David," or Messiahs born of David. They were anointed on the forehead with olive oil by the High Priest, which was symbolic of enlightenment. But during the Jewish captivity in Babylon, the prophets Isaiah, Daniel and Ezekiel prophesied that two of these descendants from David would be anointed with the Holy Spirit not by a High Priest, but by God Himself.

Jesus, being descended from David through King Solomon's brother, was the first of these two prophesied Christs. The meaning of the word Christ, therefore, is a lineal descendant of King David who has been anointed. And the second of these prophesied Christs, or Saviors, has been said to appear much later, causing world peace and human enlightenment, and reigning for awhile in a time of utmost destruction and chaos.

These two Christs, presumably descendants of David's line of sacred kings, are not the same. And the one who is to appear later is not the Second Coming of the original...

As ACTING PRESIDENT of the United States, the first thing the Antichrist did was figure out whom to contact within the constantly changing political structure of the one-time ruler of the Soviet Union and the largest country on Earth.

The President of the Russian Federation was dead, and so were all the members of the Russian Security Council. Mabus could contact their Federal Assembly, which was the current Parliament of Russia. There might be better luck there than trying to deal with what was left of the Communist Party leadership, which had grown in strength over the past year by being in the forefront of the Arab-Israeli war. They had been the ones most responsible for making that conflict into the start of World War III.

The Russian Federal Assembly consisted of two chambers, the Council of the Federation and the State Duma. The Federation Council had the jurisdiction of declaring war, and also ending it. The Chairman of the Council was its head, and was not a member of the Communist Party. This seemed to be the best bet for whoever was currently in charge in Russia. But Mabus had a small problem with this being the right person.

"What do you mean, she's probably not the one really in power just because she's a woman?" Barbara cried indignantly when the Antichrist called her to the Oval Office.

"You know Russians. They're very male-dominated. If everyone else on top is dead, probably some men in the Federal Assembly will try to wrest power from her. Or maybe the Supreme Commander of the Federation Armed Forces has already taken control. I have to call this lady's office and find out. Please back me up, Barbara, in case I need a woman's opinion. I'm going to determine the fate of the world today."

Barbara sighed permissively, settling in as Mabus made the international Presidential phone call to the Russian Federal Assembly's main switchboard. They immediately sent him over to the Chairman's office, and a female voice rang high and clear over the line.

After about an hour, Mabus hung up. He immediately turned to Barbara. "It looks like you were right, honey bunch. She does have enough power in the government to help us, although everything over there is pretty chaotic nowadays. At least she believes that I'm not the one responsible for the poisonings. And I further said that America's probably not to blame either, as many of our high-ranking federal officials have also died. It helped immeasurably that I called and backed up all the reports they've received."

Mabus picked up the "football" and handed it to a security aide. "Get Air Force 666 ready. We're flying to Moscow in fifteen minutes to meet with the Russian Federal Assembly. C'mon Barbara, we have to pull an all-nighter for this one."

On their long flight to Russia, Mabus and Barbara made up for lost time. For so long, Mabus had been kept busy by his undying drive to control the world. He hadn't really kept up his end of the relationship with Barbara. But now, even amid the papers he was being handed, he talked to her as a friend and a lover. They chatted, over as romantic a dinner as you could have on a specially modified 747. Finally, Mabus took an interest in Barbara's rapturous wedding plans, and she, for a change, went on and on about their prospective china patterns and towel colors.

They made it to the Kremlin quickly, and Mabus was soon shaking hands with the Chairwoman of the Council, a dark, raven-tressed and mature-faced woman. She was half-Evenki, of a Northern Chinese and Eastern Siberian people who inhabited Russia. She ate deer on a regular basis.

Chairwoman Agdy was deeply impressed with the Antichrist's credentials, even though she had been an animist before converting to atheism. This change was largely due to Mabus's many statements that there was no such thing as a divine God or Jesus, combined with the several phenomenological miracles that he had been publicly displaying. Most of these were regularly shown on worldwide television.

Nowadays, the Chairman was a true believer in the lordly and miraculous works of the charismatic Antichrist. She had even witnessed his slaughter and his shattered head growing back, in close-up and living color. She would soon prove to be a very good friend, and a most powerful ally.

Agdy was also the unofficial head of the Liberal Democratic Party of Russia, and had steered the LDP far away from many of their right-wing positions, either in spite or because of the continuing war. Thankfully, she had a great deal of influence over the Communist Party of the Russian Federation, which would have a lot to do with containing the spreading conflict. In a few minutes, she had arranged for the Antichrist to speak before the Russian General Assembly later on that evening, at around midnight.

After a brief consultation with the Foreign Minister and the acting Supreme Commander of the Armed Forces, it was agreed that every attempt would be made to push Mabus through into both the office of the President and that of the Prime Minister. This would take place as soon as the major Communist Party heads and other important Russian dignitaries had agreed to Mabus's terms and conditions regarding ending the war and establishing a new Federation government based on his sole rule.

"I always lusted to be the head of the Federation," Mabus joked to Barbara, humming the high-pitched music of the original *"Star Trek"* TV show. "That's a lot more than Captain Kirk ever did. After I finish up here, the next move is to hit Beijing and convince them to let me take over Red China. After that, the rest of the world should come easy."

But it was not to prove to be all that simple. At midnight, Mabus faced down a sea of folded arms and tight lips at the General Assembly, which now held quite a few empty seats. After yammering on for about an hour and feeling like he wasn't making any real headway, he looked into the audience and saw a familiar blonde head making its way between leaders of the hard-line Communists and members of the Liberal Democratic Party. It was Eva! It was difficult for him to understand how a NASA spokeswoman could be parleying with the Reds, but he imagined that she had ruthlessly moved up in the world since her television broadcasts decrying him. She was stirring up dissension among the ranks, trying to get these two venerable factions to block Mabus's prospects. He was amazed, but angry, and it was in this spirit that he tried for a Hail Mary.

"My documentary has secured me over sixty billion dollars, counting video and charitable sales, residuals and other contracts. Immediate world peace is much more important. Therefore, I am willing to submit my largesse as the world's wealthiest man. I am going to hand over to the Russian government the equivalent of twenty billion dollars in rubles."

Barbara, who was sitting in a seat ordinarily reserved for Pravda's journalists, gasped. She knew that would translate to roughly 66.6 billion rubles in their currency. Mumbling, gulping and head shaking were occurring among the rest of the seated crowd, and the Communist Party members seemed especially excited and energetic. Eva stalked off and disappeared into the crowd of legislators making their way to the restrooms.

By the wee hours of the early morning, Mabus had hammered out a simple deal and main set of rules concerning his complete takeover of the Russian Federation, its military, the various Ministries of Russian government and the Central Bank of the Federation, which basically held total control over all of Mother Russia's financial enterprises and dealings.

"I understand you are planning to centralize your world power structure, much as we used to do it, Mr. Antichrist. Will this new government be a capitalist one, socialist, or will it be communist?" inquired the curious Estonian Minister of the Russian Economy. Their ministry functioned to coordinate state policies for attracting international investments.

Mabus merely smiled broadly at this, then shook his head. "Sorry, none of those," he said in perfect Russian. "The seat of my government will be in the country now known as Palestine.

"Aside from what's going into rebuilding New York City, and whatever else I may need to procure the attention of the Chinese people. And as I stated before, much of your governmental structure will remain in place, but there will be some sweeping changes.

"First of all, I'm disbanding the Communist Party forever," Mabus firmly stated, causing much gasping and groaning from that group's "fat cat" officials. "I thought I'd let you know now, rather than getting you to sign my charter and then telling you. But some of you can stay on, if you can prove you're worthwhile enough. I'm forming a new political party in Russia, the US and China, to be called the Antichrist's 666 Party.

"That's exactly how many members it's going to have in each country that it governs, and it will have basically the same local structuring worldwide. This will serve as your truly centralized governing organ, and will be answerable only to me. Every nation on Earth will soon use the 666 Party as its sole ruling government, and each sub-nation, such as the territories, will have a similar complementary structure for its government.

"Members of the 666 Party will not be elected. They will be chosen by me from those who deserve to comprise it. The 666 Party will always be split into three main departments, one executive, one legislative and one judicial. And the legislature will be split into two congresses: the Senate, and the People's Congress.

"The latter is the one to which I will be most answerable, and where ordinary people will bring their disputes, struggles and problems before my special committees. The former will be composed of those public officials I deem to be most suitable to continue in their governmental structures…" **Mabus continued, droning on well into the night.**

Barbara simply fell asleep in her chair, to be gently kissed awake by her loving man. And so she was, when the early light of dawn broke through the window.

"Time to hit the jumbo and head for China. It's all taken care of. It didn't take long to get this bureaucracy-ridden bunch moving, amazingly enough. Russia is completely pulling out of the conflict, and they're resuming talks with the Islamic world leaders. Only this time, instead of begging for land concessions and places to stow their weapons programs, they're going to begin talks to end the whole war, and allow the Israeli people back into part of Israstine. We're going to evenly divide that area of the Middle East into equal portions for both the Jews and the Palestinians. I know exactly how to do it."

"Do you know how to wake me up?" mumbled Barbara. "It's nine o'clock in the morning, their time. I think I haven't slept for over twenty-three hours. Wake me up, darling."

Mabus leaned into her face with a broad grin. "After we convince the Red Chinese, we're going to fly back to Vatican City and get married in a little old-fashioned rustic chapel."

"I'm wide awake!" shouted Barbara as she threw herself into Mabus's strong arms. He carried her that way, running swiftly up the ramp into their huge modified Boeing 747 airplane.

"What's the name of this small chapel?" asked Barbara breathlessly, looking at Mabus's perfect face and form with true love beaming from her deep brown eyes. "And who are you getting to marry us? I'm betting it won't be a religious ceremony."

"An old friend of mine called the Pope," **Mabus answered.** "It won't be any Catholic production, and I'm going to have to make some new arrangements about that sort of thing in the future when it comes to marriages. But you'll really enjoy getting hitched in La Cappella Sistina. It's not much, as it's only the same size as King Solomon's…"

"The Sistine Chapel," Barbara heavily breathed, gazing at the glowing Antichrist in stark staring amazement. After all that had happened, he was shocked that she was surprised.

"But first, China. We'll bed down in a Beijing hotel for today. And after I gain total control of the People's Republic, we'll make you into an honest woman. I'm kidding—you already are, Barbara. You'll become First Lady of the Earth, that's all. Rest assured, this is going to be one magnificent and, uh, expensive wedding ceremony."

A short distance away, Thaillo, who always traveled with Mabus and advised him on important issues and matters of international complexity, loudly coughed.

"Don't worry, old man, you're invited," Mabus exultantly reassured Thaillo magnanimously, taking out a ten-carat diamond ring and placing it on Barbara's trembling finger, on top of her engagement ring. Her old, tiny, cheap jewelry was long gone, and her new engagement ring held three two-carat perfect rubies, divine symbols of their love and infinite time together. For a flawless ruby also signified beauty, charity, passion, power and most especially, royalty.

But the wildly triumphant Antichrist was peering closely at Thaillo's face. It was darkened, and obviously his mentor had something distressing to say about their wedding plans.

"I'll give you the bad news when we finally leave for home," Thaillo told Mabus, who was frowning. But Mabus smiled again when he saw the enraptured face of his bride-to-be.

Red China's People's Government took all of three days to convince. Eva was nowhere to be seen; perhaps she had learned her lesson in Russia. Mabus and Barbara decided to linger in Beijing for a whole week, to chase away the blues of what Thaillo was going to announce to them about their marriage. They couldn't stay much longer, as Mabus had to get back to America and begin carefully arranging his plans to install a new worldwide government in the heart of the Middle East.

The loving couple, content for now, anonymously strolled the paved grounds of the Temple of Heaven, a sight that Barbara especially had wanted to see before they left China. They had strolled along the Great Wall and briefly toured the Forbidden City, but both of them had wanted to experience the beauties of this special place.

The Temple of Heaven was larger than the Forbidden City, but smaller than the Summer Palace, with an area of about three million square meters. The Chinese Emperors, or "Sons of Heaven," dared not build a temple bigger than their own large dwellings. The Temple was built in 1420 AD during the Ming Dynasty, to offer special sacrifices to Heaven. It was enclosed with a superlatively menacing wall, engraved with Chinese characters in gilt, and its northern part was higher than the southern. This design showed that Heaven is high and the Earth is low, and it also reflected an ancient Chinese maxim stating that "the Heaven is round, and the Earth is square."

"Fancy that," noted Barbara. "The Chinese believed in a flat Earth, too." The two of them linked arms as they strolled through the circular palace. A few heads seemed to turn in their direction, but Mabus was wearing the black cap and dark glasses the Antis generally affected, hoping he would thus be rendered inconspicuous. It did appear to be working.

"Yeah. They also believed in the principle that light and darkness, man and woman, and good and evil are in an exact balance of directly equal proportions. Actually, when it comes to that, they actually happen to be…"

"You are the *Antichrist*! Chu, this is the Antichrist! Please sire, may we take your picture? You are not a 'gweilo' (overbearing Westerner)! You are our friend and master!" ardently begged a young man, obviously a college student, who was touring the Temple with his friend.

Mabus sighed, and penned his entire official title in Mandarin, as that was the student's mother tongue, on the napkin the eager lad had shakily handed him. But suddenly, Mabus looked up, staring around as if searching for something important.

"We'll treasure this forever!" both the avid young men cried, almost simultaneously.

"I'm afraid not," Mabus grimly stated as the first shock of a giant earthquake hit the building. He grabbed Barbara and raced out of the Temple, carrying her as he sprinted outside, faster than a speeding 'Vette on the freeway. The entire ceiling crashed down solidly behind them.

The roof of the Temple of Heaven had been covered in black, yellow and green-colored glaze which had represented Heaven, the Earth and everything else in the world...

Deeply worried, Mabus and his companions stuck around for another three weeks, helping Chinese officials take care of the crippling damage being caused by the massive earthquakes racking their entire country. Air Force 666 wasn't able to leave China for quite a while, anyway, as the average quake registered magnitude 7.0 on the Richter scale, and there were always multiple severe aftershocks.

And China wasn't alone. The entire planet was suddenly being beset by these ordinarily periodic large-scale natural disasters. It seemed like every land area on Earth was suffering intensively from an alarming number of human casualties, and millions of dollars in property losses. California was especially hard-pressed, as every skyscraper in the city of Los Angeles had tumbled permanently to the ground during a two-day-long 9.0 upheaval. Most of the City of Angels now lay in smoldering, crumbled ruins. The Bay Bridge in San Francisco was now under water forever. And the dozens of tsunamis generated by this great earthquake had flooded Hawaii, the Philippines, and Japan, being but the merest presage of far more perilous events destined to occur in the near future.

Mabus was faced with the second major crisis of his personal career. The Illuminati took advantage of this crisis to mount another attack on Mabus's powers and reputation. Although most of the TV channels were already under the 666 umbrella, and wouldn't broadcast material conflicting with the Antis' political doctrine, Eva could be found on late night cable TV infomercials, blaming Mabus for the natural disasters and the deaths that came with them, and exhorting people to go back to their religions and obey God's word. Many men tuned in the infomercials to get a good look at the beautiful Eva, even while they turned the sound down.

As Emperor of the World, Mabus gave a calming speech on the 666 International TV Network in China. Translated into all the world's many languages, Mabus promised that he would devote all his personal resources to relief, doing what could be humanly done for the globe.

"For the world's sake, I will become a pauper, living solely off the goodwill of my friends and concerned others. I will work to ensure the peace and safety of those under the dark clouds of war, disaster and deprivation, making sure that all are fed, clothed and housed. I will send forth international troops, the Peace Corps, and the Red 666 to all corners of the globe. And what is otherwise not fundable under present means will be paid for in full."

"There goes all our money," Barbara told Mabus on the plane to Italy. They had decided to go ahead and fly to Vatican City, as Thaillo was remaining rather close-mouthed about his problems with the marriage ceremony. The Pope had been contacted, and was quite agreeable when it came to performing the ceremony, even though it would have to be done for no fee whatsoever. For Mabus, who had briefly been the world's richest man, was now officially the Totally Broke Antichrist.

"I've really gotta take care of this money thing. Say, Barbara, do you still want to wear a long white gown? I know it's traditional, but black is more the color of our administration."

"I'd feel like I was at my funeral," Barbara quipped, which made Mabus laugh. They were soon entering Vatican City by cab, and passing by La Cappella Sistina.

Built between 1475 and 1483, in the time of Pope Sixtus IV della Rovere, the Sistine Chapel was rectangular in shape and measured 40.93 meters long by 13.41 meters wide, the exact dimensions of the Temple of Solomon as written in the Old Testament. It was 20.70 meters high, and roofed by a flattened barrel vault, with little side vaults over the centered stained-glass windows.

Its architectural plans were made by Baccio Pontelli, and the construction work was supervised by Giovannino de Dolci. The first Mass in the Sistine Chapel was celebrated on August 9th, 1483. And it wouldn't be long before the last Mass would be held there, too.

The Chapel's magnificently intricate wall paintings were by Pietro Perugino, Sandro Botticelli, Domenico Ghirlandaio, Cosimo Rosselli, Luca Signorelli and their respective workshops, which included Pinturicchio, Piero di Cosimo and Bartolomeo della Gatta.

Michelangelo Buonarroti was commissioned by Pope Julius II della Rovere in 1508 to repaint the curving ceiling, completing the work from 1508 to 1512. He painted the Last Judgment over the altar between 1535 and 1541, having been hired by Pope Paul III Farnese. This monumental fresco covered the entire end wall of the chapel, and neatly obliterated the frescoes with a star-

spangled sky painted by Piero Matteo d'Amelia at the time of
Pope Sixtus IV. But Michelangelo's exquisite fresco was a thousand
times more wonderful, continuously inspiring awe in the Chapel's
many daily visitors.

"It's so… beautiful," Barbara whispered as they performed the
rehearsal walk-through.

"This is where the College of Cardinals used to hold their
conclave when choosing a new Pope," Mabus whispered back.
"When I took over the Church, I ended that practice."

All the heavy Chapel doors had been roped off to tourists for
this very special occasion. The bride wore a simple black dress to
accommodate her Mabus. But as she discussed with the Pope
how the Antichrist was altering the Liturgy of the Hours to make
it into an elegantly spiritual blessing, without mention of God or
Jesus, Thaillo drew Mabus aside.

"What is it?" Mabus angrily growled.

<Use your thoughts,> Thaillo commanded with his mind.

<So where's the problem? You want my girl yourself, you
jealous or something?> Mabus thought.

<I'm afraid there's no way you can ever be married.>

<And why is that, Thaillo?>

<The High Commission of the Anti Militia has decreed that
only you and twelve Antis are to leave the Earth on *Noah*, so
your marriage has been rendered pointless. Also, it interferes with
the needed Biblical injunction concerning the Antichrist's lack of
regard for women.>

<Yes, but that's plural! I don't want a bunch of naked ladies
swooning over me. Barbara is the only woman I…regard. We're
deeply in love, and I don't desire any other such company!>

<I'm sorry.>

Mabus reflected on this for a moment. <I know what I'm
going to do,> he thought.

<What?> thought Thaillo. Mabus knew that Thaillo could
always tell whatever he was thinking. To himself, he was slowly
learning how to guard his innermost thoughts from Thaillo just
as his mentor often did from him.

<I'm Emperor of the World. I'll disband the High Commis-
sion!>

<Even if you do so, Barbara is merely human, and cannot travel
with us back into the past. I am very sorry, my Divine Master, but
that is simply the way it is.>

<But if she stays here on Earth, she'll die…>
<Yes. That's precisely what's going to happen.>

Chapter Twenty

"NOTHING," MABUS ANSWERED.

"Don't tell me nothing's wrong. I know when something's bugging you," Barbara said. "What's wrong? Tell me."

They lay on their palatial bed in their private White House chambers. Barbara tried to distract herself by thinking of who else had slept where they now lay—presidents, wives, mistresses, children, pets. But her fear nagged her, and she had to ask.

"Darling, am I going to die?" she blurted out.

"Barb, that is the one question I don't know, and don't think I wanna know. My old friend Boone taught me something that's stuck with me. You see, his wife was diagnosed with cancer shortly after their son was born. The doctor said she had two choices: she could try chemotherapy and meds to prolong her life for two years, or she could take no treatments and have six months to live. She didn't want to burden Boone, nor could she bear the pain of him and her son watching her decline slowly. Boone wouldn't have it. He demanded that they employ whatever means were available to save her life. He pleaded with her to do the chemotherapy and she agreed to it, saying she just wanted Boone to be happy.

"This was a decision Boone greatly regretted. He wished he'd done as she asked—she might have died happy and with dignity. The treatments quickly began to take their toll on her. Boone watched as she declined daily, constantly incoherent from the medication and painkillers. Boone said that the drugs didn't allow her to live longer; they only allowed her to die longer.

"So, if you're asking me to open that Pandora's box, I'm not
gonna do it. But sweetie, I can assure you this: for as long as I'm
alive you'll be safe, I promise! My immortal heart beats for you
and you only. When you're close to me, my blood stands at
attention. It is sustained by your presence. As long as this blood
pumps through this body, I am your slave."

Barbara rolled into Mabus's arms and began kissing him. As
their passion grew greater, their kisses became ever more intimate,
when suddenly Barbara stopped and pushed Mabus down onto
the bed. She straddled him and slowly began opening her silk top.
Her nipples were hardened by the coolness of the silk as it glided
off her skin, as if the silk were hovering above her radiance. She
leaned in to kiss his lips, dry from his jaw having dropped at the
sight of her increasingly ardent affections. He was definitely getting
lucky, and she knew he knew it by that grin. With the wedding at
hand, there was no reason to wait any longer.

She slowly worked her way down his chest, kissing him with
her wettest kisses. He grabbed her head and pulled it close. They
slipped into a frenzy of erotic passion, their bodies growing damp
with sweat. The moisture glistened off his muscles, arousing her
more, intensifying the passion of the Antichrist and his Harlot.
They clung together like wet latex, flesh sliding against flesh in a
rhythmic motion. Soon their bodies welded together into a solid
mass of muscle and sweat, flowing gracefully.

As he thrust into her flesh she absorbed him and devoured all
she could within herself, begging for the next thrust of the intense
hardness of his body. The nanobots had made him bigger, harder,
and more responsive than any man in history. Barbara slid her
body across his in a self-fueling perpetual motion. The wetness
created a thin film between them that tantalized their senses.
She cried out "Oh, You! Oh, You!" And with each thrust, Mabus
could feel her body release a restrictive tension and transform it
into a liberating relaxation. Each time she would absorb all of his
blows with all of her body at once.

As Mabus's fingers combed through her hair, supporting the
back of her neck with a firm grip, her body became limp with
submission. Her head fell back, allowing Mabus to penetrate her
to her very soul. Once inside, he danced around tickling her inner
being. She was so aroused that she could only breathe sporadically.
Her lungs heaved, as she still found it hard to gasp air. An explosion

of emotions overcame them: happiness, sadness, joy, fear, triumph, pain, suffering, and embarrassment, all at once. Their hearts were tapping on each other, merely separated by their flesh.

When Mabus peeled his chest from hers, and her firm breasts softly came to rest, a peppermint coolness attacked the fronts of their bodies. It was like millions of tiny pins, poking at their skin. Oxygen quickly filled their sweat-filled pores. A bead of sweat gathered and flowed down Mabus's chest, and as he exhaled, the bead fell in a endless drop that splashed at the crest of her nipple. The droplet triggered a trembling between her thighs that Mabus could feel. Relieved by her satisfaction, he retreated to his side of the bed. Barbara lay flat on her back trying to catch her breath, when suddenly she cried out "Wow!" "Wow," she repeated. "Now that was worth waiting for."

"Well, I can't take all the credit. I did have a little help from my friends, the nanobots."

"No way, lover. When I'm with you, I feel so secure, so in love. I'm sure even if you didn't have nanobots, it would've been just the same. Besides, it was our love that fueled the passion, not the nanobots. If I died right at this moment, it would be my happiest one. But I do feel safe when I'm with you, Mabus. You make me feel womanly. You're strong, and smart, and godlike. Which reminds me, this doesn't make me the 'Whore that rode the Beast,' does it? Mabus?"

Mabus could not reply, for he was fast asleep.

Barbara cuddled close into Mabus and covered them both with the blankets that had worked their way down to the foot of the bed. "My heart belongs to you eternally," she whispered in his ear.

THE NEXT MORNING Mabus awoke to Barbara's voice.

"Wake up, honey. Did the comet ever hit Jupiter?" Barbara asked Mabus.

"Yes," Mabus said, "It happened thirteen minutes ago. Believe it or not, it's finally June 6th. Wanna catch it on the news?"

They went to the living room of their suite and turned on the channel of utmost chaos, Worldwide ACC News on Infinite Cable 666AC. "Good morning, this is Casey Rupart reporting live, for ACC News. We're here today witnessing the explosion on Jupiter. Just minutes ago, the planet suffered an asteroid collision. As you can see, the brightness from the ignition of the planet's gases has outshone the sun, turning the sun a blackish, grey color. We're unsure how long this planet's overpowering brightness will last, but scientists estimate up to a week. Back to you, Cathy."

"Thanks, Casey." An Asian woman wearing a loud pink blazer had taken the screen. "Scientists say that when the fire burns down all that will remain is a thin cloud around the surface of the planet. This cloud of dust and debris will begin forming the basis for the multitude of rings now surrounding the body we currently acknowledge as the planet Saturn." The announcer read: "Primitive at first, it will gradually coalesce into Saturn's 250,000-kilometer-wide six layers of spectacularly bright and famous rings over many millions of years. And Jupiter, which has a mostly amorphous surface, will then be much smaller and will slowly reform itself through its own very strong magnetic field and intense gravity into the smaller body of Saturn."

"Breaking news, just in. There seem to be mobs of people taking to the streets destroying everything in sight. The people of the cities, worldwide, are looting and rioting. Most seem to be attacking the govern…"

The sound of fists pounding at the door. "Unlock the door before we knock it down, Lord Antichrist!" he heard one of their bodyguards bark. Mabus leaped off the couch and toward the door in a smooth, catlike motion, as Barbara scrambled for her robe. She covered herself just in time, as Mabus unlocked the door. Five men dressed in full AC 666 black riot gear stormed in. "Sorry for the intrusion, but we gotta get you outta here! The people are rioting and they've attacked the White House," said the same one who had barked from the door.

"Don't you hurt any of them!" Mabus yelled.

"Of course not, Antichrist! We have helicopters on the roof. We're evacuating you and your staff. We can't control the crowds without killing them!"

Mabus looked at Barbara. Her robe barely covered her breasts, and her messy hair fell in her face, but the militia's men didn't seem to notice. A guard now stood at either side of her and grabbed her by the arms. Her feet searched for the floor as if she were riding a bicycle. Mabus saw her dark hair flick the doorway as the men practically carried her toward the stairwell. One man stood posted at the door while the other two grabbed at Mabus. He scanned the rumpled bed for his underwear, then grabbed the sheet and wrapped it around his waist as the men scooted him out after Barbara.

Barely a minute later, Mabus looked out the helicopter window. The White House plummeted away, growing smaller and smaller as the craft ascended. Mabus now understood why they'd been evacuated so quickly; thousands of people flooded the lawn of the building like ants as they broke in the windows and climbed the gates. It looked like a human tsunami. They'd made it out just in time. Mabus turned to Barbara, looking stunned as she sat strapped into the seat next to him. "Where are we going?" Mabus yelled over the sound of the engine. "Nevada!" the pilot yelled.

Chapter Twenty-One

ABUS AND BARBARA HAD SETTLED into their temporary underground quarters in Nevada. They would be safe there, at least for the time being. In the two days that had passed since the White House had been stormed, the citizens had completely destroyed it, gutted it, and set it ablaze. Once the home of Presidents, it was now a charred shell.

The people had been even more efficient at destroying the NASA headquarters—they had bombed it and destroyed it completely. The site lay in ruins.

Soldiers and police, completely disillusioned with the rules they had worked to enforce, had turned from their oaths to "serve and protect" and had joined in the rioting. Worldwide, people pillaged whatever government buildings they could find, and burned pictures of their political leaders.

And after Mabus had pledged all his money, he was shocked to see videotape on the news of citizens burning big piles of it in the streets. With currency swiftly losing its foothold, people were turning to looting and hoarding food to stay alive. No one was working anymore, so food deliveries and gasoline deliveries and access to everyday supplies ceased. There were more and more reports of elderly people being found dead, starved in their homes, isolated, with no access to food. All government programs had gone belly-up. Pretty soon people would be killing each other to stay alive.

Eva's propaganda broadcasts had by now gotten plenty of converts. While the Illuminati encouraged mass destruction, murder, and mayhem, her infomercials blamed all of this on the Antichrist. She blamed him for hyperinflation and the shortage of food and supplies. Although Mabus's world government tried to stamp out these broadcasts, they were as difficult to eliminate as the Spice Channel; the resources of the Illuminati ran deep. Evil always finds a place to hide on cable television.

Meanwhile, soot appeared and turned into visible striped rings around the planet—multicolored and pencil-thin. The scientists engaged in the study of air quality and climate change had discovered Asian pollutants hanging over New England and the Atlantic, one of the early surprises of research aimed at clarifying how smokestack and auto emissions traveled and changed in the atmosphere. Many more people died.

"This discovery was the first observation of Asian pollution plumes over the East Coast of North America, and it suggested that improvements in American air quality could be threatened by Asian countries. And thus, dear Barbara," finished Mabus, "I have discovered how I 'threaten' Asia. They are actually threatening us, and it is the other way around. That's pretty much par for the course with me."

Chapter Twenty-Two

"And he doeth great wonders, so that he maketh fire come down from heaven on the earth in the sight of all men. And deceiveth them that dwell on the earth by the means of those miracles which he had power to do in the sight of the beast; saying to them that dwell on the earth, that they should make an image to the beast, which had the wound by a sword, and did live."
—Rev. 13:14

"IF YOU'VE NOTICED THAT ANOTHER red dragon has already appeared in your skies, bravo. It has indeed, and it is the Pleiades," Mabus said in his now-daily worldwide speech.

"It's now the winter of 2006, and you're are still hanging in there, and although you all have your differing individual opinions regarding what we're all going through, you are at least alike in having them. Indeed, for now and further into the future. But I have much yet to teach you; so far, we have discussed only asteroids and comets, and forsaken meteors completely.

"Please bear with me, Dear Ones, while we get to the *classic* part of this. Meteors are nothing but free-flying stones, everywhere, small and compact, jetting here and there. They are small points of light in a supremely infinite space from another dimension and manifesting in another universe, they're sometimes called 'shooting stars.'

"The human brain, meanwhile, is but a mere tool, split in three, and to it, whatever is out there is unquestionably open to debate. We are small and insignificant creatures, but no one thing alone created the entire 'universe,' and even small things have the chance to burn brightly. And meteors can sometimes be the brightest objects in the night sky. For being dwarfed by the scale of the universe does not mean that we are pathetic, futile, or immutably doomed to die. The diminutive meteors are the smallest bodies in the solar system that can be observed by the naked eye.

"Wandering through space, debris from the explosion of Jupiter is finally making it to its destination, Earth. Meteoroids enter the Earth's atmosphere, are heated by friction, and for a few seconds streak across the sky as a pinpoint of eternal life with a glowing trail, steady and strong. These are the lights you are seeing now in the skies. Remain calm; although they look terrifying, most of them are harmless, even though, as you all can see, some have been penetrating and creating mass destruction. Although we did what we could in preparing for this disaster, the looting and rioting wasn't anticipated. The only thing we can do now is to remain calm and to address the areas that are being devastated by these meteors, as best we can.

"People are dying in the masses. We need volunteers to help in the relief efforts. The Antis and I are doing all that we can, but we can't do it all. We need cooperation from the people. The riots and looting are making it tougher for our rescue teams to get into the disaster areas. We must all pull together to survive these tragedies. We are low on supplies and can't hold out much longer. Especially with the beginning of winter, the harsh weather conditions are not helping. We'll all be dead before 2012. Is that what everyone wants? Do we want to burn out like a candle flame in the wind, or do we want to protect a legacy of humankind in which we can all take pride? Wake up, people! Can't you see what we are doing to each other?

"We are all equally scared of the situation, but we need to stop the violence or we may wipe ourselves out before we can be saved. The most devastating chunks of debris have already impacted Earth, yet behind the shower of immense pieces, a mist of smaller ones are heading straight for us. People of Earth, you need to find cover. Although the atmosphere will burn up most of them, many golf-ball-size meteors will shower Earth for a week or so. This is the fire from the sky I warned everyone about in my 'Talkumentary.'"

Mabus pleaded with the people to help in the efforts, and a few people did, but many sour apples had spoiled the pie. Many who volunteered had died trying to rescue others. The speech had helped somewhat, but people were still dropping like flies. Mabus felt that drastic situations called for drastic measures.

Chapter Twenty-Three

"And he causeth all, both small and great, rich and poor, free and bond, to receive a mark in their right hand, or in their foreheads: and that no man might buy or sell, save he that had the mark, or the name of the beast or the number of his name."
—Rev. 13:16-17

MABUS AND BARBARA WOKE TO the droning of a voice from ACCTV:

"The Antichrist has ordered the abolition of all monetary systems in the world, and is setting up his own system, involving a nanochip mark that will be placed on people's right hand, if they so choose. Everyone who doesn't go along with this is destined to die of starvation and deprivation, although the Antichrist doesn't want them to. This new system is necessary for our survival. The Antichrist will be addressing the world tomorrow explaining his purpose for this system. Please tune in tomorrow, at five o'clock."

"When are you going to the hospital?" Mabus asked Barbara.

"Soon," Barbara said. "We're getting another shipment of food and medical supplies from the Antis, and we'll need to distribute all that."

"You're a natural, Barb," Mabus said, "I knew I could count on you to head up the relief efforts there."

"Well, thanks to you for putting me in charge. The outpouring of help and supplies is amazing, but it's a hell of a lot of work to organize it all."

"Well, it'll keep you out of trouble, then. You just keep telling the Antis what to do, and they'll do it. Remember, they know who your lover man is," **Mabus said, drawing Barbara close.**

MABUS WORRIED ABOUT the people of the world. Though help was pouring into many locations, like the hospitals, Mabus couldn't deny the gnawing feeling in his gut that all the relief efforts wouldn't matter if the world's last days were punctuated with chaos and looting.

In his worldwide broadcast the next day, Mabus explained his plan. "I know you all have worries. Things are changing; the world is changing before your eyes. Things are not what they used to be, and nothing feels secure. I hear your thoughts: 'How will I get food? What will my children eat? What is going to happen?' Well, I have a plan that will give everyone—and I do mean *everyone*—an equal opportunity to have whatever they need. Worry no more!

"No one wants to die, but that fate is, we know, inevitable, due to the asteroid headed toward Earth. As you know, I am pre-destined to survive this tragedy, with my mission to Venus. If I could trade me for all of you, I would. But I can only choose twelve people to travel back with me. This is an opportunity for life, but it does not come cheap. Each of you will be provided with a nanochip implant, on the back of your right hand.

"Each nanochip will have a unique identification number to identify you, its owner. Don't worry about money; you will no longer need any of it. If you need milk or bread, all you need to do is go to the store and get what you need, as you always have. Only you won't have to pay for anything; the cashier won't accept payment from you, but will instead scan your nanochip and record your number. We can prevent abuse of the system this way. You can gain points by doing everyday normal productive things like working. You will be placed in a job that best suits your skills and physical ability.

"Everyone must work a minimum of six hours a day, six days a week to prevent themselves from losing their right to have a nanochip implant. Thursday will be a day of rest; no one will work. Thursday will be a weekly holiday in which we, the people of Earth, will worship the people of Earth. We will pay tribute to all the accomplishments we achieve in our minds and our individual dreams. People can earn more points by working more hours, except on Thursday.

"Every time you help someone with a good deed, you will gain points. If someone is hungry, and you feed them, you will gain points. The twelve people with the most points by August 1st win!

"The twelve who will be chosen will be twelve very special people, because of their unselfish good nature. All of you must go on with your daily routines. There will be no chaos, no rioting, no looting, no hurting or killing one another. Anyone who misbehaves will have their nanochip revoked, and they will lose their currency privileges and be excluded from the lottery.

"On the bottom of your screen right now, you should see the name of the nearest location where you can get your nanochip, and an Internet address and toll-free number if you need more information. No one will be turned away, and we won't stop implanting the nanochips until everyone has gotten one; we won't run out. These nanochips can be installed very quickly; we expect to implant everyone within forty-eight hours.

"Treat others the way you would have them treat you! This is the key to your success!"

Mabus wrapped up his address with some comforting sentiments. He'd said a lot, and the people would have a lot to digest. <That's enough for one day,> he thought. <Keep it short and sweet.> As he said his daily goodbyes to the camera, he noticed out of the corner of his eye that the television studio secretary, who usually kept herself sequestered in the front office, had crept in and whispered something to Charlie, the stage manager. He went pale as he gave Mabus his usual "5-4-3-2-1" finger countdown to signoff. The red light on the camera went dark, and Mabus took off his clip-on microphone and sensed something was wrong—very wrong. By this time, everyone in the studio was quiet and was staring at Mabus.

Charlie swallowed and crept up to where Mabus stood at his podium. "There's been a disaster, my Antichrist," he said softly.

It took a full hour for Mabus, led by guards in full riot gear, to weave his way through the maze of rubble that had once been the Immaculate Conception 666 Hospital. There had been a bombing, and Mabus had already begun formulating who was responsible. <Heh, there go the first ones to be knocked off the

lottery list,> he thought bitterly. He would use them as examples, that was for sure. Dust and debris lay everywhere, and the stench of death permeated the air.

They found Barbara's body in a storeroom under a pile of rubble, amidst boxes of sterile saline solution and syringes. "All those medical supplies, and none of them helped Barb." Mabus winced at the irony.

The guards, with unusual care and deliberateness, freed Barbara from the debris, brushed the dust from her face and hair, and stood back respectfully as Mabus knelt and cradled her head tenderly. He did not weep, though, for somehow her death did not surprise him; as much as he had tried to block it from his mind, he knew it would happen, just as Thaillo had predicted. In spite of all of his miraculous abilities, in spite of the presence of doctors and nurses and orderlies, in spite of everything, she must have *desired* to die, or it wouldn't have happened.

<You knew this was gonna happen, didn't you?> Mabus thought to Thaillo.

<I promised you, old friend. I promised you that I wouldn't tell you. You made me tell once before, and Barb died a miserable death. But worst of all, she died sad and lonely. The other time I told you of her death, you refused to marry her, knowing she was gonna die. Believe me, this was the best way for it to end. She was very happy.>

<Please, leave me with my thoughts. I'm very confused. Why couldn't you help me save her?>

<Trust me, Mabus, we have done this thousands of times before. We saved her from the bombing before, by holding the lottery a week sooner, and she suffered a painful, heart-wrenching death because she wasn't allowed to go to Venus with you. You had to abandon her due to the complications.>

<What complications?>

<Well, we tried over and over again to get her to Venus, but in each and every scenario she died a horrible death. We've come to the conclusion that the aliens are involved in some way. For some reason she is not allowed to go back with you. I'm sorry, buddy. If there is anything I can do, please let me know. I'll make all the arrangements just as you'd like them. I'll take care of everything.

You just need some time to work it out. You always do. Trust me, old friend, this is the happiest way she can die in this existence. You chose to have it this way, for her sake.>

Mabus couldn't sleep at all that night. He was trying to think of any possible scenario that might have been better for Barbara. He had none. He lay awake, with a hot, sweaty, yet chilly feeling, almost feverish. The different scenarios were eating at Mabus. Morning crept up on him like a kitten. Yet, still, he had not slept a wink. Thousands of scenarios played and toyed with his emotions, which almost seemed as they were leaking into his memory from the other timeline. All had come to this. This was the destiny in which Barbara was truly happy when she passed away. Mabus realized that he was finally at peace with her death.

He heard a knock at his thick metal door, "Go away!" he shouted.

The producer of ACCTV spoke muffled through the door, "It's time for your morning news update, Lord. You have been very consistent in making a daily announcement. We don't want to let the people down."

The door flew open and Mabus headed out for his daily duty. After he was done with his announcement, he met with Thaillo.

<Thank you, Thaillo. You were right,> Mabus thought.

<Don't you even think twice about it. I'll set up funeral arrangements for the church you were going to get married in. Sistine Chapel, where you were going to get married. The Pope said he would do the honors. Please, Mabus, understand, if there was anything I could've done to change wha...>

<You know what, Thaillo? You don't have to explain. I understand there was nothing that we could do. I do want to thank you, though, for not saying anything, and for keeping your word with me. And once again, I'll ask you please, next time, no matter what I say, it is important that you keep this a secret from me. Because you are right. If I had known, things would have been different.>

<So, are there any other secrets you are hiding from me?> Mabus smiled.

Thaillo frowned, <Actually, now that you've asked, there is something I've wanted to tell you, but I haven't really found the right time. 'Fred Thaillo' is not really my name. My real name has no importance at this point. By your decision my name would be Fred Thaillo for eternity, as a constant reminder of how important

the loyalty in our relationship really is. Please, old friend, once again, forgive me for my mistake.>

<About the 222nd time through the time bubble, I mistook someone else for you. Oh, the effects on the timeline were almost fatal. I recruited the wrong person to the position of the Antichrist. I don't know what went wrong, or how I could've mistaken him for you. Maybe it was his persuasive charm, or his overwhelming ambition, but it was a mistake I would regret for eternity. It almost wiped out everything. The man's name was Adolf Hitler. Fred Thaillo is an anagram, a scrambled combination of the same letters as in the name Adolf Hitler.>

<I hadn't given him the nanobots yet, but I did let the cat out of the bag. I told him too much information. Once the persecution of the Jewish people started, I knew this was not the peace-loving Mabus I knew. Hitler became obsessed with becoming the Antichrist, so much so that he tried to fulfill the prophecies by himself. Not only that, but he was literally trying to destroy you, in order to protect his spot as Antichrist. Rumors had it that the Antichrist might be Jewish, because Jesus had been Jewish. Knowing this, Hitler tried to erase your bloodline, by eliminating as many Jews as he could by the millions.>

<This was all my fault. You thought twice about selecting me again as the vessel for your nanobots but you gave me a second chance, renaming me Fred Thaillo as a constant reminder of what my incompetence has created.>

<We sure had those aliens scrambling. I had created a heck of a mess for them to clean up, to get the timeline back on track, especially for you to make your flight to Venus, and it was sure a close one. Sometimes, especially times like these, I'm glad the aliens are there, but sometimes I feel like a puppet. Truly, they are in control of our destinies.>

Chapter Twenty-Four

HE LOTTERY SEEMED TO BE working. People all over the globe were helping others left and right. The sight was almost strangely uncomfortable. Was the only reason they were so persuasively beneficent to help themselves in the long run? You bet your ass. But it worked. Here, suddenly, was the utopia that humanity had always aspired to. Had the Antichrist created a working system of world peace?

Remarkably, there was no crime whatsoever. People were helping others. Lines of people who wanted to volunteer at the hospitals formed. Suddenly, there was an abundance of food and supplies, in spite of the many natural disasters still happening. There was a 100 percent employment rate. Many would work double shifts every day they could, just to rack up more points. Eva's broadcasts began to fall on deaf ears.

Although the world's economic problems had been fixed, there was nothing the Antichrist could do about the Earth's climatic changes and eruptions. The people were more productive then ever in dealing with these traumas, because everyone was so eager to gain points. People flocked to help others. Militias started forming, strictly looking for disasters as an opportunity to gain more points.

Some people were still skeptical about the trip to Venus. The comet was soon to hit Venus, but until then, the conditions on Venus still couldn't support life. Some believed it was a suicide mission.

One morning during his daily announcement, Mabus addressed the issue of his theory still only being a theory. The fact that Jupiter had been hit and had formed the same rings as Saturn wasn't enough. He didn't take long to answer their cries for proof. He reminded them that the Egyptians built pyramids so that we could see them on Mars. "We, too, can build a pyramid, and test the theory once and for all. Building a pyramid is the only way that mankind itself can know for certain. This will have to be the grandest pyramid this world has ever seen. The location is very crucial also. I'm assured by the AC666 Department of Labor that we have plenty of supplies and manpower to facilitate such a project. But this is something that is directly up to the people of Earth. I don't find it equitable for me as a ruler to make you work at such a project at my decree."

Just as the Egyptians had not been enslaved in order to build the pyramids in Egypt, these people were to build their temple with a purpose. The Egyptians took a deep spiritual pride in their work and it showed. From accurately laying each stone with flawless precision, to the artwork still extant today, this meticulousness proved that the builders of the pyramids were not slaves.

The people loved the idea of a new pyramid, doubly wanted to know the truth, and agreed that this was the only way. So the decision was made and the project was a "go."

"I have eyes, and I can see," became the mantra of what was left of the entire Jewish population of the planet Earth. All the Jews began to break down and admit that theirs was an imitation religion, taken from the Egyptians, signifying hard work. But now slavery was meaningless forever, and they all signed onto "The Antichrist's 666 Pyramid Project" with a single voice; they looked upon their neighbors, and they finally found themselves. They were suddenly without an identity, and the Antichrist hatched a simple plot.

"It's time," he said, communicating with them in Hebrew. "Life is for suffering, and your people have that as a basic tenet in your 'religious preference,' as it were. Come, and do some hard work for me as we begin the razing of your old and fruitless temple and the reconstruction of your... *new* one."

Mabus considered telling the Jews what Lucifer actually was—that he represented the dark side of Transhumanism. Lucifer was the embodiment of reason, of intelligence, of critical thought. He stood against the dogma of God and all other dogmas. He stood for the exploration of new ideas and new perspectives in the pursuit of truth. He was an archetypal iconoclast, rebel and adversary.

He even had a truly wicked sense of humor. Satan was the adversary of all mankind, as contrived by God. He was the angel charged by God with the task of proving that mankind is an unworthy creation.

According to the Romans, Lucifer was none other than the Morning Star, the star of both morn and evening, or—in other words—the planet Venus. Lucifer was simply the name the Roman Empire managed to concoct about that planet, which was nothing more than a primitive version of ours, caught in the cosmic timeline, and ready to be inhabited. And if you think about it, it sounds like a female name.

And it figured. Where, after all, would you go back for safety and comfort, but to a female? Namely, your Mom, right? Man is fragile, now and forevermore will always desire love.

Chapter Twenty-Five

ABUS STUDIED AN AERIAL PHOTO of the Temple Mount in Jerusalem showing the Proposed Northern, Central and Southern Sites for the First and Second Temples.

"As the navel is set in the center of the human body, the land of Israel is once again to be the epitome of the Earth, situated in the center of the world, and Jerusalem is in the center of the land of Israel, and the sanctuary is in the center of Jerusalem, and the holy place in the center of the sanctuary, and the ark in the center of the holy place, and the foundation stone before the holy place, because from it the world was founded. Yes, my dear Jewish people," Mabus announced on ACCTV. "That is from the Midrash Tanchuma, *Qedoshim*," he added.

"This is where the pyramid is destined to be based, in biblical prophecies, and most importantly it's the best place, because of the geological location of our view on Mars." ACCTV gave the world daily updates of the building of the pyramid and its effect on Mars, though as they were building the structure, nothing showed up until the project was completed. They had to build the temple fairly quickly, and Mabus was able to help them completely by using his special Ouroborean powers of telekinesis and mental telepathy.

The workers of the projects were unusually high-spirited, and they worked a lot of overtime to get it done in time. The workers showed the same enthusiasm and preciseness as the ancient Egyptians. They took a deep pride in the work they performed. And like the Egyptians, they were split up into work crews. These crews were like teams, so that they could compete with one another for several reasons: the productivity was maximized this way; people also had a way to earn more points; but most importantly, the workers could have the enjoyment of playing a game, rather than the pain of grueling labor.

During the building of the pyramid, a strange entity appeared in the sky. It appeared to be a gigantic fiery ball with a long tail following behind it. The people feared it was the asteroid that was destined to destroy them, and this created much confusion across the world. An emergency update came over the television screens of the world.

Mabus appeared, "People of Earth, it has come to my attention that there is a comet in the sky. Please remain calm. This comet, although it will be coming considerably close to Earth, will not collide with it. This comet is on a direct path to the planet Venus. This event is a blessing in disguise. The result of this comet hitting Venus will allow Venus to have water, which will ultimately form the atmosphere needed to sustain life on the planet. Ladies and gentlemen, today we will witness the birth of life as we know it. Today, Venus will mature into our precious giver of life."

People were awed at the magnificent light show that occurred when the comet struck Venus. The sky turned a glowing red and everyone stood in amazement. People's hearts were jumping, knowing they would soon be facing the same fate. Even though they were witnessing the most important event of their existence, it was hard to find joy in it, knowing they were doomed to extinction themselves. Ironically, the comet brought happiness to Venus, but for Earth it brought a mixture of joy and grief.

Mabus was now living a charmed existence. So everything was almost perfect when they finished building his elaborate shrine. It took from mid-2007 to August of 2010 to complete the Temple.

Oh, the Temple would be built, and soon they would see if it appeared on Mars. All that would take was a telescope. But it was worthless without Barbara. He would have killed himself, but there was too much that he had to do.

For he had discovered that to the left of the "Lion's Face," which must have been the Sphinx, there lay an area with lots of pyramid-like structures, called the "city." From the smoothness of the terrain around what was once "the Sphinx," you could conclude that it had once been on the bottom of a sea or a large lake. The approximate coastline could be easily discerned, and the "islands" also included clues to the former sea level.

Finally, Mabus and his many fans stood and observed the event via the Illuminati-created Mauna Kea telescope. The 4,200 meter high summit of Mauna Kea in Hawaii housed the world's largest observatory for optical, infrared, and submillimeter astronomy. Mabus used everything there, but that damnable pyramid had indeed appeared on Mars, and had never been there before at all.

The people finally had their Temple in Jerusalem, and now they could figure out what they wanted to believe once and for all. The whole world was proud of the accomplishment, and felt great unity for once. They didn't have to rely on anyone to shape their ideas for them. They could see for themselves that the Antichrist's Single Orientation Theory of the Planets was undeniably true, and make their own judgments accordingly. How liberating it was for them to make a decision that wasn't based on the influence of others!

Chapter Twenty-Six

"And all that dwell upon the earth shall worship him, whose names are not in the book of life of the lamb slain from the foundation of the world."

–Rev. 13:8

LL AROUND THE WORLD THE twelve chosen winners were being collected, for the winners had been chosen and placed in the book whose cover read "Book of Life."

It was a week before the launch date, and the people of Earth were beginning to tense up. People were anxious to find out the results of the lottery. At the same time many were trying to stay optimistic, trying to cope with their impending demise. People were treating each other as if it were their last day alive. In a sense, this helped to set the tempo for what the world needed. It seemed to be a calm, nostalgic groove the world lay in, and seemed to have a therapeutic effect on the prevailing air of sadness. Many felt they had been cheated of their existence. "If only I had been born a hundred years sooner, I might have lived out my full life."

"Mister, could you hold this?"

"Sure, lady, I'm sorry. I was dozing off," said Thomas as he held the bandages tight to his leg. He had just injured himself saving a child from a falling piece of debris from a skyscraper. Thanks to his leap to shove her out of the way, it missed the girl. But he wasn't as fortunate. The heroic act earned him a lot of points, but also a broken leg.

"A hundred years ago! You wouldn't have been here to save this girl's life," said the elderly lady, trying to help Thomas with his injury.

Just then a vehicle pulled up and two Antis got out. "Is your name Thomas Jeffery Cowan?" asked a guard of the Antis. "You need to come with us."

"I'm not going anywhere! I just broke my leg!"

"I will assist you. And we'll get you to the proper medical attention. It is imperative that you come with us now." The Anti guards grabbed him and loaded him up into a shiny black bulletproof Hummer, with the "666" logo gleaming on its side. The rear window mirrored the confused face of the helpful bystander who had bandaged Thomas's leg, as the truck drove away.

THE CRYPT UNDER the US Mint was humming with Illuminati activity. All over the country, work crews led by Illuminati agents were digging colossal bunkers deep underground, fitted out like the bomb shelters of the 1950s. Meanwhile, here, the finest minds were puzzling out the future of their cabal. "Now that there is no currency, our efforts to manipulate currency are fruitless. We are wealthy, yet penniless. We all live on the sufferance of the Antichrist," one hooded figure said, looking at the nanochip on the back of his hand. "Indeed. Our attempts at governmental control have become ridiculous, now that there is one world government," said another figure. "These last million years have certainly been a waste of time. I'm going to take up model rocketry while there's still time left." "Fools!" burst in Eva. "There is much that we can do. This is no time for a failure of nerve. I'll show you who wears the black, cowled robes in this conspiracy!" "What is your bright idea, Eva?" said the leader. "Your television appearances have gotten lousy ratings. You're getting killed by late-night reruns of 'Star Trek.' You've gotten lucky by capitalizing on the disasters, but, truth to tell, you're a lightweight."

Eva took umbrage at this remark. She stopped herself from taking out her alien gun and vaporizing the lot of them. She said, icily, "What if I told you I had a plan?" and the ears of the Illuminati pricked up under their hoods. By the end, everyone was smiling in agreement; soon, the aliens were going to have a little surprise on their hands… and Mabus would, too.

MEANWHILE, ON THE other side of the country, in Texas, a man collapsed from heat exhaustion, and his partner scurried to help him. "Y'all all right?" asked his friend, as he grabbed him, pulled him up, and began wiping the sweat from his unconscious face. "He needs water. Someone get me some water. This man needs water. Are you OK? Can you hear me? Jacob, are you with me, buddy?" Someone from the crowd handed the man a half-filled bottle of water. "Here, drink up, man. I told you, man, it's not normal for a man to work twenty hours a day six days a week like that. Now you're gonna have to take a break. I told you this was gonna happen! Who cares about some stupid plane to Venus, we ain't gonna git to go, no how! You know how those guys are. They don't even care 'bout us workin' folk. You gotta stop, man, you're killin' yourself. Can you hear me, old buddy?"

Suddenly, the people who had gathered to see the ordeal looked up, and noticed in the horizon, beyond the hazy heat waves, a cloud of smoke bellowing closer toward the crowd. It was a vehicle, kicking up dust from the dry dirt terrain of the desert. A glossy black bulletproof Hummer with the sign of the beast drove up, almost unaffected by the dust. The door opened and two Anti guards got out. "Is this man Jacob Lanphier?"

"Yes, what's the problem?" his friend replied.

"We will be taking him with us."

"What for? He's wore out. He needs to get some rest!"

"Sir, he needs medical attention. He's suffering from heat exhaustion; if he doesn't get help soon he may die."

"What are you stand'n there fer? Help me with his legs and we'll load him up!" The three men loaded up the lifeless body into the truck. And just as the Antis had showed up in a cloud of dust, they departed just the same. His buddy couldn't help to wonder what they wanted with him. Then it came to him. "Holy crap. You've won, Jacob! You've won."

SOMEWHERE IN THE Great Northwest, a counselor comforted her patient. Her office wasn't as conventional as it used to be. Because of the chaos, looters had stolen the brown leather couch and computer that used to be there. But the soft velvet green couch was better than the old leather cliché anyway. People would instantly associate the leather couch with insanity. The green couch gave them a sense of ease and comfort, kind of a homey sense. The pictures on the wall were abstract and would often break the ice in the conversations she would have with her patients.

"Marie! Helllooo, Marie? Hey, you spaced off there. Are you all right?"

"Yes. I'm sorry, you were saying?"

"Oh yah, I just can't get over the fact that this Antichrist guy gets to pick who goes, and why is he so special? I'm frustrated! I just feel like... like, screw it. The end's almost here. I'm ready to end it now. It's killing me inside. It's driving me crazy, what should I do?"

"Alex, your life is very valuable even in a time like this. We need you. I need you. Little Sarah! What would she do without you watching over her?"

"Oh believe me, Sarah is everything to me. That's why I'm still here. I'll never forget the desperate look in her mother's eyes. That face still haunts me today. When I first saw her, Mount Rainer just blew its top. There were ashes and rocks falling everywhere. She and her mom lived there, at Tent City. Some of the people were able to find safety under a bridge.

"There was a terrible hail of rocks, and the bridge had been damaged from previous earthquakes. The area had been pummeled with debris and ash, which progressed to more rocky golf ball sized bastards. And those suckers hurt! Finally the bridge gave out. I barely made it out alive. I looked over and saw her mom holding her daughter's limp body. I wanted to help her but the place was gonna go at any time.

"I had to find cover. The rocks were striking my head. It was everything I could do to stay conscious. I was able to find a garbage can lid, and run for cover. After I seen what happened to the bridge, I thought it was safer out in it than getting buried alive. I soon came across a Hummer that belonged to the Antis. The driver was dead just outside of it. I jumped in and drove as fast as possible back to the bridge, to see if the lady and her daughter were still there."

"When I had gotten there, the bridge had fully collapsed. That's when I saw Sarah lying next to her mom, hugging her. I ran to her and snatched her away from her mom's lifeless grip, and placed her in the front seat of the Hummer. But when I went back for her mother, I saw that she was not alive. I retreated back to the truck, and the rocks still were getting bigger. When I got to the Hummer, I just drove. All I could think about was her poor mom. I should have done something when I had the chance. To this day, Sarah doesn't know I could have saved her mother. Please don't say anything. Like I said, the only reason I go on, is for her."

"Oh no, I'm not gonna say anything. You shouldn't be so hard on yourself. You know, you did the right thing. Even the professionals are trained that if your life is endangered, don't attempt to save someone else. Because if you're injured, now there are two people that need assistance. So you did the right thing. If it wasn't for your various smart actions, Sarah wouldn't be here today. You're a true hero. Quit beating yourself up!"

"I didn't think about it that way. You're probably right. I'm so thankful I have Sarah."

"Quit thinking about dying, Alex. It's time you started thinking about living. It's not how long you live. It's 'how happily did you live?' Enjoy what time we have left; use it to absorb Sarah's childish laughter, and it will ring eternally in your heart."

"That was beautiful, Marie. You're the best counselor I've ever met. How do you hold the weight of the world on your shoulders like that? Especially in these times. You're one special person. Say, who do you go to when you're in crisis? Even you have to have issues, what with all these disasters we faced."

"Truly, Alexander, it's not the way it looks. Actually, I'm selfish. I depend on your weakness to find my strengths. I can relate to all my patients. We all can relate. We're all going through the same fate. When someone has a problem, I set into place tools that I've learned in my profession. When I drum up these tools for my patients, I get to wrench on myself a little bit also. That's why I've dedicated every bit of my time to serving these people in need. I selfishly need their problems, to get me through my problems. We should wrap this up. I have an appointment in thirty minutes and I haven't eaten."

"I definitely appreciate what you've done for me, Doc."

"No problem, and thank you, Alex, for sharing your story. And tell Sarah to come see me soon."

Marie followed Alex out of the old battered building, and they went their separate ways. Alex went to pick Sarah up at the park and Marie headed to the town center for a sandwich. As she was walking, she noticed two guys who looked like Secret Service agents. They seemed to be following her, so she began walking faster, and they pursued her. She ducked around the corner, and slammed into another one of the agents. Due to his size, he hardly budged from the impact of little Marie's frail body. She recognized the Anti badge, and was relieved. "Are you Marie Dickerson?" the agent asked.

"Yes. What's this about?"

"You need to come with us."

"Where are we going?"

"The Antichrist would like to see you."

"Me? What does he want to see me for? I've got a one o'clock."

"You better call and cancel," the Anti said, as a black armored Hummer pulled up to the curb.

ON A ROAD through the creaking swamp near Cape Kennedy, a black limo carried Eva and a hand-picked squad of Illuminati commandos toward a government installation that appeared on no maps. Even its launch tower was painted with a photographic reproduction of the terrain below, so that it could not be viewed by spy satellites. The sides, meanwhile, were covered with billboards for Lil' Debbie Cakes and Pennzoil. Eva turned to the commandos in their black ninja suits. "You know what to do, right? On no account are you to damage the spacecraft. If so much as a…" The commandos were not listening; they were dozing off after their fifteen-hour trip from Washington, DC. She raised her voice, and adjusted her black chiffon skirt to show a bit of knee. "You know what to do?" she yelled at a commando. Awakened, he stuttered, "Uh, yes, ma'am. Secure the spaceship. Kill anyone who gets in our way. Don't scuff the spaceship." "That's right," said Eva. "And you do know what will happen if you *do* scuff the spaceship?" "Uh, you'll feed us to the walruses." "Good boy," Eva said, without a hint of levity.

IN MELBOURNE, AUSTRALIA, two Anti guards were about to pick up another lottery winner.

"This guy's a scientist, huh?"

"Yah, I guess he's been working hard to maintain devices that are keeping a lot of these people alive. These hospitals haven't been efficient, since the economy went to shit. But yah! This guy's been in this hospital, working on these life-support machines for the patients. He doesn't stop. He's locked himself in and hasn't come out. People say he's a little strange."

"Strange? What do you suppose they meant by 'strange'?"

"Well, they said he might not come along so willingly. So if he refuses, we may have to sedate him. But hopefully it won't come to that."

They entered the hospital and saw the nurse at the front desk. The place was packed with patients due to the recent tsunami. The Antis approached a nurse, but she ignored them, being entirely preoccupied with helping patients. One of them spoke up.

"We're looking for Dr. Jonathan Wagner. Do you know where we can find him?"

"He doesn't talk to people. He's usually where people aren't. The old parking lot downstairs, all the way to the back, you'll see a workshop. Check there!"

"How do...?"

"Down the hallway, to the right, and take the stairs down."

"Thanks." The two men slowly approached the room. They were amazed. The room was filled with all sorts of gadgets and tools, and equipment stripped of parts. The men decided to wait it out, and they were successful: the scientist entered briefly. They were a bit taken by his size. They expected to see a tall, lanky, skinny guy. Instead they were looking at someone who appeared to be a defensive lineman.

"The nurse upstairs said a couple of agents were lookin' me up. What's the bloom'n problem?"

"We need you to come with us, uh, sir," the guard said, slightly intimidated.

"I don't think that's gonna be possible, mate."

"No, I don't think you understand, Dr. Wagner. We can't leave without you."

The other Anti pitched in. "You're one of the lucky winners. Don't you wanna escape the fireball?"

"I could give a koala's ass about your lottery. Push your scam on some other gent. I'm not interested, mate!"

"Listen, pal, there's a lot of people who would die to be in your shoes right now. Take me, for instance. I dedicated my life to serving the Antichrist, who requires me to save your candy ass. I don't wanna die. I'd love to be in your shoes right now!"

"Trust me, mate, you don't want to be in my shoes." The doctor's face grew pained. "Six years ago, my wife was attacked by some looters during a riot. I brought her here. Because of all the anarchy, the hospital had no power, and was already down to two generators. Instantly I knew what I had to do. It was up to me to fix the generator. I stole parts from one of the broken generators to repair the other, and was able to get it running, so the doctors could put her on a life support system. Although she never recovered, she stayed in a coma for six weeks. I stayed here the whole time, right next to her bed. Then the doctors told me that we had to free up the plug for a more savable candidate. So do you wish you had been in my shoes that day? Well, mate? Ever since that day this is where I've been. Keeping the maintenance up on these babies. Because you never know who's gonna come through that door and need this equipment."

The Anti looked embarrassed. "Look, man, I didn't mean to blurt out what I said. You won the lottery, so that means you deserved to win more than anybody. You've earned your spot."

"I understand, mate, but you don't understand. I made an oath to this hospital. I'm not leaving. If you think I'm comin' with you two, you're smokin' eucalyptus leaves."

"I'm only human, you got to look at it from my point of view. I don't get a choice, and neither do you." As one guard sprayed a knockout gas in the doctor's face, the other guard caught the collapsing body, and they carried him to the Hummer waiting outside.

BACK IN SEATTLE, two Antis found Alexander at a park with Sarah. Each nanochip implant was hooked up to GPS, so rounding up the winners wasn't as tough as it might have been otherwise. "Good afternoon," said the Anti, as he took a seat next to Alex on the bench. "Today's your lucky day!"

"Oh yah. Why's that?"

"Well you've been chosen to go to the New World. You're in the B.O.L."

"B.O.L.?"

"Yah, the Book of Life. You're in it."

"I don't wanna burst your bubble, but I can't go. I don't wanna go. But I know someone you should take."

"Sorry, only you can go, it's your name in the Book of Life."

"Well, I'm not going anywhere without Sarah!"

"Thank you," said Sarah.

"Sarah?" He looked at the little girl. "It says here you never married or had children."

"Let's just say I'm her new dad, due to the circumstances."

"Well I was told, no one is allowed to be accompanied by family members. But I'll call and check for you." The Anti pulled out his voice-activated cell phone and said "Thaillo." The phone automatically called Thaillo, and rang twice.

"Hello."

"Yes, Sir, sorry for bothering you, but this is Mr. Jeremy Hunnel from Section N.W.1. I've run into a complication with one of the winners. Let's see, an Alexander Lujaque. A little girl named Sarah…" Before the Anti could even ask, Thaillo replied in a cheerful voice: "Did you say a little girl, named Sarah? It has been so long. Yes, silly. Yes, bring Sarah along. Bring them straight to me, I'll prep them myself."

"Yes, sir."

The Anti shut his cell phone, turned to Alex, and said, "Today is your lucky day. The boss gave it the okay Let's lock and load. I have a car waiting for us just this way." When the two saw the car, a rush of memories and sadness overcame them, but they only felt a sense of security when they entered the cab of the Hummer. They remembered that the same exact type of Hummer saved their lives. It seemed as if the vehicle might do it again, at least for Alex.

IN CANADA, THEY found the next winner, just outside Vancouver. A doctor by the name of Jeremiah St. James had converted his home into a full-time hospital where he treated people in distress outside the city's boundaries. He had a full-time staff of five people in addition to himself. Together, with his leadership, they aided anyone who suffered from a medical emergency but couldn't make it to the city hospitals. As they were doing their routine procedures, the doctor noticed the dog outside was barking. He went to the window to see what the commotion was and his heart started racing, as he saw two men dressed in black approach the door. "Ding dong," the doorbell rang, just as Dr. St. James opened it. "Good afternoon, gentlemen. Do you have another patient for me?"

"Sorry, man, not today. Today we've come on a different matter. We need you to come with us. The Antichrist has you on his need-to-see list. It's very confidential. Can you come with us?"

Unnerved by the unexpected visitors, he paged one of his subordinates over his P.A.: "Timothy, report to my office, stat!"

Soon after, Timothy arrived. "Yes, Dr. St. James?"

"I have to go away unexpectedly. Can you take over my duties till I get back?"

"How long will you be gone?" Timothy asked. St. James glanced at one of the Antis for answers. The Anti just shook his head, as if to say he may not return. He was shocked at the shortness of notice and a bit irritated at the secrecy. He said his goodbyes to his staff, as the Antis escorted him to the shiny black Hummer parked outside.

THE ANTIS WERE now in pursuit of the leaders of the militias, which had been set up strictly to help people in distress. The leaders had no idea that they had scored more points than anyone else. Many relief expeditions were organized by these leaders, and everyone involved donated their efforts and generated points for themselves, but every deed they did also scored points for their leaders. This was like the pyramid scams or get-rich-quick schemes. The guy on top makes all the points. But no one knew this was happening. The two leaders had been in something of a competition. They argued over whose group was more efficient at saving lives, and whose militia was better. Almost like the gangs in Compton, California, or New York, New York, these men preyed on people in distress. They would help people just to help themselves gain more points.

Deshawn, who was still quite young, had made a prominent position for himself as leader of "The Crusaders," dedicated to truly serving and protecting the public, searching the streets daily for people in need. Deshawn made his way up through the ranks of the Black Panthers, from whom he learned a lot of tricks of propaganda. He also learned how to speak with energy and passion, to motivate young prospects to join his cause. His role models were Dr. Martin Luther King and Malcolm X. He wanted to lead, and lead he did. He was soon the NAACP official spokesman for the entire West Coast of the United States. When the Antichrist began his reign, Deshawn was inspired, and felt there was a more important battle to be fought. He set up a very organized group that vowed to protect and serve the endangered people of the world. And these vigilantes did exactly that. When the lottery started, more vigilante groups started forming, competing with one another for work. They called these freelance heroes "Point Pirates."

DESHAWN'S MAIN COMPETITION was a group called, "The D.R.'s", short for Disaster Relief. The man heading the group was Michael Holbrook. This man was your everyday G.I. Joe, freedom fighter, ex-military, in his early thirties but still in great shape. He felt it was his duty to reverse some of the bad karma he had created fighting man's wars. He felt he owed something to the people, but most of all, he was an adrenaline junkie. Even for his age, he gave the biggest and strongest a run for their money. Michael and Deshawn were constantly at each other's throats, competing for first rights at disaster sites all over the world.

Because of the severity of the world's disasters and the abundance of needed rescues, there was plenty of wealth to spread in the occupation of heroism, as far as points went—especially the way these militias were operating, better than any army forces that had ever existed. Because of the deep motivational drive to gain points, this occupation was held by one-quarter of the lottery winners. These people were rescuing people more productively than ever. Their highest-ranking officers in these militias were next down in the pyramid of superiority. Stefan O'Rand had served under Corporal Holbrook for five years. Taken under Holbrook's wing, he idolized the Corporal for everything he stood for. He had vowed to stand by his commander's side to the end, and now he would be able to keep his promise.

There was room for Deshawn's first officer Craig O'Rand also. Craig joined Deshawn soon after his brother enlisted with Corporal Holbrook, just because of his deep-rooted competition with his twin brother Stefan. The two were complete opposites and clashed in everything they did. This became a constant game of cat and mouse for the two, always toying with each other for superiority, each trying to outdo the other. Their childhood was a constant fight for glory over the other, and now their battle could rage on.

Little did these four know that they were going to be seeing a lot of each other. They were all rounded up and were eager to claim their prize, but were very dissatisfied to see that their competition had made it also. Misery loves company, though, and from the looks of these four, this wasn't going to be a dull journey.

THE ILLUMINATI LIMOUSINE pulled into a hidden drive guarded by a pit of hungry-looking alligators and a variety of high-tech sensors. "What is the password?" asked a voice from the trees. Eva stuck her head out the window—a laser crosshairs appeared on her forehead—and said, "Skcus hsub egroeg." "The voice said, "You bet! You may enter." Eva pulled her head back into the limo, and said, "Drive. Gentlemen, I would like to remind you about the walruses. If you fail…" She left the ominous end of the sentence unstated. The commandos gulped. The concealed hangar drew near.

"WHO'S NEXT IN the book?" one Anti asked another as they staked out a building in their Hummer.

"Mrs. Jordyn," replied the other Anti.

"What's her story?"

"Ever since her husband died five years ago, she's been housing juveniles from the streets."

"And where do we find her?"

"Tijuana, Mexico."

"TODD! PUT THAT down, help Sissy set the table, and wash your hands. Breakfast everyone! Chop, chop. Wash up, everyone."

"Hey, Mrs. J. We need another addition built. Should I go get some two-by-fours at the lumberyard today?"

"No, it would be a waste. There is only a little time left. You and Jeffery should bunk up with the other children. One of you in each room—they'll feel more secure knowing you're in there. It's getting close to the last day."

"Okay," said Pedro.

Mrs. Jordyn ran an orphanage close to the US's border with Mexico. A lot of Americans of all races had migrated south to escape Earth's temper tantrums. There weren't many children left, and the ones that were left had been separated from their families. The Antichrist had made an exception to the nanochip mark as far as children were concerned. He was a lot more lenient with the children. No children could be turned away, even if they had no mark on their right hand. And many ran amok, but not the children in Mrs. Jordyn's house. These were the most disciplined children. Even though they all had suffered great tragedy, they all seemed to find an inner strength to go on as productive members of society.

Mrs. Jordyn ran a tight ship. There was no laxity when it came to Mrs. Jordyn's house. It was her way, or the highway. She taught these children how to cook, clean, sew, learn, and play, and she didn't have to do all the work. She organized a system in which the children did all the work themselves. This house was run better than some of the hospitals in the area. These children expressed deep pride in what they accomplished, and it showed. Pedro and Jeffery both had been with Mrs. Jordyn for five years, and owed their lives to her. They had stepped up to the plate and taken responsibilities to help her help more children.

Miraculously they housed thirty-six children, all different ages. Pedro was twenty- one now, and Jeffery was nineteen. Mrs. Jordyn's doors were open to the public and to anyone who needed help. Not just children, but adults also. She would only board the children, but during the day these children ran a pretty efficient shelter, which served up fresh lunches and fresh dinners to anyone who showed. It was a sight to see. It looked like a fast food franchise, like one of those multibillion-dollar corporations controlled by the Illuminati, except all run by teenagers. She built up those skills, ironically, working for McDonalds for ten years as a manager. She even had training videos for her children. The doorbell rang, and the children ran up like bell-hops. They greeted two Anti officers at the door.

"Come on in. Can we take your coat?", asked Suzie. She had been with Mrs. J for two years and loved to sing while she worked. While humming a tune, she light-footedly danced around the guards, peeling their jackets off.

"Here, sit." Two children scurried up out of nowhere, set two places for them, and pulled their chair out for them.

"Oh no. We're not here for lunch. We're here for ..."

"Sit."

And before they could say another word, two hot steaming plates of the finest meatloaf and mashed potatoes arrived. The guards looked at each other. "Well, I guess we could have just a taste. It *is* lunchtime."

"Here's your water," said Angie, as she set two ice-filled glasses of water down. She asked the guards, "Do you need any salt or pepper?"

"Yah, sweetheart, that would be nice." She ran into the kitchen still wearing her morning Onesy, which she had slept in. Angie was a five-year-old who had suffered severe burns in the volcanic eruption of Mt. St. Helens. She escaped with her life, but she was badly scarred. She was rescued by the D.R. militia. Corporal Holbrook headed the mission and rescued five children and three hundred adults. The Point Pirates had to escort these survivors over the border and into Mexico, where they found refuge in a camp. The Corporal dropped off the children at Mrs. Jordyn's shelter. Mrs. Jordyn and the kids fed them and nursed them back to health. After a one-day rest, the men were off, back to the scene to search for last-ditch survivors. These guys were almost as aggressive as the children in Mrs. Jordyn's house. Even the Corporal had commented to Mrs. J. that her army was in tip-top shape, and had passed all his military criteria. She said, "Thanks, I think."

"Here yah go!" said little Angie, as she ran back from the kitchen. "I brought my favorite."

"Oh, yah? What's that?"

"Ketchup."

"Man, I haven't had ketchup on meatloaf since I was a kid. Man, this is great! Thanks, kid! Oh, I almost forgot, do you kids know where Savannah Jordyn is?"

"Mrs. J? Oh, yah. She's out shopping for inventory. We're running low on supplies."

"When will she be back?"

"Not for a while. She just left. Enjoy your lunch, and if you need seconds, just ring the bell, and I'll help you," said Angie, with her cheeks still puffy from baby fat.

Pedro and Jeffery walked in from the garden and noticed the Antis. Their eyes lit up as though they had seen a movie star. They ran to the table and pulled up a chair. They stared at the guards as they ate. The guards began to feel a little unsettled from the children's gawking at them. "So, are you guys out saving people today?" asked Pedro.

"Not today! We're here for Savannah... uh, I mean Mrs. J."

"Oh, what do you need with her?"

One of the guard said, "She won the …" The other guard kicked the guard under the table, giving him a hard blow. Then the Anti realized he was about to let the cat out of the bag.

Suddenly the door flew open, and the Antichrist himself was there. The two guards jumped up and brushed themselves off. "Sorry, boss, she wasn't here and…"

"Stop! Just take care of the next people in the book. I'll handle this one."

"Are you sure, boss?"

"Go!"

Mabus took a seat next to Pedro. Pedro's eye was fixated on Mabus's flawless face. He idolized the Antichrist, as most kids did, and always dreamed of meeting him. All the children ran from every room and huddled around Mabus as he started to tell the children about the new world and the ideas of harmony.

Jeffery interrupted, saying, "Cut the shit! You're here for Mrs. J, aren't you? She won the lottery, and now you've come to take her away!"

The eyes in the room teared up instantly; suddenly you could hear a pin drop. A fog of sadness was heavy in the room, as the children realized that the Antichrist was there to take her away.

"Yes, Jeffery, that's exactly why I'm here. But I need you guys to do me a favor. I need you to do Mrs. J a favor. She's not going to want to leave with me and abandon you children. But you see, she won the lottery. She won because she took all of you children in and impacted your lives. It's time you impact her life. We need to show her you can run this place without her. Pedro, Jeffery: you're in charge."

"Yes, sir."

"Angie, we may need you to drum up some alligator tears."

"Aye, aye, captain!"

"All you children, you know your jobs. Let's give Mrs. J. a warm goodbye!" shouted Mabus.

"I'll get a cake started!" said Suzie, clapping her hands together.

The children all jumped into their work, synchronized like a finely-tuned machine. They cleaned and decorated, hanging a banner which said "Congratulations, Mrs. J." They hung streamers in every direction. Then they turned out the lights, and waited. "Here she comes, shhhhhh!"

"SURPRISE!"

She nearly fell backwards when she entered. She was shocked. She had never had a surprise party. Tears instantly welled up in her eyes. All the children were lined up, from small to big, and they were all dressed up in their best clothes. Even their hair had just been freshly combed. As she looked down at each one and hugged them, she made it to the end, to Pedro and Jeffery.

"What have you boys done?"

"Congratulations, Mrs. J! You won the lottery!"

"Lottery?" she said. "What?" looking at Mabus and smiling.

"You're gonna be leaving. They need you now. We can handle this gig. We were taught by the best. Pedro and I are going to step it up, and take over your duties. Please, you need to go. Don't worry about us, we'll be fine. This is the most important thing for you. You're done taking care of us. It's time you take care of you. Please go. We believe in you. And we all love you."

"Oh, Jeffery. You've made me so proud. You've come so far." Tears welled up, in both their eyes this time; a special bond was about to be broken.

"Sorry, Mrs. Jordyn. We must go now," said Mabus as he put his hand on Mrs. J's shoulder. His touch sent a shiver down her spine. She said her goodbyes and they headed out for Anti headquarters. The children watched as the black Hummer faded into the night and slowly disappeared.

EVA STROLLED DETERMINEDLY through the hangar, as peals of automatic gunfire echoed in the background. Stepping daintily in her Ferragamos over bloody corpses splayed in her path, she approached an oddly-curved semi-spherical object, thirty feet in diameter, covered by a gray tarp. She heard a noise and turned around; there was a guard who had her in his sights in one corner of the hangar. Eva blasted him into tomato purée with her alien gun. Now, she called for her commandos. They had finished securing the installation, and came running. "Get this tarp off!" she ordered. The men complied. What remained after they did was a sight to behold: a glistening silver flying saucer, styled after the 1950s much as the *Noah* was styled after the 1930s. Unlike the saucer at Groom Lake, this one seemed to have all its parts. It looked as though it had been cast out of one piece of metal, and glittering highlights chased each other across its burnished surface. "Magnificent," Eva breathed. "No walruses for you, gentlemen."

"THIS NEXT GUY we're lookin' for has had it bad," said one Anti to another, as they shared a lunch break of chili dogs and French fries.

"Oh yah? Why's that?"

"He lost his legs. Well, I guess you could say he didn't lose them. Apparently the guy was performing a concert when the coliseum collapsed, trapping fifteen thousand people inside. Many were hurt, but not as bad as Rich Davis."

"Rich Davis," the Anti interrupted, "That name seems so familiar."

"An enormous pillar collapsed on his back. The survivors were able to free him, but when he awoke, he found that he had lost all feeling below his waist. It says here that it took three weeks before they were rescued."

"Three weeks! How did they survive three weeks without any food?"

"I'm gettin' to that! The guy couldn't feel his legs so he let the survivors eat his body to survive."

"You're shittin' me!"

"It says here, 'He allowed them to eat his buttocks and his legs because of the plentiful amount of meat.' That ain't it. Get this: they were rescued twenty-four hours after they ate his body from the waist down. I guess it did a real number on his mind."

"I bet!" replied the other Anti, who was now pale as a ghost. "Suddenly I'm not so hungry. This hot dog's not settling right with my stomach. I would be messed in the head also. I don't know if I could do that, for anyone. I know why he was picked," the other Anti said as he threw his half-eaten lunch in the trash.

"Actually you'll be surprised. He racked up enough points with his music. It says here that he would have won anyway. His music inspired millions of people to find strength in this horrible reality."

"Yah! Didn't he write that song, 'I'm Not Gonna Die. Not Until I've Lived?' I've wondered what happened to that guy."

"I guess after the incident, the guy hasn't been the same. He sits alone all day playing his music on street corners. He plays a flute that some kid carved for him while they were trapped in the building. I guess the kid felt he owed the guy something. He keeps it with him all the time, even wears it around his neck."

"What a strange deal."

"So where do we find Mr. Davis?"

"I'm picking up his GPS marker at the corner of Fifth and Pike. "There he is," the first Anti said, as they stared at the blinking light on the screen of his laptop. "Let's go."

IN A SMALL storefront on Lido Island, in Southern California, a designer worked with her seamstress. The designer's name was Parim Bakhtiari, a petite, beautiful thirty-year-old woman from Iran, who had fled persecution to come to the United States. She worked harder than most, even given the number of people who were working double shifts under the Antichrist's lottery regime. She had a business designing dresses for society matrons and their daughters, mainly for weddings, using the most expensive fabrics from Europe. In her store, a yard of Armani fabric might sell for $320. But what most people didn't know was that she spent her nights designing dresses with her special flair for events in the lives of the poor and needy. Although the Newport Beach police did not like the idea of poor people parking at night near an exclusive shopping district, the flow started at 7:00 P.M. and did not end until midnight. Out of more economical fabrics, she constructed dresses to make poor unappreciated women and girls feel like princesses for one day in their lives—dresses for weddings, graduations, and quinceañeras. Her seamstresses were busy around the clock. Once the black armored Hummer pulled up at her store, she looked at the Anti guards coming to her door, and swallowed hard. When they came in, she pleaded with them:

"I swear, I'll pay those parking tickets!"

One of the Anti guards said, "It's OK. The Antichrist has forgiven them. Now we need you to come with us."

Parim could tell that this was for keeps. She told her seamstresses to finish up any dresses they had started, and then to give the fabrics in the shop to her most deserving customers. Then, she departed, for the great unknown.

BACK AT ANTI headquarters, the rest of the lottery winners were almost all rounded up. Thaillo greeted these people and geared them up for their mission. He lodged them in separate rooms. Each room was prepared with a video about the process that they would need to undergo before their flight to Venus. Because space travel had long proven fatal to astronauts because of the low gravity in space and the flares of solar radiation, nanobots would be injected into each person, giving him or her the power of immortality.

The videos explained the quick and painless process for their mind-enhancement surgery. Most of the new Antis were pretty motivated to do the process. Once the surgery was through, they no longer had any fear. They had experienced total enlightenment. For once in their lives they were at peace with themselves, nature, and each other.

THE ANTICHRIST RAN into the Antis's control room.

"Where the hell is Thaillo? He said it was important!"

One of the female technicians was the one to tell him: "Jesus has returned to Earth."

Mabus sat down on a spare chair, clasped his head, and moaned, "Jesus fucking Christ!"

"That's the one," said Thaillo, strolling in. "Cheer up, Mabus. We've been preparing for this eventuality for the last two thousand years. There's nothing to worry about."

"But he's supposed to come in on a white horse, pull a sword out of his mouth, and rout us and all we stand for."

"Mabus, old friend, that's his PR machine, written, directed, and funded by the Illuminati. Let us take care of it."

"What are you going to do?"

Thaillo smiled. "Nothing."

"Nothing?"

"We own all the media, now—television, radio, newspapers, the works. We are simply are not going to cover him at all. Let him try to get airtime on the Illuminati infomercial."

EVA SMILED CHARMINGLY. "I'm very pleased to have the honor of introducing my very special guest, King of Kings, Lord of Lords— give it up for our Savior, Jesus H. Christ! Jesus, before we get started, what does the 'H' stand for?"

"Horatius. My mother liked the general."

"And what's that tattoo on your thigh? Let's see if we can get it on camera."

"It says, 'King of Kings and Lord of Lords.' In Aramaic."

"Very interesting. Now, you've come back to Earth to judge and save mankind. How's it going, so far?"

"It is rather difficult, my child. All around me are the Works of Perdition. It seems as though the Antichrist has done my work for me. I have turned loaves into fishes and water into wine, but the Antichrist's hellish and perverse rationing system has deluded mankind into believing it has found its sustenance in bread alone. I can walk on water, but the Antichrist has regularly scheduled hovercraft service across the Sea of Galilee. I can heal the sick, but the Antichrist has enough hospitals for everyone. I can even bring the dead back to life, but since people have begun believing the foul lies of the Antichrist, they no longer fear death. Besides, the aliens—"

"Moving right along," Eva said hurriedly, "Why do You feel uniquely qualified to be mankind's Savior?"

"Well, Eva, as you know, I am the only-begotten son of God. Surely that is qualification enough. I am mightier than the angels and more powerful than all the kingdoms of man. I have sat at the right hand of my Father."

"What can You offer our viewers?"

"An eternity of peace, love, and blessing. Except if they do not believe in Me. All those who follow the Antichrist shall die at the point of my sword, that which I took out from My very Mouth. Then the birds shall eat their flesh, and their souls will be cast into a lake of fire."

Eva smiled into the camera. "A terrible penalty for those who follow that false prophet. In our next portion of the show, we'll go over highlights of Jesus's career, with commentary from the Source, the Way, the Truth, and the Life."

"That's a wrap. The rest's on tape."

Jesus got down from the dais, clad only in a loincloth, and asked Eva, "Could I get a glass of water?" She rolled her eyes. "There's some vinegar in the closet. Make the water yourself."

THAILLO SUMMONED ALEXANDER and Sarah. He wanted to do their orientation himself, just like when he did Mabus. "And you must be Sarah? I'm Thaillo. I'll be helping Alex with his orientation but you can join us if you like," as he held out his hand.

Sarah took his hand and instantly a bond was formed, almost as if it were already there. As they walked down the corridor to get to the surgical department, Alexander crossed paths with what

looked to be his counselor, Marie. As they walked passed each
other their eyes locked on one another and they grinned. Each
was pleased to see that the other person had won the lottery as
well. "Here we are. Right this way," said Thaillo.

"THANK YOU FOR letting me stay with Alex, sir," whispered little
Sarah to Thaillo.

"You don't worry your pretty little head. You and I have a lot
more in common than you think," he murmured as he strapped
Alex into the chair.

"We do?"

"Oh, yeah. Here, let's let the doctor do his thing, while we
wait in the lounge. We'll be right next door, Alex. I'll get you
some hot chocolate, Sarah." They entered the lounge, a room with
ten or twelve vending machines and a long table in the center. He
pulled out a chair for Sarah. She sat as Thaillo warmed up some
hot chocolate for her. He began, "We're both losing someone
special. Mabus has been my friend for thousands of years. Can
you imagine the bond we have? Unfortunately for us, we can't go
to Venus. Everything is the way it is. We can't change destiny, but
we can find strength in knowing that our loved ones will be
carrying our legacy through time. If my Mabus, or your Alex, isn't
successful with his mission, then the human race may cease to
exist. Or even worse, it may cease to have ever existed. It's pretty
complicated, sweetheart, but we are actually pretty lucky. We're
lucky to have these special people in our lives."

"I don't want Alex to go away, but I don't want him to die
even more," Sarah said with a sad look.

"So you see, Sarah, we must be strong not just for ourselves,
but for these people we love. Leaving us behind is harder for
them than letting them go is for us. These people need our support,
so that they can complete their mission, not for themselves, but
for all of us who live and have ever lived. All shall rise again,
thanks to these heroes. So you see, we can't put our own needs in
front of the needs of civilization. Do you understand, sweetie?"

"Yes," she sniffled. "If it weren't for Alex, I wouldn't be here. I
owe everything to him. Oh, Thaillo, I'll miss him so much." As
she hugged him, tears poured down her face.

"Everything is going to be fine, sweetie. Don't worry, I'll be
here for you." As they hugged, they were interrupted by an Anti

knocking at the door. "We're all done with Mr. Lujaque," the Anti said, without opening the door. "Okay. Thanks," he replied. "How are you? Are you going to be all right?" She nodded, but Thaillo knew the pain wouldn't go away that easily. "Come on, let's go get Alexander."

LATER, MABUS AND Thaillo inspected all the stats on the twelve Antis. <These are the future, huh?> asked Mabus, inspecting the line-up of winners. <Yep,> replied Thaillo as the screens revealed the actions of the twelve Antis in their quarters. <We had some interesting results on the one called Richard Davis. The nanobots did something completely unexpected. The nanobots are pro-grammed to repair damaged cells from the existing tissue. Everything from the man's waist down had been amputated, so there wasn't any tissue to recreate. So the nanobots restructured his lower half with nanotubing.>

<So, he'll be able to expand and shrink,> thought Mabus.

<He will be able to change shape. At least the bottom half of his body will change shape. The nanotubing is hard-wired right into his mind, so his mutations will take shape consciously.>

<What do you mean, mutations?>

<Here, look for yourself.> Thaillo turned the monitor toward Mabus and pressed "Enter" on the keyboard. Mabus watched in amazement as the guy, tormented by his mutation, was trans-formed into a half-bull, half-man. He resembled nothing so much as the Minotaur of ancient Greek legend. But this bull had nanobots, making the strength of his legs one thousand times greater than that of steel. The creature began to tear into the holding chamber as though it were the Cretan Maze. The struc-tural-steel-paneled room was, in short order, dented like an aluminum can.

<When he runs, his body naturally responds, and the nanobots change their tasks and take a more efficient form. Just like your body used to naturally sweat as soon as your heartbeat increased. His body will react in the same way. If he jumps into a body of water, his body will mutate into that of a shark. He's not taking the change too well right now. We have him isolated in a steel room where he seems to be letting off a little steam. It hasn't held up very well. We can't keep him contained.> Realizing that he'd torn the place up, Davis stopped to get his head straight. His

massive body pulsated with immense energy. <Get these things out of me!>, he exclaimed with his mind, looking up at the camera and straight into Mabus's soul.

Mabus used his strong telepathic ability to calm the… man.

<Go ahead, say it! Freak! That's what I am now. These things have a mind of their own. I'm just a puppet now!>

<My dearest Richard, what you have is a gift. You are immortal now. What's done is done. You can't be destroyed. Remember, it was you who inspired people to find a lighter side in darkness, and to see good within evil. Can't you see the capabilities of your new temple? You are an artist. Now you can express yourself in a way no other can. You are a creature of superior beauty. I envy your capabilities. You have inspired many to see the positive side to a negative existence. Can't you find happiness?>

<Where's my necklace?!>

<Necklace?>

< It was around my neck. Where is it?>

<Richard, all your belongings are in your room. If you're ready to see reason, we can show you to your room.>

<Well, you do have a point. This is much better than that skateboard I was strapped to.>

<Mr. Hunnel, show Mr. Davis to his room.>

"Right this way, Mr. Davis."

The necklace and flute were waiting for him on his dresser.

<So we've got our work cut out for us. These people who are pure of heart—how can we ensure that these people won't go back and ruin everything?> thought Mabus to Thaillo.

<Hey, once you guys leave, it will be all up to you to ensure this timeline makes it to the present. Trust me, you'll do just fine. But be careful, old friend, because you know that at some point you will be betrayed by some of these folks. There is nothing we can do, it's the way it has to be. Now I must not reveal too much, because of the risk of a paradox. You see, what I tell you affects your decision making. It's vital that the decisions you make greatly alter our next future for the better. At any time you could change your mind, and decide to enslave the planet under your rule. But you don't. You won't. You're incorruptible. That is why you are here. Not many people have what it takes inside to ignore power and greed, but you do, Mabus. You are indeed the ultimate

humanitarian. Your efforts have always been toward the greatness of mankind, rather than the greatness of yourself. I will miss you, old friend. But soon we will reunite, and I will be patiently waiting for you. Which reminds me: sometime before the time of the pyramids, when a little boy steals your shoes, don't be so hard on him.>

<What shoes?> asked Mabus.

<Uh, never mind,> replied Thaillo.

Chapter Twenty-Seven

"And the beast was taken, and with him the false prophet that wrought miracles before him, with which he deceived them that had received the mark of the beast, and them that worshipped his image. These both were cast into a lake of fire and brimstone."
                                                                —Rev. 19:20

O N THE DAY MABUS WAS TO leave Earth, he addressed his people once more. Mabus had never had children, but on this day he had never felt more fatherly.

That morning's live broadcast was not from the usual studio, but from the cockpit of the spaceship. Mabus had chosen this backdrop not so much for dramatic purposes but rather for reasons of practicality—he and his small crew would leave Earth the moment the broadcast was over. He wanted nothing to impede their escape.

"Good morning, my human beings," Mabus said somberly. He paused and cleared his unusually dry throat. He had rehearsed what he would say on this day so many times over the past few months, but now that the moment had come, it all seemed so surreal.

"As you know, this will be my last daily broadcast. Much has happened in the twenty-four hours since yesterday's broadcast, and my Antis will fill you all in on what has transpired.

"Most importantly, the lottery has been completed. Yesterday afternoon, under cover of armed guards, I personally oversaw the computer selection of the twelve winners from the lottery. I flew my personal jet, aircraft AC666, to transport each of them to a top-secret facility in what was formerly the Southwest United States. Their identities will remain guarded for the time being, but will be released after my spacecraft has ascended."

"I apologize for the secrecy, but I hope you all understand that our survival as a race depends on my spacecraft's quick departure as soon as I end this broadcast. I simply cannot take any chances on chaos erupting and impeding our departure. What I will disclose about the identities of my shipmates is that each of the twelve lottery winners will be my apostles on our new planet, and we have a great task ahead of us ensuring that we all can live again."

Mabus paused. There was so much more to say, so much more he could say, but he knew he shouldn't. Knowing most things, Mabus knew that Jesus and the Illuminati were, at that moment, escorting a large group of carefully selected people down to secret underground shelters to await the coming of the meteor and the end of the modern world.

But Mabus could not tell everyone everything. He could not give all that he knew away. He was leaving his children behind to die and he wanted them to die without any unnecessary knowledge that would only make their final hours more torturous.

"I…I am the true Lord Christ," he stammered. "You are all my followers." As he said this, he did in fact depict himself as the innocent lamb—white skin, clear azure-blue eyes, and sandy brown hair arranged perfectly in place. Only he was also filled with an untold number of carbon nanotubes.

Mabus sat for a few long seconds, staring at the cockpit camera, wordless, and pointed to the ship's Earthtime clock. Mabus had to sign off—now the comet was coming.

"I bid you all farewell. Go to sleep, my children, for when you wake up, you will be alive again almost instantly. You won't remember a thing. But your precious seed will bloom once again. So close your eyes and go to sleep; tomorrow the sun will shine brighter for you. I promise, I won't let you down! Fear not death! Death is but an instant! We will live again! We will live eternally! I promise you all!" Mabus shouted. His television image faded to black and the transmission ended. <Goodbye, old friend. I will miss you,> Mabus thought to Thaillo. Mabus squeezed his newly blue eyes shut and listened to the sound of the engines as they prepared for takeoff.

<Farewell Thaillo,> Mabus thought. <I'll see you on the other side.>

<Goodbye, old friend.> Thaillo replied. <This is the part I always hate. So let's keep it short,> Thaillo said as a lump built up in his throat. <We're all counting on you, old buddy.>

Thaillo picked up Sarah, as they watched the ship leaving the atmosphere from the safety of 666 headquarters. <Sarah, you're the best thing that ever happed to me. If it were up to me, you would be sitting here right now,> thought Alex. <I may be immortal, but without you in my life, I would never have truly lived. And for that, I'm eternally grateful. Goodbye, Sarah. You'll always be with me for eternity.>

Chapter Twenty-Eight

IVE HUNDRED MILES AWAY, SIXTY-TWO-YEAR-OLD Mabel Sullivan clicked off her television set, laid down the remote, and stroked Gem, the cat in her lap. "The cancer would've taken me within a year anyway," she said to Gem as he purred. "It's just as well for me." A red dot in the sky caught Mabel's eye through the window of her mobile home. It grew quickly in size as she squinted and pushed her bifocals up on her nose. She realized she was looking at Chiron, the asteroid, as it zoomed straight for her and right into what would become the future planet Mars. The red ball was now a torpedo of flame, growing at an exponentially increasing rate. Gem hissed as Mabel balled her hand into a fist, unintentionally pulling on his fur. "Oh, my *God!!!*" she gasped, seconds before she and Gem were vaporized.

New York City died a most ignoble death, similar to Los Angeles. The Earth finally swallowed both cities, harbingers of American civilization, whole. But as usual, some of the screaming people were left alive. And the surface and subterranean upheavals, horrifying as they were, kept themselves away from a huge, flat, dry, arid acreage of desert land in Nevada.

The children of Mrs. Jordyn's shelter huddled in the living room, which they filled with all their special belongings. They wrote notes to family who had passed away or were going to pass away, and celebrated life with one last slumber party. They closed all the blinds in the house so as to ignore their deadly fate. They didn't want to die with fear in their hearts. They wanted to die remembering the joys of their lives.

When Mabus signed off, and the people of Earth saw the spaceship leave, the people ceased their labors. But there was a peace that remained among them. The torment of the threatening disaster was worse than the fate itself. The torment was over. Most people felt relieved at the sight of the great fireball in the sky.

No one, not even Mabus, knew that another spaceship was counting down to launch. As Illuminati technicians scurried about the hangar, Eva adjusted her psychotronic helmet and sat down at the control nexus, cursing the fact that the aliens had buttocks far smaller than her size-six posterior, as well as the fact that there were no cup holders. The ship, the *Nephilim*, was just about ready to go. The technicians jabbered worriedly among themselves, wondering if they would get to the shelters on time, but Eva didn't care. She was ready. With the launch of the *Noah* over, she was the most powerful woman on Earth. The *Nephilim* moved out of the hangar and shot up into the sky at twice the speed of the asteroid, and soon was less than a speck in the reddened Florida morning haze.

As QUICKLY AS man appeared on Earth, he became extinct. Scientists say that if the span of Earth's age were compressed into an hour, mankind would have existed for less than a second. The people all cherished that second together. Within that brief second, the miracle of their lives existed.

As the Antis left the Earth's gravitational pull, Mabus switched the ship into deep space mode. The ship instantly became ten times bigger, with plenty of room for their long journey. As they headed toward Venus, the Antis could not stop staring back at what had been Earth, nor could they help recalling the memories of what they left behind. From their view, the debris from Earth began to take the shape of Mars's second moon. Venus's moon was also forming before their very eyes. They didn't believe something so massive could be formed so quickly.

Mabus's concentration was broken when a song, "I'm on a highway to hell!" by AC/DC, began blaring over the intercom. Suddenly the crew broke into laughter. Immediately, the twins strummed their air guitars to the song. Thomas followed in with some air drums while Jeremiah broke into a horrific singing lead. Even with his technological enhancements, he couldn't carry a tune in a wheelbarrow. Deshawn and Holbrook embraced each other and began to dance around the ship. Mabus had never seen a polka dance to a heavy-metal beat, but they were pulling it off. Mabus was amused by the show performed by the crew, and spirits were up.

Chapter Twenty-Nine

HE TRIP WAS TAKING LONGER than expected, but the crew didn't mind, fearing that they might get there too, soon before the planet was even inhabitable. Most of the crew spent the time reflecting on loved ones left behind, while Mabus realized he was supposed to learn some important information Thaillo had mentioned. He found a disc hidden in the pocket of his suit. It wasn't labeled, and Mabus put it into his computer in his quarters. Thaillo appeared. "If you are watching this, you are halfway home, buddy. I prepared the DNA fingerprints, stored on this disk, of every living creature on earth, plants and animals. This will help to provide food when you first get there. Unfortunately I can't tell you much because of the paradoxes, but beware, old friend, loyalty cannot be taken for granted. It is up to you and you only to get us back again. You must not forget your objective. The only thing that separates us now, old friend, is time."

Suddenly, Mabus's senses, which were hooked up to the ship's sensors, registered something unthinkable – a spaceship moving towards the *Noah* at a tremendous rate of speed. To Mabus's surprise, it was a craft looking very much like the small cannibalized one he had seen at Groom Lake. Then he heard a voice in his mind—one he had never expected to hear again. Eva was *thinking* to him. <Let me aboard your ship, or I will destroy you.> <How the hell could she do that? For that matter, what was she doing aboard an alien spacecraft?> He tried to conceal his strategic thoughts while Eva was waiting for a reply. Mabus wasn't sure whether Eva was bluffing or not, but he instructed the ship to turn on and then jettison one of its nuclear rockets in the saucer's direction. The rocket blazed and sped towards its target, but at the last moment, the saucer twisted forward and to the right, and the rocket sped harmlessly into space. It had never been designed for use as a weapon, and now Mabus knew why. The saucer zipped forward and tried to ram the *Noah*, but Mabus was able to flip the ship out of the way.

The *Noah* and the *Nephilim* played cat and mouse for about twenty minutes; Mabus and Eva were of similar skill levels as pilots, and each was able to cancel out whatever the other did. Mabus was getting sick and tired of this, though, so he thought, <We're even. Can we stop this game?> <We can, if you'll let me come aboard.> <Why should I, when you've threatened to destroy me?> <That was just to get your attention.> <Still, no.> <All right. Then take *this*.> Suddenly, Eva's mind had penetrated his. It was scooping up facts and memories, while at the same time it was pressing down upon his will with a single message: <Obey.> Mabus quickly attempted to erect his own defenses, and to see whether he could get behind the lines and read Eva's mind in turn. He was not completely successful. Although he could more or less squelch the order to obey, he could only get very selective information from Eva, including that she had slept her way up the Illuminati hierarchy, and that her handyman—actually a crack Illuminati assassin—had killed Boone at the orders of her father, Senator Salvatore.

Amazed, Mabus tried to rid his mind of her entirely, by directing his thoughts entirely towards the contemplation of a soothing torus: a donut. Mabus tried to make his mind like the donut, with no center and no end, looping around in perfect continuity. It seemed to work, for Eva was out of his mind, but now she was up to something completely different. She was playing upon the nanobots integral to the ship, using her mental powers to persuade them to make something. Mabus only realized this too late; she was a step ahead of him, and out of the solid bulkhead, as if walking through a waterfall, came Eva. Her blonde hair fell to her shoulders, and her blue eyes twinkled. She was wearing a cropped T-shirt that exposed a navel pierced with a charm of Ourobouros, the tail-eating snake; low-rise blue jeans that hugged her toned legs and pert bottom; and low-heeled Via Spiga slides.

"Surprised to see me, aren't you?" said Eva. "The ship's nanobots were most obliging, and replicated me here."

"You can't do that. There are supposed to be thirteen people on this ship, no more."

"That's no problem." Eva whipped out her alien gun, set it to "annihilate," and vaporized Jacob. She countered the crew's gasps of horror by waving the gun in their general direction. "Oh, stop whining, already. He was the one who was to betray you. Now, there are thirteen again."

"Not to state the obvious, but you seem to have come into possession of some nanobots yourself," said Mabus.

"That is correct. I am your equal in every way. If you are the Antichrist, I am the Whore of Babylon."

"But how did you get the nanobots?"

"We harvested them from your late fiancée's reproductive system."

"You mean you dug Barbara up and cut her open?" Mabus gagged.

"Indeed. There were over two thousand nanobots, which you transmitted to her when you last—how shall I say?—made love. They shut off, naturally, when they realized they were in the wrong person's body, but we gave them an electromagnetic pulse that made them forget all that, and they replicated back to full strength within my bloodstream."

"But you haven't had the mental surgery! You don't know what you're doing!"

"Ah, but I do. It is necessary that I come to exist within your timeline. It is inevitable, and you may even come to like it."

"What do you mean?" asked Mabus.

"You structured your lottery to come up with the twelve people with the highest point scores, yes?"

"Yes. And I'd do it again."

"You are, as usual, sweet but misguided. You selected nine men and three women. Would you not agree that, in order for reproduction to occur, the ratio is a little lopsided, your way? So, you need me in order to even things up a little. I will bear your children, and together, we will reign over this new planet."

"Wait just a minute! Let me get this straight. Your organization had me raped and left for dead… "

"That wasn't us; those were the Rosicrucians."

"Never mind that. You seduced me and then dumped me. You spoke out against me. You tried to kill me. You've tried to undermine me at every turn. You dug up and carved open my dead fiancée. You've just murdered a member of my crew. You've been completely evil. And now, you expect me to practically marry you?"

Eva looked at Mabus with her sparkling, mesmerizing blue eyes, and smiled sweetly.

"In a word, yes."

Mabus stood with his jaw hanging open.

"You can't destroy me. You can't get rid of me. As your wife, I would get up to less trouble than I would otherwise, and perhaps I would absorb some of your... good influence. In the meantime, I would get back something that I threw away when I was seventeen: your love. That's why I visited you, years later. I wanted to make you one of us, but I also wanted to warn you of the dangers you would face. I spoiled that opportunity, too. And then I hated you, and everything you stood for. Yes, I worked against you. But you were the most desirable man on Earth, and I desired you. I didn't kill Barbara—the aliens made sure of that—but once she was gone, I felt your full power, and it filled me with hope. Now, I am in turn the most desirable woman in the solar system—no offense to you girls." She gestured towards Marie, Parim, and Mrs. Jordyn, then turned her attention back to Mabus. "And I want you."

Mabus didn't know whether to smack her silly or to laugh in her face. This had to be the most preposterous line of bullshit he'd ever been fed. All his life, the adults who should have loved him had instead caused him pain, and now, Eva was asking him to submit to more of the same.

Eva thought to Mabus, <My mind is open. See for yourself.> Mabus ventured into her consciousness. He saw their teenage sexual encounter, through her eyes; she had been patronizing, but she had truly wanted him, and had become, not only angry, but grief-stricken when he had not responded in the way she had hoped. He saw that she was indeed trying to warn him when he was in his twenties—smugly, egotistically, but in some sense sincerely. She had been brought up to be her father's girl, privileged and powerful, well-groomed for a bright future. But she had not thought about the consequences, just about power, and had acted accordingly; everyone around her was doing the same, so it didn't seem wrong. Over the years, she had committed many injustices and crimes, including murder. Mabus felt a surge of triumph when he knew for certain that she was connected to his assassination. But she had also felt empty inside, in a way that could not be satisfied by mere power. She needed authenticity—she needed Mabus—and suddenly, he was all that mattered. People were still a means to an end, and her killing of Jacob was no different. She just couldn't see that it was wrong.

Mabus slowly nodded. "This may be the worst mistake of my life, but I think that, given that you've now made a complete hash of the timeline, we might as well make things worse. Perhaps the aliens envisioned this, and perhaps Thaillo couldn't really tell me about it. Barbara is dead, and although that marriage would have been ideal, sometimes successful unions have less-than-auspicious beginnings. It will be a pairing based on mutual distrust and suspicion, but, then again, many Earth marriages were like that. I've seen the best and worst of you, and though I despise the worst, I appreciate the best. There is nothing more to say than 'welcome aboard.'"

The crew was very, very slow to applaud when Eva wrapped her velvety arms around Mabus and gave him a long and sensuous kiss. Mabus broke free of her arms, clasping in one hand the alien gun. He had grabbed it from off of Eva, out of nowhere. "We won't be needing this where we're going, my dear," he said, and crushed it into a lump the size of a Brazil nut. Now, finally, the crew cheered.

Chapter Thirty

HE SHIP FINALLY DIPPED INTO the planet's atmosphere. The thirteen passengers gazed out the front of the ship in amazement. It was the most beautiful sight. Earth had never looked as luscious as it did right then. Literally, it was the Garden of Eden. The ship reentered the new Earth's atmosphere. Mabus set the ship on feather mode, to slow it down for safe reentry. The craft gently landed, without a single bit of turbulence. The thirteen people didn't take long to pile out. One by one they took in the fresh air and rolled in the grass. Like children on their first day of summer break, they all ran in different directions, taking in the amazement of all the vibrant colors nature had to offer back then. The flora seemed ten times more intense than our typical foliage. There were yellows so bright you had to squint, and there were more blues and reds than anyone would expect to see.

No people were anywhere to be seen. They were expecting to land on the original African savannah, but this garden of earthly delights was something far more than they had anticipated. It seemed to be the actual Eden. Had they run off-course by a thousand miles, and landed in the vicinity where the Garden of Eden would once stand in ancient Mesopotamia? Had a time paradox been introduced into their voyage? Mabus wandered and wondered to himself, briefly touching a gigantic glistening green cycad. Then it dawned on him: this far in the distant past, the entire Earth was all one Garden of Eden.

Mabus's reflexes were a hundred times more efficient, and his senses seemed to almost radiate from him. He could hear the sound of a drop of water being released from the edge of a leaf.

He could actually hear the wind from the leaf flapping slowly as the weight of the water droplet released the leaf from its gravity. He calculated the time the water droplet took to hit, and realized there was a large embankment just ahead.

The eleven Antis and Eva hiked toward the embankment and on the way there, they frolicked playfully chasing each other. They looked like children in an Easter egg hunt. Davis's legs had changed into the four legs of a horse. He galloped in front of the pack of superhumans. His muscles radiated the independence he felt. This was the dawn of a great civilization. Their minds raced with ideas for their perfect oasis. What could they do with a new Earth, and eternal powers and knowledge?

Davis retrieved his flute from around his neck, and played a tune for the celebrations. The harmonious sounds enhanced the visions that danced in their heads. Laughter filled the background like a chorus. Their heads were spinning with ideas. This was the beginning of the thousand years of peace the Bible had prophesied. They all thought about how glorious it was going to be.

"Why only a thousand years?" Mabus began to ponder. As he looked at the faces around him, he remembered what Thaillo had said about being betrayed by them. His number-one problem was Eva, but if the prophecies were true, she wouldn't begin to be a major threat until the thousand years were up. He was aware that his mission was to keep them all from destroying mankind.

ANCIENT GREEK MYTHOLOGY used to tell tales about the gods living among humans. They called themselves immortals. Some of these gods would mate with the mortals and have children who were half mortal and half immortal. Could the old folklore from the past be tales of our future? These gods were known to send mortals on grueling journeys, for their mere amusement. Mabus thought, "Could these eleven Antis be the gods of Ancient Greece, tormenting mankind?" As he stared at Davis, he now realized that he was witness to a real-life centaur. Man had no logical explanation for this technology. "Is that why it was passed down through time, as folklore?" Mabus shook his head and thought, "Nah."

THE ANTIS, EVA, and Mabus, the Third and True Antichrist, continued their supernal voyage, journeying through a cycle of 1,000,000,000 Earth years each time, over and over, evolving further with each iteration they took over billions of years until they finally became the tall, grey, big-eyed aliens of mythology and folklore who had originally saved the Antichrist so that all their plans to preserve humanity throughout eternity would be achieved.

And the above story remains to be written, for indeed, it is based on reality. These are all events that have been occurring and which continue to occur even now as you are being told of them. For this is the history of an infinite universe, and of an infinite number of galaxies as well.

<IT IS TIME,> thought one Grey to another Grey, who merely nodded.

ABOUT THE AUTHOR

THE ANTICHRIST VERSION 666 is partly based on a true story with the author's life intertwined within the storyline.

Cloise Orand II grew up in an abusive family and found himself living on the streets at the young age of twelve. Kidnapped at thirteen and brutally attacked, he was found DOA from several knife and gunshot wounds. The paramedics were able to miraculously revive him. Thankfully, at the age of fifteen, with the help of a loving foster family, he was able to turn his life around.

Today, Cloise is a devoted husband and father of four. From a homeless child to a multi-millionaire, he owns several successful businesses in which he includes his family and friends. He loves to shark dive, surf, skydive, play the guitar, and take on demanding challenges. Cloise firmly believes that a positive attitude enables a person to achieve anything they desire regardless of their past. He now resides in Kitsap County, Washington.

He is a member of The Heartland Writers Guild, The National Writers Union, and The National Writers Association.